*The Stones of Bothynus Trilogy*

BOOK TWO

*Minimize*

*The Stones of Bothynus Trilogy*

BOOK TWO

# Minimize

*by*

D.K. Reed

Purple Finch Press
1087 Elm Street, Suite 306
Manchester, NH 03101
603.770.5282
info@purplefinchpress.com

Printed in the United States of America

ISBN-13: 978-1-54561-492-1

# Contents

# PART ONE

# *Annie and the Cave*

*Quote from* <u>Hypnerotomachia Poliphili</u>:

*Oh delycate and heauenly Damosell, whatsoeuer thou art,*
*thy forcyble loue hath set me on fire, and consumeth my grieued heart;*
*I finde my selfe all ouer, burning in an vncessant flame,*
*and a sharpe dart cast into the middest of my breast,*
*where it sticketh fast, hauing made a mortall wounde vncurable.*[1]

CHAPTER 1

# Annie's Summer on the Farm

## JUNE 15

Annie was beginning to regret agreeing to stay all summer with her grandmother in Tennessee. As her mom drove south on Interstate 81 hour after hour, Annie only spoke in monosyllables when her mom tried to draw her into conversation. She felt gloomy and just wanted to listen to rap and old rock tunes she'd downloaded to her iPhone, her only link to the real world she was leaving. She was abandoning modern suburbia and going to a real working farm.

She looked to see if anyone had texted. Nothing. She had gotten her iPhone for Christmas the year before. Wow—she couldn't believe that was less than six months ago. So much had changed. The mystery of Uncle Alistair's disappearance had been solved—mostly by her older sister, Red. She couldn't help but admire how Red had managed to turn the tables on a bad situation, finding out that Uncle Alistair and his graduate

3

student, Erik, were not dead after all, but stuck in transformed states that made them invisible. Well, Erik was invisible; Uncle Alistair had just been tiny. And Red had certainly made off like a bandit on that whole deal—going from some crazy chick in love with a ghost to the luckiest teenager she knew, with a hot grad student head-over-heels in love with her. Red would undoubtedly be having an amazing summer—how could she not? Certainly a far cry from her own summer, unless some hot apparition was waiting in the wings to shake her own world. She silently snorted at the absurdity.

"Annie, honey, you seem awfully quiet. What's on your mind?" her mom prodded.

"Nothing, Mom, just listening to music."

"Well, I want you to know how grateful I am that you were available to help my mom this summer. You're a real hero, you know that? I mean, if the timing had been different, if it hadn't happened just before school was out, I don't know what we'd have done. There's no way Mom could have managed the farm alone this summer with a broken hip. Serendipitous, I'd say."

"Yeah, how convenient," Annie muttered under her breath, feeling defeated.

"What was that, honey?"

"Nothing." She dropped her head back onto the headrest and squeezed her eyes closed, chiding herself for being so negative. She did love her Mamaw. Mamaw was sweet. She thought briefly of the name Mamaw—a colloquialism of the Smokey Mountain region. "Mom, why do we call her *Mamaw*? I mean, Carrie had never heard of that name."

"You know, Annie, I don't honestly know. I mean, 'Mamaw' and 'Papaw' are just what people call their grandparents where I grew up. I don't know what language or culture gave rise to them. Maybe that's something you could learn this summer. My dad had a lot of books."

Annie didn't answer. She turned her head toward the window and watched the world go by in a blur. Trying to look on the bright side, Annie thought of the money she'd be earning this summer. She'd been a little jealous that Red had earned money as a counselor at her tae kwon do studio even before turning sixteen, the age requirement to get a job at the mall. Annie had earned a little money in previous summers doing odd jobs for her mom; she'd painted the living room in their old townhouse last summer. But that was different. Anything earned from one's parents didn't count for bragging rights. Still, it was something, and she would save most of the money to use for gas when she got her license.

Annie knew part of her gloom came from not getting to see much of her best friend this summer. In previous summers, she'd either traveled to visit Carrie or Carrie had traveled to be with her. But this summer, Annie had been disappointed to learn that Carrie was tied up with summer camps, leaving only one week at the very end of the summer. Carrie had always been part of summer. They'd lived in the same townhouse complex and had been inseparable until third grade, when Carrie's dad, who worked for the State Department, had been transferred first to Japan, then Finland, and now Israel. Annie and her friend had kept in touch over email, even for a time visiting by webcam every day. Their summer visits since third grade had been for at least two weeks and sometimes as much as a month, and Annie had gotten to see a lot more of the world than if Carrie had stayed in Maryland. This would be their first summer without a visit.

Annie mulled over her situation, now admittedly feeling sorry for herself. She knew her disappointment at not getting to spend time with Carrie had been only part of the problem. But coupling that with Red's immersion in all things Erik all winter and spring, and then learning that her new friend Nyah would be visiting her own grandparents for most of the summer—she felt abandoned. She'd tried not to let this show and had adapted a don't-care attitude. But that attitude had been the reason she'd reacted impulsively when her mom had asked if she wanted to earn money by being Mamaw's helper this summer.

She remembered how nonchalant she'd felt when responding. *"Sure, whatever,"* she'd said.

Being impulsive wasn't like her and she now regretted it. And it was only after this agreement to imprison herself in the boonies for the summer that she'd realized the implications and how much she would be cut off from her friends. She wouldn't even have Internet access. She was struck by a sudden horrible thought—what if there wasn't any cell service?

She was almost afraid to ask. "Um, Mom, is there cell phone coverage there?"

"Annie, of course there is. Well, some, anyway. You can usually get a couple of bars."

Annie sighed. "What about cable?"

"Well, no-oo, not exactly," her mom said slowly, seeming to catch her drift.

Annie sighed.

"She does have a satellite dish," her mom said, obviously trying to sound chipper.

"Is it one of those huge ones in the yard?"

"Well, yes. But you know, Mom's eightieth birthday is coming up soon and the new dishes are smaller and some are even able to supply Internet service. What if we have one installed for a birthday present?"

Annie felt a small ray of hope threatening to break through her wall. "Yeah, that'd be good. But Mamaw doesn't have a computer. I brought my laptop, but wouldn't Mamaw need to have a computer if we put her online?"

"How about we stop off in Morristown and pick up something for her as part of the gift? Maybe a Notebook?"

"I think we should get her an iPad. Something simple. I could set it up for her and show her how to access games and email."

"Tell you what, kiddo, when we stop, you can go in and pick out something and while you're doing that, I'll call and arrange to have someone install one of those small satellite dishes with Internet service." Her mom seemed excited now.

"Okay." Annie knew she'd been being snarky, but this was a great relief. At least she'd remain in communication with her friends this summer.

Annie gazed out the window again and thought about the summer with a little more enthusiasm. Now that Internet service was assured, she thought of the other thing she'd done to save her sanity this summer: she'd provided a potential escape route by bringing something with her that no one knew she had, though she wasn't sure she'd have the nerve to actually use it. Before leaving Maryland, she'd swiped one of Uncle Alistair's special remote controls that he'd fashioned into a STAG control.

The control, which stood for Snap to Alternate Grid, was a truly amazing device he'd made from the Stones of Bothynus, ancient artifacts he researched that had the capacity to alter one's molecules. Generally, he was very careful with the STAG controls, keeping them locked away in a safe at Georgetown University, where he did research with them. But he had a few he kept in drawers in his basement, and she had heard him complaining to himself one day about not being able to find one of them.

This had given her an idea. She knew one of her special gifts was that she was so ultra-organized she had a talent for finding things. She just had a sense for materials and their physical locations. Anything that wasn't in order bugged her and stuck in her mind. She'd remembered seeing an old remote control among a disarray of books and papers on a table in the basement. Sure enough, it was the missing STAG control. At the first opportunity, she'd retrieved it and hidden it in her room.

She knew this was a little like stealing, but she was pretty confident he thought it was merely lost and would never suspect she had it. If anything, he probably suspected his graduate student, Roy, did something with it. Roy was no longer possessed by a demon, the way he had been for months until Alistair, along with a group of priests and a psychiatrist, had performed an exorcism, but he'd still probably be the first person they'd think of, especially since he supposedly had ties to an Italian cult. Now that she thought about it, though, Uncle Alistair might think the cult had the control and freak out. Annie felt a twinge of guilt. Still, whatever her uncle thought, she was pretty sure he didn't suspect she had it. And she knew she wasn't going to do anything bad with it, so it was okay.

Annie thought briefly about the cult, *Tyrannus-Novum*. Red had said it was led by demonically possessed people. She shuddered and wondered if they might still be looking for the stones. She wondered if part of the reason her mom had suggested the idea of her spending the summer with Mamaw was to get her out of harm's way, then quickly dismissed the thought. Uncle Alistair was back, and she was pretty sure he'd dealt with the cult, or would deal with them if he had to. She preferred to think the danger they'd been in the year before was behind them. And it would make her mad if she let herself think her mom had arranged this summer imprisonment on purpose. She turned up her music and tried not to think about that any more.

They arrived at Mamaw's in time for dinner. Delicious aromas wafted from the open door at the head of the freshly built, plywood wheelchair ramp. Mamaw looked so fragile in her wheelchair that Annie felt a little guilty for begrudging her. Mamaw's arms still seemed strong though; she raised them in greeting when Annie stepped through the door. "Come on in," she said, beaming with delight.

"Hi, Mamaw." Annie bent to kiss her cheek and received a kiss in return.

"Mom, you really shouldn't have cooked. Annie and I came to help, not to be waited on," her mom scolded Mamaw as she bent to kiss her.

"Oh, it's not much, just some green beans and potatoes," she said, brushing aside any potential compliment.

"And is that cornbread I smell?" asked Annie, suddenly feeling her stomach growl.

"Yes it is, and it's gettin' cold."

"Well, Mom's right, you shouldn't have."

"I just wanted to have a little somethin' ready after your long drive. Your mom said you were a vegetarian now, so you came to the right place. We've got a freezer full of vegetables from last summer and plenty more in the garden."

Annie surprised herself by saying, "Well, I'm here to help with that. And what about animals? You still have cattle, right? And do you have chickens or pigs?"

"Just cattle since your papaw died. But you won't need to worry with that because one of the neighbors tends them for me."

As Annie carried her luggage to her assigned bedroom, she couldn't believe she was actually here and would be farming all summer. She understood that in earlier days, the farm had produced beef cattle, swine, poultry, eggs, and milk, as well as vegetables. Annie thought she might not object if her Mamaw still raised animals, like she did to factory-farming—she was sure Mamaw would be kind to the animals.

Annie hadn't realized how hungry she was until she bit into the warm cornbread. She was surprised at the yumminess of the corn, green beans, and mashed potatoes and didn't bother to join in the animated conversation going on between her mom and grandma.

She looked at her plate. She'd never before considered how amazing it was that such a frail little woman could still plant a huge garden every summer, harvest it, and cook such a delicious meal. And this year, she'd be the one doing most of it. She couldn't help but sigh a little at the thought.

At least Mamaw had already planted before breaking her hip. Annie was pretty sure a large part of her job would be to tend the garden. Annie feared her idea of what this entailed might be somewhat naive, having never spent an entire afternoon in the hot sun, leaning over a row of plants, doing the same repetitive motion hour after hour. But she tried to put this out of her mind right now—after all, this was how her ancestors had lived, and if Mamaw could do it, so could she. And if she survived it, she'd probably learn a lot.

That evening, however, Annie's slightly more upbeat mood began to wane again. She felt panic rising in her throat as the three of them sat in Mamaw's living room, watching game shows. She hoped she'd feel better once she could get online.

"Mom, when's that guy coming for the you-know-what?" Annie glanced toward her grandmother, who was seated in an overstuffed armchair, her fingers working ceaselessly on a huge quilt attached to an oval frame in front of her.

Annie's mom gave her a look of consternation and formed her lips into a silent *shhh*. Annie knew this was supposed to be a secret, but what was the big deal—Mamaw would know soon anyway. What was one or two days early?

"Who's comin', Kaye?" asked Mamaw.

Annie smiled—nothing escaped this small enigma of a woman. She would have to keep that in mind this summer.

Annie's mom gave Annie a smirk she took to mean, *why couldn't you keep your mouth shut?* Annie felt sheepish.

"Mom, it's a surprise. But I guess now that little Miss Can't-Keep-Her-Mouth-Shut has let the cat out of the bag, I'll tell you this much. Since you turn eighty this year and this is a special birthday for you, Annie and I want to give you an early birthday present. It's from Red and Yates, too. But we're going have a little pre-birthday party tomorrow—just us three. Annie and I will bake a cake and present you with a surprise, and the man coming on Monday is part of the surprise. That's all I can say for now."

"There's a man coming Monday? What kind of man?"

Annie laughed. "Not a man popping out of a cake or anything like that. You'll just have to wait and see. And I think you'll like it."

Her mom added, "This, of course, doesn't mean that we, or at least I, won't come down for your actual birthday, like we did for Dad's eightieth. Remember that, Mom?"

This suggestion launched Mamaw into a discourse of memory. She'd been a widow for eight years and seemed lonely, Annie thought. But she knew Mamaw had too much mountain folk pride to agree to move in with them.

She knew her mom worried over Mamaw being so isolated in the old farmhouse. She'd begged her to come live with them. There were two neighboring farmhouses that could be seen from Mamaw's house, but neither was within shouting distance. Her mom had worried Mamaw would fall and injure herself even more and be left to die alone, in misery and pain. Of course, Annie couldn't see how this could happen, since her mom called Mamaw every night to check on her, but still, her mother worried.

Annie watched a man on the television reveal what was behind door number two. Trying not to get sucked into the flashing lights of the old game show, Annie wondered if by the end of the summer, she, too, would be hooked on game show reruns. She glanced at her mom, who was now in a lounger with the footrest up, reading a mystery novel.

At eleven, Mamaw suggested that Annie might need to go to bed after such a long day on the road. Annie took this as a grandmotherly way of saying that she, herself, was sleepy, and rose to help her to bed and wake up her mom, who was snoozing in the recliner. This was her first night in Mamaw's house and she had no idea what to do.

Her mom didn't seem to know much more than she about how to help Mamaw get into her nightgown, but somehow, the three managed. Annie knew she'd have to do this on her own once her mother left.

The next day, she and her mom cooked a large meal for lunch, as well as a cake for their special birthday celebration. Her mom showed her where all the food and cooking utensils were kept to save Mamaw the trouble. Annie would be cooking for her as part of her job.

Annie felt good watching Mamaw enjoy the cake, but sensed she was trying to force enthusiasm about the iPad. She was obviously a little wary of the new gadget and not sure what she was supposed to do with it.

The next day, a man came and installed the new satellite dish. Annie set up an email account for Mamaw, along with several apps for the iPad.

She realized the generation gap was pretty wide when she tried to open new worlds for Mamaw by teaching her to surf the web but she kept asking what she was supposed to do next.

"Whatever you want, Mamaw. What do you want to know more about? Like, if you wanted to know what movies are coming out this summer, you could type in *movies new releases* and press Enter. And look."

Annie showed Mamaw the screen, but she didn't seem all that interested, saying warily, "But I haven't been out to a movie since your mom was small."

Her mom laughed at this. "That's right, Annie, Mom probably hasn't been to a movie since I was young enough to watch full-length cartoons."

"Well, they closed the theater in town."

"Maybe try to find an online almanac," her mom suggested.

Annie attempted this without much better luck, but at least Mamaw did seem to like the Solitaire app she showed her next. Annie sighed. She'd have to work on that this summer.

Annie was a little nervous the next day as her mom drove away, saying she really had to get back to work. Annie suspected her mom wanted to leave before she could change her mind about staying the summer.

She decided to keep busy to avert her gloom. She began by making a list of daily activities so she could plan out her time. She felt hopeful when she showed Mamaw the list and Mamaw nodded with approval. "Yeah, this is good, cooking and cleaning and helping me with my bath. And harvesting the vegetables."

"You'll have to tell me when I need to do the harvesting."

"Yep, that's a ways off yet."

"And what about watering? Do I need to do that tomorrow?"

Mamaw laughed indulgently. "Well, that's one thing you won't need to do. We get plenty of rain here most years."

Annie was starting to feel like this might not be so much work. Then, to her dismay, her grandmother added, "But the garden does need to be weeded every couple of weeks. I planted just before I broke my hip and this is peak growing season. It's pretty much a constant race against the weeds now."

Annie took a breath and tried to stay optimistic. "Okay. So I'll start weeding right away. How should I do it? Didn't Red and I help you chop weeds with hoes when we were little?"

Mamaw laughed at the obviously pleasant memory. "That's right. And remember that your papaw or I tilled it first? That removed the weeds between the rows and then the rest of the family used hoes to chop the weeds from within the rows, and sometimes we had to stoop down and pull the weeds from the smaller plants, like carrots. Well, that's what we still do."

Annie was beginning to feel overwhelmed. "Okay, so do I need to drive the tiller tomorrow?"

"Oh no, one of the neighbors does that for me now. He'll come and till this week and again in two weeks. You'll need to hoe the garden each time after it's tilled."

Annie thought of how huge the garden was and knew this was going to be a lot of work. Still, her almost-eighty-year-old grandmother did it; so could she.

Her grandmother must have sensed her unease. "Annie, I feel bad asking you to do all this work for me. And if it's too much, just leave it be. It's just a garden."

"No, Mamaw, it'll be fine." Annie forced herself to smile. "I've been trying to think of ways to get in better shape, anyway, and just think of the tan I'll get."

That afternoon, after the dishes were done, Annie had a moment of alone time while Mamaw napped, sitting up in her easy chair, her sewing project in her lap. Annie went to her bedroom and fell onto her bed, staring up at the ceiling. What had she gotten herself into? This was so *boring*. Hoeing a garden all day and watching game shows in the evening? There was the new Internet connection, but it was almost too slow to bother with. Annie let out a hopeless sigh.

There was only one thing that intrigued Annie now—and that was the STAG control tucked safely away in her suitcase. She wondered if she would get to use it and felt goose bumps rise at the thought. To use the STAG control, she knew she'd need to find someone to help her, which meant she needed to develop a friendship with someone. There was no way she'd zap herself without having someone to unzap her. She might be eternally lost in some alternate dimension. Heck, she really only knew how to use the minimization button, but she also knew it was capable of other types of transformations.

She really, really wanted to be free to play with it, though. She'd been tiny just once for a few minutes, a birthday gift from Uncle Alistair. She'd inherited her dad's adrenaline craving, and Uncle Alistair's gift had been truly awesome—she'd never forget the thrill of being minimized. She could envision herself swimming among the little minnows and tadpoles in some mountain stream. That was another reason she needed help, she thought; not only to return her to her regular size, but also to rescue her if a crayfish tried to eat her.

She'd be on the lookout for someone she could befriend and trust, she decided. She'd offer to exchange the favor and allow that person to also minimize. How could any red-blooded, adventurous teen refuse?

The first candidate presented himself the following day, when a neighbor boy arrived to till the garden. He must've been at least sixteen; he drove up in a pick-up truck. He steadied a wooden board between the truck bed and the ground and propelled a tiller off the truck.

She went out to greet him and convey Mamaw's instructions to please till the corn first because Annie needed to train the running beans to go up the corn stalks.

He seemed to know the garden; clearly he'd done this before. Annie learned his name was Billy, he'd just finished high school, and this was his summer job—taking his dad's tiller around to local farms and tilling the ground. He'd done this for two previous summers and had been allowed to drive the truck since he was fourteen, he boasted.

Annie had heard her mom talk about the fact that the huge county only had a sheriff, a couple of deputies, and a very small police force. So with all the methamphetamine crime that had encroached in recent years, minor traffic laws weren't something that got much attention. Interesting, she thought— it was very different from her home in Potomac, Maryland, where you'd get a ticket if your seatbelt wasn't buckled. Maybe she could work on learning to drive this summer. But first things first—she was more interested in getting to use the STAG control.

Billy was tall and skinny, his hair bleached from the sun and his skin bronzed, though it was hard to tell for sure because his skin and clothes were covered in garden dirt. He had a rustic charm and looked like he might clean up good. He seemed shy and intent on his work, though. To her disappointment, she got little opportunity to speak with him before he finished the last row, reloaded his tiller, and was gone. *So much for him being my new friend.*

Annie was sweating by the time she went in to make lunch for Mamaw, so she took a quick sponge bath and put on some dry clothes. No point in having a full shower if she'd be going right back out again.

By the end of that first day, she had blisters on her hands from the friction of the hoe. She applied bandages for her second day out and spent more time stooping and pulling weeds rather than using the hoe. At night, she dropped into bed, exhausted. But somehow, she made it through the week. She was amazed that this was what her grandmother not only did, but enjoyed. Mamaw frequently stated how she missed being in her garden. Annie didn't get it, but didn't have the heart to complain about it or to question her grandmother's sanity in enjoying it.

Mamaw had a strict policy about not working in the garden on Sunday, apart from harvesting something needed for a meal that day. The nice thing about this was that Annie really did need the break. She'd soaked much of the soreness out of her muscles the night before in the bathtub, but she felt the need to stretch her legs to loosen the muscles. Her whole body felt sore, but also curiously more alive and strong, lean and mean from all the work.

She mentioned to Mamaw that she would like to take a walk after the lunch dishes were done on Sunday, and Mamaw was delighted, recommending several nice treks around the farm. Annie knew Mamaw would love nothing better than for at least one member of the family to fall in love with the farm and move back to tend it and live off the land. Annie did see some attraction in this life of simplicity, but her thrill-seeking needs were a definite complication. She was excited about going to college one day and learning more about the world. She wanted to learn about ancient Egypt, asteroids, Greek mythology … and she wanted to save the planet from those people who didn't care about loss of rainforests or endangered species. Still, she could see her summer didn't seem as bad as it had her first day.

Annie continued this reverie as she set out to explore. She was on a mission. She needed to find and strike up at least one friendship so she could do some real exploring—hopefully in an unchartered realm. She was determined to find a way to explore the micro-flora and fauna of some enchanted mountain stream by minimizing herself.

# CHAPTER 2

# New Friend and a "Smokey" Mountain Adventure

Annie decided to walk down the dirt and gravel road to another part of the farm. Today's destination would be to a place where she and Red had spent many hours as kids—the Swan Hole.

The Swan Hole was a deep pool in Kingfisher Creek with a waterfall that made a hollow churning sound. The waterfall wasn't visible from the dirt road—she would have to walk up the creek from the small bridge where the road crossed over the creek. The creek defined the property line between Mamaw's land and the neighbor's. The land rose steeply from the creek on Mamaw's side, so it was much easier to walk up beside the creek on the other person's land.

Annie arrived at the bridge and was relieved to see the path she and Red had used when they were kids was still there. It was a barely-visible footpath alongside the creek. As she walked, she wondered if she'd be disappointed. The pool was probably some tiny thing, embellished by her childhood memory. When she was little, she used to look for swans, but never saw any, and remembered the disappointment when she learned from her mom that the pool got its name not from the graceful birds, but from a boy with the last name of Swan who had drowned there. But her mom more than made up for the name thing by telling her about the legend that the pool was a bottomless pit and that a horse-drawn carriage fell into it once, disappearing beneath the falls. If the legend was to be believed, it must be a pretty deep pool.

When they were younger, she and Red had only been allowed to walk to the Swan Hole accompanied by an adult. Apparently, her grandparents believed the legend, or at least the story about the boy who drowned. They'd always refused to allow the girls to swim in that pool. She wondered what the real story was of the Swan Hole. She suspected the horse-drawn carriage disappearance was just a country legend. Still, in her Google searches before coming on this trip, she'd discovered the whole region was considered a limestone-karst region, which meant it was prone to having caves because water eroded the limestone and formed underground tunnels. Maybe there was a cave entrance lurking under the pool. She got goose bumps just thinking about it.

She was surprised to find a travel trailer standing at the edge of the field to the west of Kingfisher Creek, hidden from the road and just beside the path. She vaguely remembered hearing something about this land having been sold and divided after the death of an old farmer who'd owned it. There was now a housing development of starter homes up the small valley that ascended from the road, but she was surprised to find a trailer so close by. It stood alone, but was surrounded by a small, tidy flower garden bordered by short plastic edging. Someone had tended the garden with loving care. She saw tire tracks on the other side of the field.

She felt a little uncomfortable trespassing on the land now that she knew it to be occupied. As she approached the dwelling, a side door swung open and out stepped Billy, the sun-bronzed youth who had tilled the garden for Mamaw. He jumped when he saw Annie, obviously not expecting to see anyone walking between his front yard and the creek.

"Billy?" Annie called. "It's me, Annie, Mrs. Jefferson's granddaughter."

He relaxed, still reticent, but friendly. "Oh, sure, no problem. What brings you here? Does Mrs. Jefferson need some more work done?"

"No … I mean, I don't think so just yet. I was walking up to the Swan Hole. I hope you don't mind me coming up your side of the creek—Mamaw's is so steep."

"Of course not. Any time."

Annie noticed a pretty young woman peeking through the window of the front storm door. The wooden door was open wide, she realized, and the glass on the storm door was raised, leaving only the screen on the bottom part of the door for ventilation. Did this young couple not even have air conditioning? Annie had heard that travel trailers, which were made of metal, got really hot in the summer without air conditioning.

"Hello," Annie called to the shy young woman peeking from the door. "I'm Annie, Mrs. Jefferson's granddaughter."

The door opened then and the young woman came forward, warm but nervous. "Pleased ta meet you. Billy said you were stayin' with Mrs. Jefferson to help out while her hip heals. I'm Missy, Billy's wife." With this, she gave a bashful glance to Billy, who, shirtless, had begun to sharpen some type of farm equipment, a long metal arm with what looked like large metal shark teeth attached along its length. He looked up as Missy introduced herself and smiled at her. It was sweet, Annie thought. The couple was so very young, not much older than her, yet they were married already. She remembered her mom telling her how this area had a custom of marrying young. The

21

girl looked to be about her own age—Annie doubted she'd graduated from high school yet.

"I was just walking up to the Swan Hole. Do you want to come?" Annie liked this shy young woman. She reminded her of a sturdy farm lass of old, with strong hands, a warm heart, and maybe a bit of a wild streak to match her wild mane of hair. Annie realized that Missy reminded her of her own mother. Annie warmed to her right away, feeling a kinship—like maidens of old in a hunter-gatherer society.

"Okay," Missy said, seeming interested. "Let me grab my sandals." She disappeared and then reappeared in a few seconds.

Annie snapped out of her reverie, her edgy attitude returning. *Boy, she must not get out much.* Then she smiled.

The Swan Hole was only about fifty yards further up the stream. Annie enjoyed their chat as they strolled up the path. She told her about Maryland and her high school. In return, Missy told her she'd finished high school at the only one in the county. She'd finished in three years and was enrolled this fall at a community college in Morristown. Annie figured that made her a year or two older than herself.

Missy explained that she'd have to drive across Clinch Mountain three days a week to attend the college, but it was all her family could afford. She wanted to study nursing and work at the small hospital in Sneedville. "Billy and I like living in the country so much. We'd never consider moving into a city," she said. They were trying to design their lives so they could take advantage of the local opportunities, she said. Billy's dad had bought them this piece of land and their used travel trailer. No, it didn't have air conditioning, but it was okay for now, she said. They had fans and sat outside in the shade on hot evenings. "Billy just wants to farm. He works for other people to earn money. We're saving so we can buy enough land to live decently," she said. They might buy one of the houses on the nearby hill at some point, she said, if she could supplement his income by working at the hospital in a few years, though they might have to sell this field to help pay for it.

Annie didn't envy them their hard lives, but they didn't seem to mind. In fact, she'd have to say they seemed very happy.

Upon arriving at the Swan Hole, she was pleased to note that it really *was* spectacular. It hadn't just been a childhood fantasy. She peered into the pool and failed to see a bottom. Okay, that was promising. She scrambled on the rocks, skirting around under the overhanging ledge supporting the curtain of falling water. She was surprised that Missy seemed just as eager to explore. Annie suspected she'd never had a lot of time to play.

It was a very pleasant afternoon, sunny but not too hot; a light rain that morning had refreshed the earth. Annie removed her sandals and dangled her feet in the cool water. Missy did, too. Annie was surprised at how much she enjoyed the waterside chat with her new friend. Her ears really perked up when she heard Missy say there were many local tales of little people and "*haints*" throughout the county, and she was pretty sure her grandmother had mentioned the Swan Hole in at least one story.

"Did you ever swim in the pool?" Annie asked.

"Oh, no. It ain't safe. Ain't you heard that it draws ya under?" Annie hid a smile, wondering if her fearful attitude had something to do with the isolation of this remote countryside.

"My mom told me. I suspect there's a cave under the pool."

"My mamaw said there used to be a little cave openin' under the falls, but some rocks fell and sealed it closed," reported Missy with much animation.

"Hmmm, really?" Annie's attention was definitely captured—maybe that was where a *haint* lived. She felt goose bumps. "Did your mamaw ever say anything about where the opening was located?" She rose and began to climb around the rocks on the back of the waterfall.

"No, she just said under the falls." Missy was now following Annie.

With Missy's help, Annie searched all the crevices beneath the falls, but didn't find an opening. They began to move around the rocks that could be moved. At one point, upon moving aside a rock the size of a football, Annie thought she saw blackness, perhaps a hole the size of a tennis ball, like there was a space behind it, but before she could speak, she was startled by a splash. Missy screamed and the girls heard laughter from above the falls.

"Oh, that silly Billy," Missy said, giggling. "Billy, you're gettin' yours, son!" Annie giggled as she watched Missy scramble out from behind the falls into the pool, scoop a handful of water, and try in vain to splash Billy, who was laughing as he skirted around the pool just out of range. He raised his palms in surrender.

"Hey Missy, don't you think it's gettin' to be about suppertime?" he asked hopefully.

Annie didn't think Missy would deny her man anything. "Okay, sugar. I'm a comin'." Annie loved her mountain accent. "Annie, this was real fun. I gotta go, but let's do it again."

"Absolutely. I'm here all summer. I'll come back the next chance I get. Definitely Sunday, but even before if I can."

"I'm here most of the time this summer. I'm takin' two classes online but other than that, I can come out most any time. Your mamaw's got our number. Call, or just drop by like you did today," she said. "Oh, and tell your mamaw that I've got extra cherry tomato plants if she wants some."

"Okay, will do."

She waved goodbye and watched them go. She knew she should get going, too; Mamaw would need her soon. But she just had to see if that black area under the stone might be a cave entrance. She went back to work at that spot, moving a couple more boulders as far as she could, which wasn't much.

Sure enough, there was definitely a black space. But was it an opening? The boulders blocking the space were too big to move, so there was no way to be certain. But the more she examined it, the more convinced she became that this was an opening to a cave. She could hardly contain her excitement. How could she stand to wait until next Sunday?

And how would she know whether she could trust Missy to let her in on her secret? She knew she needed an accomplice to operate the STAG control but also knew she must proceed slowly and cautiously. Anyone she let in on the secret was a risk. But without another person, she couldn't transform back. Still … if she could just shrink herself and a flashlight small enough to fit inside the opening, she'd be able to see if there was a cave beneath the falls. She knew she was becoming obsessed with the idea.

Over the next few weeks, Annie developed a routine of working in the garden for a couple of hours in the early morning and another couple in the evening, during the coolest parts of the day. During mid-day, she helped Mamaw indoors with cooking and cleaning.

Though she sometimes wished that Mamaw would give her more space, she mostly enjoyed these interactions with her maternal ancestor and learning how to live largely independent of the outside world. It was a simple life, but satisfying in a way.

Annie was an avid reader and though she and her peers were all very much into the super-hero theme, she also secretly loved the classics. During mid-day, she imagined herself in the kitchen at Wuthering Heights; while in the garden, she pictured herself as a Thomas Hardy character, like Tess, slaving away at digging turnips. Her imagination made the work bearable, maybe even enjoyable.

Another item of interest was that Mamaw tried to teach her about gardening by moon signs. This was somewhat intriguing to Annie, though it seemed out of character for Mamaw—pagan, but she imagined it was part of agrarian history the world over. Annie thought perhaps, in a way, this valley was simply frozen in time. Overall, it had a charm for Annie, though she didn't think she'd like to be permanently confined here like Missy.

She visited Missy every chance she got, sincerely liking her bright, warm personality, but also feeling a little guilty because she knew she had an agenda. She intended to cultivate a friendship sufficient to be able to trust Missy with her secret of the STAG control; hopefully, they could explore the cave, either separately, or maybe even together if Billy could also be trusted with the secret and be the one responsible for zapping them back to normal size.

Annie walked to the Swan Hole once or twice during each week, and always on Sunday afternoons, when she could count on free time. Missy seemed thoroughly and sincerely pleased to see her coming and never failed to join her if she was at home. Annie dared not come any more often than she did because she feared it would arouse Mamaw's suspicion that she was up to something and also because she didn't want to wear out her welcome with Missy.

Annie, often with Missy's help, overturned or scooted away as many stones as she could lift, but the two of them didn't discover any additional prospective cave openings other than the one spot Annie had identified. She and Missy also spent some relaxing time wading in the edge of the pool or sitting in the shade, dangling their feet into the cool water. It wasn't difficult to refrain from actually swimming because the water was so cold, likely originating from a mountain spring.

Somewhere around the sixth or seventh visit, Annie learned that Missy and Billy each had a vice. *Now we're getting somewhere*, thought Annie. Billy's vice was to sneak an occasional drink of whiskey, though he tried to never overdo it. Annie didn't think this unusual. Missy's vice, however, did shock Annie, though she thought she was prepared for anything—pot, even cocaine. Missy's vice was cigarettes, something Annie had always shunned, knowing an addiction would likely lead to lung cancer—the thing that had killed Papaw some years earlier.

Missy pulled out a pack of Virginia Slims and lavender lighter and offered a cigarette to Annie. She hesitated. Under any other circumstance, Annie would've shunned the suggestion that she have one. She had no desire whatsoever to try a cigarette. Pot, sure, but cigarettes? Definitely not cool. But she wanted to cultivate a deeper level of friendship in a hurry so she could share her secret, and so she complied. She also reasoned that once she tried it, she wouldn't seem so condescending when she tried to talk Missy out of smoking. So she tried to convince herself this was self-sacrifice rather than a totally manipulative maneuver.

The first puff felt pretty much like she'd imagined—hot, choking smoke burning her throat. She coughed and gagged.

Missy giggled at her attempt. "No, just take it into your mouth and try not to inhale for a while. Like this." She demonstrated.

That worked much better.

"Watch this," Missy said, and puffed out a perfect smoke ring.

Annie did find that kind of fun. She focused on not inhaling, but practiced using her tongue to eject smoke rings. The whole time she felt guilty, however, remembering the anti-smoking information from health class, and sincerely hoped that if she only had one cigarette, or a couple if needed, she wouldn't cause too much damage.

As she walked back to Mamaw's that day, she was aware that she reeked of cigarette smoke, and upon entering the house, went straight to the bathroom and brushed her teeth. She also washed her face and arms and then went to her bedroom and changed clothes, stashing the offending garments in a plastic bag and making a mental note to do laundry very soon.

She was relieved, but at the same time dismayed, to discover when she next met Missy that the smoking of a second cigarette was expected and that it was just slightly less unpleasant than the first. Was she developing an addiction already? She decided to waste no more time before sharing her secret. She reasoned that she'd been a good sport about Missy's secret.

So that Sunday afternoon, she took her customary walk to the Swan Hole, this time with the STAG control tucked away in her daypack.

CHAPTER 3

# *The Cave*

## SUNDAY, JULY 28

S he was delighted to see Missy's sunny face watching from the front door window as she'd done on that first day and waved enthusiastically to her. Missy waved back and then disappeared momentarily, reappearing at the side door. Annie had hinted that she had a secret to tell today and Missy trilled with excitement.

They arrived at the Swan Hole. Annie pulled an old blanket from her daypack and spread it out, along with two small, green, misshapen apples from Mamaw's orchard. Missy was busy likewise pulling things out of a small plastic cooler she'd brought—two soft drinks and a bag of chips.

"I love Mrs. Jefferson's apples. They may be small but they're the tastiest ones around," Missy said kindly.

Annie agreed. "Yeah, I think she grafted them from some collection of ancient apple limbs she got from someone. Mom says Mamaw babied those trees. A few are ready to pick and Mamaw promised to teach me to make fried apples and biscuits—I'll bring you some."

Missy popped the tops of the aluminum cans of soft drinks and then brought out the cigarettes.

Annie took the soft drink, thanking Missy, and then took the cigarette but didn't light it. Instead, with the cigarette vice clearly in the open, Annie used the opportunity to pull out the STAG control.

"What's that? Looks like a remote control," Missy said.

"Well, it used to be, but it's been turned into a scientific gadget that my uncle made," Annie said. "Listen, Missy, you shared your secret about smoking with me and I've decided to share a secret with you."

"Okay, what does this do? Make your TV show channels you're not signed up for or something?" she asked, picking it up.

"Careful," Annie warned. "Please don't press any buttons on it until I explain. But first—Missy, if I tell you what this does, you're going to have to promise complete secrecy, okay?"

"Okay." Missy was obviously enjoying the idea of some secret game.

"Well, here goes. And this is going to be hard to believe, but I promise it's true."

"Okay, you've got me intrigued."

"Well, my uncle does research on ancient artifacts and he came across these stones that can draw energy from you. And when they do that, the molecules become smaller and you transform," Annie blurted out and then watched for Missy's reaction.

Missy laughed good-naturedly. "Okay, now I get it. This is one of those role-playing games they do in colleges, right? Live-action role-playing? LARP-ing, I think it's called. Right?"

Annie smiled, gritted her teeth, and tried to think of how to explain this. "Well, not exactly. Let me try this again. This is real. The stones he found really can change molecules. Some powder from the stones is rigged up into this remote control,

THE CAVE

so that I can point it at something and change its molecules. I can make it smaller or even invisible."

Missy looked at her as if she were suspicious of her sanity. Annie realized her description sounded too much like science fiction and Missy didn't really believe her, though she obviously wanted to go along with her friend. So Annie decided to show her.

"Okay, Missy, I'll demonstrate. But first you have to promise me two things."

Missy nodded uncertainly.

"First, no matter how disturbed you are with what you see, you'll point the remote control—it's actually called a STAG control—at this spot."Annie drew a circle on the ground with a stick.

"Okay," Missy said seriously.

Annie continued, "Okay, so in five minutes—no, one minute—you point the STAG control at this spot and press this button." She showed Missy which button. "You got that?"

Missy repeated the instructions.

"And secondly, this absolutely has to be kept top secret. I know we already said that, but it's something my great-uncle's researching and if word got out, it would cause all kinds of trouble for him. So I really need your solemn promise, okay?"

"Can I tell Billy?"

Annie considered. "Yes, if you think he could keep the secret. In fact, it might be nice to tell him. That way both of us can have adventures with this. But no one else, okay?"

"Okay. Cross my heart and hope to die." Missy made the sign of the cross on her chest.

"For now, please push this button once I get situated over there." She pointed to another button and then to the spot on the ground. "But please remember, and this is extremely important, press THIS button after one minute, got it?"

"I ... think so." Missy didn't sound too sure but was being a good sport.

31

Annie wanted to be certain. "Want to say the instructions back to me so I can make sure?"

"Yes, I press this here button when you stand over there, and then this here button after one minute, with the remote control pointed at that spot."

"Exactly. Nothing to it." Annie felt relieved that the instructions were clear. "Are you ready?"

"Yep, ready as I'll ever be." Missy seemed to want to get this over with.

Anne stood on the spot, feeling a trill of excitement. "Go."

Missy pressed the button and Annie felt herself snap to a lower grid, much like at her birthday party, when her uncle had transformed her, much to the shock and horror of her family. She knew that one press of the button minimized her to elf size. Annie wished as she transformed that she'd stressed that Missy *only* push the button once. She wasn't sure what would happen if she pressed it several times; she didn't want to think about being engulfed by an amoeba.

Annie watched astonishment cross Missy's face at seeing her disappear. She moved and shouted to her, though her shout probably sounded like a squeak to Missy. She knew that at this grid, she was practically invisible unless she moved. The molecules were so small that they couldn't easily be seen, but movement could still be detected visually, though somewhat immaterially, like a mist.

She saw Missy strain to see her.

"Here!" Annie shouted and ran to the water's edge and splashed. She heard a roar and saw Missy's mouth moving; she could just make out something that sounded like a question— she assumed it must be, "Is the minute up?" She'd forgotten that she couldn't clearly hear what someone was saying when she was minimized. She saw Missy point the STAG control at the spot where she'd transformed.

Annie scrambled back to the spot just in time, tripped, and fell face first on the spot, snapping back to normal size. She quickly raised her face and laughed heartily.

The laugh was infectious. "Oh, my gosh. I can't believe this thing." Missy seemed to be in a mixture of ecstasy and disbelief.

Now that the demo had been done, Missy was all ears for Annie's explanation of what had occurred. She told her all about the stones and briefly about the other type of transformation, one her sister had experienced, that had allowed her to be invisible and to see angels and colorful essences. She thought the STAG control was also capable of that transformation, though they'd need to experiment on plants or something to see which buttons did what. She thought, too, that it worked on both living and non-living things, but not everything. She giggled when she told Missy about how the transformation Red had experienced hadn't worked on woven fabrics. Red had told her all about her experience with having her cotton clothing disappear and finding herself completely naked, though invisible to other humans. Thank goodness that wasn't the case when one was minimized.

Missy was obviously a little nervous about trying it herself. Annie understood it was all new to her and she didn't know Uncle Alistair. In fact, she seemed to think of him as a mad scientist. "I think I should talk to Billy about it before I try it," she said. "No offense, but I'd feel better trying it if I knew he had the remote control in his hand, ready to bring me back." Annie understood and thought it was sweet.

The next visit occurred the following Tuesday afternoon. Missy was happy to transform Annie again, but said she hadn't yet found the right moment to tell Billy about the STAG control. She promised to do so before Sunday. Annie, this time, instructed Missy to press the button twice so she'd be smaller than during her previous demonstration—not too fast, not too slow. Just enough to make sure that each pressing was a solid hit. One, two. And the same to be repeated upon the transformation back to normal size.

The main pool was too cold for Annie, but she found a small calm pool on the side that had been warmed by the sun. Missy transformed her to the size she'd been for the birthday party surprise. Annie could see Missy, though Missy was gigantic. She thought that Missy seemed to be enjoying this. She heard her thunderous voice say something and could just make out the words, "… so cute."

"Thanks, Missy," Annie tried to respond. It seemed clear that Missy had heard something but couldn't quite make it out.

Annie dove into the warm pool. The water was so clear she could see the cobbles beneath the pool. She was a little nervous when she saw a minnow swim below her. Thankfully it didn't seem interested in her. She rolled over on her back, letting the sun warm her face, and floated. "Ah, this is the life," she said, sighing in contentment.

Suddenly she saw an enormous shadow move and tried to focus on what it was. Before she could figure it out, she felt two snaps and she found herself sitting in the small pool, mostly dry except her bikinied bottom, which was in the water. The water molecules, she realized, were normal-sized and were therefore unaffected by the re-transformation. One of the advantages of swimming this way, she thought—automatic dryness.

"What happened?" she asked, beginning to giggle at the absurdity of sitting in the pool.

"Oh my gosh," breathed Missy in a panic. "You didn't see it?"

"See what?"

"The crawdad. It was hidin' in the rocks and started toward you. I grabbed the remote control and zapped you just as it was about to snag you. I mean, at first I couldn't really see you but then I realized what you looked like and I could just make out where you were. And so could that crawdad."

Annie's mouth dropped. She'd had no idea she'd been so close to death. "Oh my gosh. Thanks, Missy. I owe you my life.

I didn't think anything that big would be in that tiny pool." She realized she felt a little sick, thinking of how close she'd come.

"You almost gave me a heart attack," said Missy, drawing out her pack of cigarettes. She lit two and handed one to Annie. "Here, we both need this."

Annie took the cigarette, not wanting to offend such a dear friend at the moment she owed so much to her. And as loath as she was to admit it, she was beginning to enjoy the taste.

That Sunday, Billy joined the girls, though he was obviously wary. "Okay, girls, I'll do this 'cause Missy's threatened me with the doghouse if I don't, but I'm keepin' an eye on you two. If this thing really works and the two of you shrink, I'm zappin' you back at the first sign of any danger."

They did a demo for Billy to convince him that it worked, using only the first grid, but instructed him to use two button presses so they could become small enough to fit through the cave entrance. "Why don't you just dig it out and make the openin' bigger?" his practical farmer logic suggested.

"We want to do it this way, hon," cooed Missy. Billy blushed and was once again her puppet, Annie observed with a smile.

"Hey Missy, you know what I forgot?" asked Annie, suddenly realizing. "A flashlight. You got one handy? I can't believe I didn't think of that."

"Sure do. I'll fetch it." Missy stood up, brushing off her shorts, and ran toward the trailer.

"And bring my tackle box." Billy shouted after her. "I ain't goin' to let you two go down that hole without tying some fishin' line on you." He mumbled something more to himself but Annie couldn't make it out.

"Hey Billy, you wanna try it while we wait?" Annie suggested.

"Naw," he said, then hesitated. "Well … okay, I guess." He obviously didn't want to appear too enthusiastic, but Annie could tell he was dying to try it.

"One zap or two?" she asked.

35

"Let's do two, just like you ladies are 'bout to do. That way I can tell if it's safe."

"You got it." Annie double-zapped him and he disappeared. She found him beneath her, waving up to her. She thought she heard some shouts of glee, but they sounded like squeaks.

Annie strained to watch as Billy ran over to a thin vine hanging from the bank nearby and used it to climb up a few inches before letting go with a swing. He then scrambled to another vine that hung over the water and climbed up, this time about a foot. He let go and swung out over the water with a large enough swing that he was able to do a double summersault before plunging into the edge of the Swan Hole.

Annie had the STAG control ready in case a fish or crawdad appeared. Billy was so active that he was relatively easy to spot by watching for motion. She was pretty sure she couldn't have seen his misty form if there'd been a lot of other motion in the area.

She watched him surface and tread water. Then, sure enough, she saw a fish coming toward him. She quickly pressed the button twice and saw a stunned Billy standing on the edge of the pool, only his feet in the water, his arms still moving to tread water.

"What happened?" he asked with astonishment and began to laugh when he realized he was treading air.

"You almost got gobbled by a fish," said Annie, and then caught her breath enough to join in the laughter.

"Hey, you two, what's happenin'?" asked Missy, now approaching.

"You should'a seen me," Billy boasted, stepping out of the water toward Missy, apparently glad to have a new fish story to tell, if only to her. "Annie shrunk me and I swung on that vine and dove into the water and a fish, probably bluegill, almost ate me."

"Oh, my poor honey," Missy cooed. Annie wondered if this was a mixture of real concern and frivolity at the absurdness of being swallowed by such a tiny fish.

"You think that thing would zap me back to normal-size inside a fish?" Billy asked, a thought-provoking question that Annie didn't really want to consider.

"I guess it might make you both larger and then we'd have to open the fish's mouth and drag you out." She shuddered at the thought.

"Well, best we don't have to find out," said Billy. "Now, if you two go into that cave, I want you to promise me you won't go into the water. I won't be able to see whether a critter's 'bout to get you."

"Okay," said Annie enthusiastically. Missy echoed her agreement.

"You both sure you still want to do this?"

Annie nodded and was glad to see Missy agree excitedly, not allowing him to back out.

"Okay, then, let's get this done while we still got plenty of daylight."

Annie was excited to get to explore the entrance and hoped that a cave would open up behind the rocks, but found that before the exploration could begin, her patience was to be worn thin by the care taken by Billy to make sure each girl was securely tied to his fishing line. The three discussed whether to first tie on the cord, and then minimize the cord along with the girls, or tie the unaltered cord to them after they were minimized. Fearing that some change in the cord's structure might make it weaker, Billy insisted on the latter. He very delicately tied a length of fishing line loosely around their torsos, being extremely careful not to injure his tiny wife.

Once that ordeal was over, Billy had them climb into his hand. Annie was amused at the way he made his upturned palm into a scoop shape to they wouldn't fall off and then sheltered them with the other hand. It was thrilling, though, to be lifted through the air toward the cave opening. Both girls squealed, which seemed to spur him on, and he made airplane sounds and gave them a ride around the edge of the pool for a few minutes before depositing them near the opening. Annie noted that Missy giggled and squealed throughout the whole experience and Billy beamed with delight.

He then positioned himself near the opening, holding both fishing lines in one hand and the STAG control in the other. Annie felt secure in the intensity with which he watched them, prepared to act upon an instant's notice.

Missy, obviously nervous, insisted that Annie hold their only flashlight because she wanted her to lead the way. Thankfully, the rocks weren't slippery, but were covered with soft moss, giving very good traction and making a ready cushion if either fell. The fishing line was a little heavy to drag along, but no more than a large rope would've been if they'd been normal size. They crept forward. Annie made an effort to go slowly enough for their eyes to adjust, not wanting to leave Missy behind because she sensed this might frighten her. Missy held tightly onto the back of Annie's T-shirt.

Both girls were dressed in tennis shoes, T-shirts, and shorts. The uncertain footing made Annie wish they had kneepads in case they fell. Unlike the rocks outside, where traction was greatly aided by moss, the rocks inside the opening were moss-free and slippery. They could've also used some gloves. Trying to make sure that each step was secure before putting her weight on that foot, Annie found that her progress was slower than she would have liked. Especially for Missy, who didn't have a light to aid in the placement of each foot. Annie tried to shine the light first to see where to place her foot, and then back so Missy could see where to place hers. There was water inside the opening, adding to their difficulty. Both girls were so focused on their footing that they hadn't yet looked ahead to see if the cave opened up.

Annie screamed as she felt her foot slip on a stone. She teetered for an instant before she fell on her bottom in the pool of water. At least she managed to hold the flashlight up out of the water.

"You okay, Annie?" Annie could tell that Missy was becoming a little giddy from the adrenaline. This triggered Annie's own giddiness and she burst out in laughter at being once again seated with her bottom in a pool of water. This, in turn, seemed to trigger Missy's giddiness further and both girls had a good laugh.

"You know what, Missy? As the light swung around I thought …" she shone the light all around now. The light encountered much blank space. Both girls gasped. It did open up—a lot.

"Wow, Missy, there's a cavern here. Look."

"But, Annie, there might be a drop off, too, if there's a cavern." Missy's voice began to sound shaky. "I don't like it. I want to go back out."

"Come on, Missy. Just a couple of steps more and—"

"Annie, you don't know what's in there. I'm not goin' one more step." Missy's voice shook.

"Okay, just let me look for a minute." She sighed and moved forward some more, shining the light around.

Unsure of what she was looking at with such a tiny beam of light, she stood momentarily transfixed as she found herself staring at what appeared to be the interior of an elaborate palace, complete with columns, terraces and statues, though the light was insufficient to see what the statues represented. She thought she also saw the flash of sparkly jewels. She exhaled slowly at the sight. She felt dazed with excitement and almost let out a squeal.

"Wow, Missy, are you seeing—" she looked back at Missy but realized Missy hadn't been looking nor listening, and hadn't likely heard her over the sound of trickling water in the cave. Her words died on her lips as she watched Missy, who'd already turned back, unsteadily picking her way over the stones toward the light that streamed in from the opening.

Not sure what to make of the amazing architecture she'd just seen, she thought about trying to entice Missy to come look at it, to share her excitement. But then something inside her hesitated and after a moment she decided to keep what she'd seen to herself. Visions of Cudjo Caverns, caves that had been turned into a tourist attraction in a neighboring county, danced through her mind; her mom had taken her once, and Annie remembered all its neon signs and the gift shop with little boxes that mooed like a cow when she turned them over. No, she'd need to think about whether to tell anyone about this cave. Perhaps it'd be better to keep it secret until an archeologist could look at it. Feeling protective of the cave, she thought that maybe *she'd* become an archeologist and do the work herself rather than risk a tourist invasion. She tucked away the last few minutes, with all she'd seen, into the back of her mind.

She caught up with Missy near the opening. Wanting to make it a fun experience for Missy, she forced herself to be playful. "Hey, Missy," she called.

As Missy turned, Annie tried to make a scary face while spotlighting it with the flashlight. She then made a ghostly sound and Missy squealed and finished the distance to the opening.

Annie laughed and heard Missy call from outside the opening. "Hey, I'll get you back." And then she, too, laughed.

Once outside, Billy, obviously anxious to have his beloved back to normal, immediately zapped them back, first Missy, and then Annie.

After Billy released Missy from a bear hug, she threw her arms around Annie's neck. Annie hugged her back, sharing her excitement.

Annie patiently allowed Missy to tell Billy the exciting news about finding an actual cave, confirming the legend that one existed. It was apparent all Missy had seen was the large cavern and that she hadn't seen any kind of detail. To be fair to Missy, Annie knew it'd be very hard to comprehend what she was looking at without a flashlight. With Annie in charge of the light beam, Missy probably hadn't been looking at the right spots at the right moments to see the palatial sculptures. As much as she wanted to tell her, she also knew she had to think about the cave and its implications.

After the shared experience, Missy offered Annie a cigarette in an apparent gesture of camaraderie.

"Thanks, Missy, but you know, I think I'm good. I'm starting to think I'm becoming addicted. I think if I smoke any more …" She shrugged and tried to make her face appear defeated and not judgmental, hoping to not look like a prig.

"I think you're right. I should probably quit, too," Missy said regretfully, looking at the now-glowing end of her cigarette.

Annie added, "And I think Mamaw caught me last time."

"Oh, no, Annie—what did she say?"

"Well, actually, she didn't say anything. It was just kind of implied. I turned on the light in my bedroom and there was a flattened cigarette butt lying on the dresser. I snatched it up and hid it in my shoe so I could find something to do with it the next day. But then I thought, what was the use? Mamaw obviously found it in one of my pockets when she'd done the laundry."

"Well, it's good that she's well enough to do laundry now," Missy said, obviously trying to look at the bright side.

"Yeah, that's a good thing. But you know, Missy, the odd thing was that she didn't say a word about it, not the slightest hint of anything being wrong. Mamaw had obviously placed the butt there so I'd know she knew and she'd know I knew she knew. But then she'd left it to me to decide what to do about it. What the heck was that?"

"I think that's the way of the older folk around here, Annie. It sounds exactly like what my mamaw'd do. Nerves of steel, but the grace of an angel. So are you gonna say anything to her about it?"

"No, but I think I lost my taste for cigarettes. It's funny, like I just can't stand to disappoint her. Is that weird?"

Missy smiled, "I don't think it's weird at all. What do you think you'da done if she'd yelled at you?"

"Yeah, I thought about that. I'd probably have rebelled and smoked more. But as it is, I think I'm done with it." Annie noticed that Missy snubbed out her cigarette and felt relieved that'd been settled—no more shared cigarettes.

"Well, what about a cherry cola then?"

"That sounds great." Annie said sweetly, glad for the diversion.

"Annie, I gotta tell you how grateful I am for getting to do the transformation. I mean, words can't tell you how amazing it was—right, Billy?"

Billy chimed in. "Absolutely. I mean, I still can't fully comprehend what just happened. Getting to minimize and swim, almost getting' eaten, and then watching you two go into that cave. I got so much I want to say, I just don't even know where to start. But one thing's for sure, you don't have to worry about us tellin' anyone, 'cause who'd believe us?" He laughed richly.

Missy laughed, too. Both seemed to be still on an adrenaline high from the experience.

Before taking her leave, Annie thanked the two profusely for their help in the adventure. Their responses were equally appreciative of the opportunity to have such an adventure. Annie hadn't meant to make it sound like this had been their final adventure, but she knew she was starting to feel protective of the cave's contents.

As she walked home, she was torn between guilt that she should've told them and relief that they didn't know the truth about what she'd seen. After all, the cave was equally on their property, and with such limited means for a successful living, they could use all the help they could get. But this kind of desperation also made them more likely to try to cash in on exploiting the sculptures. She decided that the only proper thing to do would be to make sure that any profits obtained from the cave would be shared with this sweet couple, even if it was years down the road and the couple no longer owned the piece of land. Annie resolved not to forget this promise to them.

Aaan was surprised to awaken to the sound of splashing in the nearby pool. How long had he slept this time? How many years? Ten? One hundred? Thousands? He wondered what the world was like now. He lay still, listening for another sound. Whispers. *Maidens. Giggling maidens. Wood nymphs? I did not think those tiny dancing sprites worked their mischief in this part of the world anymore.*

He opened his eyes and could see it was daytime from the light rays streaming in through the small openings in the ceiling of his cave. He was glad the walls were still intact. No one had built anything over his resting place this time. He now moved with total silence, not difficult in his present state. He sat up and watched.

Another light beam came from the entryway. *Someone must have a torch, or one of those ... what were they called? Oh, yes—lightflashes, no, flashlights.* Only this couldn't be humans; they'd have to be much smaller if they came in through that opening. He was sure no one could've excavated a larger opening without awakening him.

He would just watch and hope this didn't mean his cave would be taken over by modern humans. He had been relatively comfortable here for a long time, left alone to sleep peacefully.

He sighed inwardly. After all, what more was there for him than to sleep the time away? Maybe someday things would change for him, but every time he had tried to live as a human, he had failed miserably. Half-breed. Not human, not angel. Belonging nowhere.

He willed his mind away from all that negativity. He should be glad he existed. No use being unappreciative. Someday, maybe it would be his turn to find a place to belong. He tried to clear all thoughts and just listen and watch.

He almost giggled with them. These joyful little creatures seemed to be having so much fun. Apparently one had slipped into the water and they both giggled. He thought their sweet giggling voices tinkled like bells. He saw the light beam brush briefly inside the cave, swinging around the walls, and heard one little voice gasp, seemingly in awe.

His dread of being discovered and having to relocate was temporarily overpowered by his pleasure in hearing the maiden appreciate his artwork. Yes, he guessed the cave must be quite a sight for a human. He had patiently molded and trained mud with dripping stalagmite and stalactite formations to achieve elaborate sculptures. After all, time had been no object—he could be infinitely patient. He had never known another artist who used the same medium—probably no one had enough patience—or enough madness. He sighed.

He had used the jewels he had collected over the centuries to embellish the sculptures; these were mostly ones he found in Africa, but also some nice turquoise from the western part of this continent.

Oh, it wasn't as nice as Solomon's temple, or even as beautiful as Michelangelo's work in the Sistine Chapel; he had watched in awe as Michelangelo's deft hands displayed his genius. Nor was his work even as nice as some he had seen in Russia before the revolution, or in Constantinople, but it was much nicer than what that silly bunch did at Mount Rushmore. He had been tempted to instigate some mischief then—how could they call that art? It was *very* big, but didn't have the whimsical appeal of the Great Sphinx of Giza.

The maidens were coming into sight. Were they elves? They were so very tiny. And beautiful. Not emaciated like so many he had seen in the bleaker places he had lived. He used to like looking at the healthy people on this continent. It reminded him a little of a much-earlier time. And most of the people he had encountered here seemed relatively peaceful—not always quivering in fear for their lives. Regardless, watching these two maidens, he saw that one seemed bolder than the other. The timid one wanted to go back, but the bold one kept trying to make it fun for her and calm her fears. The bold one seemed in awe of his artwork, now standing still, shining the light beam first over one and then over another sculpture. The timid one didn't seem to notice, having already turned back.

My, how he liked this tiny bold maiden, this water sprite. He was glad she enjoyed his artwork. He would give her something of it if he could figure out a way to do it without frightening her. He could not see her face in the dim light, but was curious to note that she was dressed immodestly for this country, at least by the standards that had been in place when he retired here, though maybe the style of dress was different now. One couldn't be too quick to judge customs—many a chaste maiden dressed more skimpily than this in other, hotter parts of the world, and so this did not tell him very much. She had a long, sun-bleached braid on either side of her face, and her bare limbs looked like they had been fair but tanned by the sun. A poor maiden, no doubt, required to work in the fields. But with that adventurous spirit and boldness, she wouldn't stay poor for long. *Hmmm,* yes, she intrigued him.

For the first time in many, many years, he found himself interested in something. He felt his limbs begin to gain energy, his whole body awakening. Yes, it was time to awaken again. His curiosity had been piqued.

He watched as the tiny enchantress, to taunt the other standing in the opening, shone the light on her own face and made what was undoubtedly intended to be a scary face. While the light was still on her face, just for an instant, he saw her laugh before the light was whisked away, and his heart leapt. She was beautiful. Not in a sultry way like Cleopatra, more like the free-spirited beauties of the earlier years.

As he watched and listened, the timid maiden screamed and ran out of his cave. The bold one followed toward the opening. He felt a flicker of regret that she was gone. He knew he would remember that sweet face, now indelibly etched in his memory. And she loved to laugh like dear, dear Zyou. He smiled for a moment in blissful remembrance of the sound of her sweet laughter. Yes, the sound in his ears was even more precious and beautiful than strains from the harp of David.

As the tiny maiden left the cave, he sighed to himself. *Don't go. Please.*

# CHAPTER 4

# Hidden Treasure of More than One Kind

Once back at Mamaw's, Annie decided to make plans for the rest of the summer. After the dinner dishes were done and Mamaw helped to bed, she went out on the front porch to view the moon and stars. The moon was three-quarters and shone bright enough here, away from the city lights, to cast shadows. Yes, this was a precious world. How does one protect things that have mutually exclusive interests, when both are priceless?

She decided she'd continue to visit Missy until the end of the summer, but perhaps they could experiment with the Angel Stone feature—the one Red had used to become invisible. And she'd cease mentioning the cave. Now that they knew it existed, she didn't think Missy would ask to go into it again. After all, she'd rushed out due to fear of a sudden drop-off. Billy probably wouldn't ask to explore it. His mind was on more practical matters, like trying to scrape together a modest living by farming. This took pretty much all his time and energy.

So she'd avoid the cave until she could talk to her mom about it. Her mom would know what to do and could advise her on whether to tell Mamaw or anyone else. Or perhaps, Uncle Alistair would have a suggestion—he knew lots of professors, at least one of whom had to be an archeologist, she reasoned. And of course she'd tell Red. They kept no secrets.

She'd keep her friendship with Missy as long as Missy wanted it. She owed her and Billy so much for helping her make the discovery. Did Missy Skype? She'd ask her.

She heard a screech owl calling from a nearby ridge—such a haunting sound. She glanced toward a nearby hill where the black form of the church stood tall and strong. She knew that Papaw was buried in the graveyard next to the little church, and this somehow suggested peace to her. It was funny. She'd have thought that if anyone asked her if she'd like to live near a graveyard, especially in such an isolated place, she'd have responded, "Definitely not." But that wasn't the case here. That graveyard that contained the remains of her ancestors and their neighbors; it wasn't scary at all, but comforting. Yes, she could see why Mamaw wouldn't leave this house to come and live with them. There was something hauntingly compelling about this place. To her surprise, she realized she'd miss it when she went back to Maryland. Who knew, maybe someday she'd move here.

Once in her room, she pulled her pocket calendar from her purse. She really hadn't been keeping up with the date or even which week it was—her preoccupation with getting into the cave had dominated all her thoughts this summer. She walked back into the small den and found the object of her interest— the daily newspaper that came by mail from Morristown each weekday. The paper still lying on the sofa was from Friday and was dated August fourth. *Wow*. There were only three weeks left in the summer.

For the next two weeks, Annie continued to visit Missy as often as before, though taking care to spend time talking with Mamaw, too, showing her some new video games to play on her iPad. Mamaw didn't like Minesweeper, but really got hooked on Spider Solitaire.

Annie never re-entered the cave again with Missy, but focused on figuring out how to achieve the ghost-like transformation that Red had experienced, what Annie now called the ghost transformation. This wasn't too difficult—they experimented on plants and finally, one afternoon when Annie was visiting Missy, a ladybug, though Annie had felt a little guilty doing this in case she lost it and couldn't zap it back.

Missy apparently was having the same thought. "Annie, do you think if we can't zap it back, it'll have to crawl around aimlessly for eternity, or do you think it'll eventually die?"

"Well, Red said her boyfriend didn't have to eat when he'd been zapped, so I guess it might live a really long time. But I think at some point it'd run out of energy from the food already in its system. It wouldn't have anything with the same molecules to eat, and so I guess it'd starve—eventually."

Both girls frowned at the same time. Annie quickly pointed the STAG unit at the spot where she thought the ladybug would be and they were both relieved to realize that they needn't have worried—it was zapped back and scurried away, no worse for wear. Realizing it had worked and they could now turn themselves invisible, they both let out an excited squeal.

"Do you mind zapping me first? I want to go first just in case anything goes wrong," Annie said.

"Are you sure? Maybe we should ask Billy to go first, him being a man and all. I mean, he'd probably want to be the brave one."

"Missy, that's sexist," Annie said, laughing.

Missy smiled. "Yeah, I guess I am a little old-fashioned that way."

"No, this is my responsibility. And besides, if something happened to me, it wouldn't affect as many people. I mean, what would either of you do without the other?" Annie said.

Missy blushed slightly and looked towards Billy, who was peacefully sitting under a tree, whittling.

"Admit it, Missy. Billy would be totally lost without you."

"Yeah, I guess."

The first time, she had Missy zap her back in one minute just to make sure it worked, same as when they'd experimented with the Elf Stone feature, and then she spent half an hour in the ghost transformation. Missy good-naturedly complied. Before they began, though, Missy had been a little shocked when Annie explained that she would have to strip before being zapped because fabrics that relied on friction to hold the fibers together disintegrated in the ghost transformation, and she'd forgotten to wear something other than cotton. So they'd ended up doing the zapping behind the trailer where Annie couldn't be seen.

During her half-hour adventure, Annie decided to try flying. Red had told her what to expect, but Annie didn't think she'd told her half the story.

It was indescribably beautiful, being able to see the essence of all things. Annie saw the guardian angels hovering overhead, but as Red had warned, her own angel disappeared instantly upon realizing she could see it. Missy's angel didn't seem to notice her, though, and so she got to watch it hover protectively over Missy for a few minutes, amazed at actually seeing something people had speculated about for eons.

She then flew up over the Swan Hole, viewing the ridgeline that traveled north to south, dazzled by the green lushness. She saw mists already beginning to rise from the valleys even though it was only early evening. She got to soar with a pair of turkey vultures looking for a meal, though she couldn't travel as fast and was soon left behind.

She knew she'd never forget this experience. She was ecstatic at having the opportunity to give this gift to Missy and Billy.

After her half hour was up and Missy zapped her back, Annie hugged Missy and practically swung her off her feet in her excitement. "Oh my gosh, Missy. I can't wait for you to see it! I'm not going to give you any spoilers, but you and Billy have got to try it."

"Yeah, I was thinking about it and do think I'd like to try it. But the clothing thing, Annie ... I'm not sure Billy'd do it. I mean if we do it together, which is what I'd like, you'd have to see us naked, wouldn't you? I don't think Billy'd do it."

"Red and Erik wore leather," Annie remembered. "I'm not really sure, but I think anything except cotton, silk, or wool would work—anything that's not woven."

"Well, I can look for something, but I don't know, Annie."

"Missy, you've got to try it. The two of you together. I think even if you wore plastic trash bags like tunics, that'd work. But I guess I shouldn't push. Something could go wrong and I'd never forgive myself. Tell you what—it's getting late anyway. Why don't you talk to Billy tonight and see what you can find to wear and I'll come back tomorrow? Then, if you want to, fine, and if you don't, that's fine, too. Sound okay?"

Missy looked relieved. "That sounds good. I'll talk to Billy."

When Annie packed the next day to go back to the Swan Hole, she decided to visit the cave again, this time under the ghost transformation. She remembered Red saying she could pass through doors. So perhaps she could enter the cave without being small.

She needed to find some type of clothing to wear. She searched through all her clothing labels and finally found a disposable plastic raincoat; thankfully, it was yellow rather than clear. It also had a large pocket on either side. She wanted to try and record as much as possible but was afraid to try transforming her cell phone, since Red had told her they thought

Erik's key, which he'd had with him when he transformed, had dissolved along with his clothing.

What about paper? She'd take a pencil, she decided; the graphite should be useable for etching over any raised designs she found. But paper was another matter. She didn't think it would survive the transition, because wasn't it just wood fibers held together by friction? She decided to pack a few pages in her pocket just in case, but wasn't going to count on it. What about wax paper? The idea struck her as a possibility. Perhaps the wax would hold the paper together. Yes, that should work. She knew where Mamaw kept the wax paper. She found a nice full roll and unwound about twelve feet, folding it and placing it in her pocket.

She arrived at Missy's and was pleased to find that she and Billy had decided to take her up on her offer to let them try the ghost transformation.

They were dressed in cut-offs. She reminded them that they couldn't wear woven fabric, and Missy said she had that covered and so they disappeared momentarily into the trailer and returned wearing some type of synthetic swimsuits, which Annie wasn't certain would work.

But they turned out to work just fine. They were gone for just over half an hour and returned from their adventure raving about their flying experience and casting loving glances to each other. They also expressed profuse gratitude at being able to see essences and glimpses of their guardian angels, both of which had ducked for cover once they realized they were being seen. Annie wasn't surprised at all to hear that.

"I mean, Annie," Missy interjected, "it's one thing to read about angels, but to get to actually see one, I feel so very blessed. Thank you so much for this opportunity. It's something neither of us will ever, ever forget."

"It's definitely mutual—I'm grateful to you, too, Missy. And Billy. Without you, I could never have gotten to explore like this, either. My Uncle Alistair, as you know, doesn't know that

I have the STAG control, and if he found out, he would be really mad because some people have been after it, wanting to use its power for evil, I think," Annie said. "So you and Billy have to remember to never breathe a word of this to anyone. Well, at least not for a few years. Maybe by the time you have kids, the mysteries will be solved and the whole thing will be common knowledge. And then you can tell them of our awesome adventures."

"Yes, agreed." Both Billy and Missy nodded.

"Well, guess I had better get changed for my turn," Annie said, anxious to see the cave again.

"You can change in the bathroom," Missy suggested, holding open the front door for Annie.

Annie emerged a few minutes later, wearing her plastic raincoat and with her tools of investigation stashed in the pockets. Upon being zapped, she wasted no time, knowing she only had half an hour and this would likely be her only opportunity to investigate the cave again before going back home to Maryland.

She hesitated just a moment, however, steeling her nerves at the idea of actually trying to move through rock. She only had Red's account of passing through objects to go by. She flew to the small cave opening. She timidly reached her fingers into the opening, then pressed her arm into it. She felt a strange sensation, kind of like her arm was soaking up water, but in this case, it was rock. *Okay, this isn't so bad*, she thought, and pushed the rest of her body into the rock bank. *Yes!* She almost cheered aloud as she entered the cavern. She felt a little giddy at first and then focused her attention on the task ahead.

She began by observing her surroundings, remembering that one of her favorite teachers used to say that observation was the first step in the scientific method. She had no flashlight, but had bargained on the glow of all the things in the cave to help light her way. Red had told her about this aspect of the transformation, and during her test run yesterday, had found it to be truly awesome and beautiful. Living things had a glow—Erik called them essences. But rocks and other materials also had a glow that could be seen in this state, probably some type of energy. She wasn't sure how it worked but she'd love to know—she could perceive some things that were usually invisible in her normal state. And she couldn't see some things that were usually visible, like people or birds, at least, not in their usual forms; rather, she saw their inner essences much more clearly than their physical forms. And this cavern glowed with an unspeakably beautiful essence.

She could clearly see every corner and nook. She didn't have to worry about falling. If she and Missy had explored the cave in this state, Missy likely wouldn't have panicked, she thought.

She began to swim-fly into the large cavern. Like a hummingbird, she hovered for a moment to view each work of art. Were these carved? She tried to feel the surface of a perfectly shaped cathedral column, but her hand kept slipping into the stone. The column and all the other sculptures glowed with a white-green glow, like white quartz with a faint green glow inside. And it sparkled. In some places, she thought there must be actual jewels, a ring of emeralds encircling the top of each column, and something that looked like rubies enhancing a flower carving above an arched shape over what appeared to be the entryway to a royal chamber. There was a throne made of stone, adorned with elaborately carved animal shapes, mostly birds, on top of the high back. And alongside the throne, there was a smooth shelf that looked almost comfortable, couch-like, though made of stone. Whoever, whatever did this obviously had a beautiful soul. It was breathtaking.

She noticed a tunnel leading downward on the right side of the royal chamber. A silvery-white glow shone from the tunnel, much brighter than the faint green glow from all the surrounding stones. She wanted to investigate, but first she wanted to methodically catalogue what she saw in this room.

She removed the wax paper and pencil from her pocket and stretched the wax paper onto one of the steps leading up to the throne. She began trying to write on the wax paper like a scroll, then quickly ripped the twelve-foot length into page-sized sections to make it more manageable. She tried very hard to make notes on the wax paper with her pencil. As expected, this was difficult and so she relied more on making impressions in the wax than actually leaving darkened letters from the graphite, which mostly just slipped over the paper, not really leaving a mark. She'd have to figure out later how to lift the etched writing from the wax paper, maybe with chalk powder, but she'd worry about that when she got back to Maryland where she had all manner of art supplies—and Uncle Alistair's lab.

She took elaborate notes and sketched the beautiful royal chamber with its columns and steps leading up to it. She inspected the area to the left of the chamber and discovered something like a plaque with an elaborately carved frame on the rock wall. She could hardly contain her excitement when she realized there was some type of writing on it. Most of the shapes looked like modern letters but she was sure it was no modern language. She decided to try doing rubbings of this plaque. She pressed a wax paper page onto the uppermost part, and, using the side of the graphite, rubbed back in forth in rapid motions, pressing down as hard as she dared without tearing the paper or having the paper press into the object, and made an imprint of about a third of the plaque. She continued with two more pages until the whole plaque was copied. She quickly, but carefully, folded these and slipped them into a pocket.

She already felt like she'd discovered the mother lode of all that was mysterious. And she felt a little self-satisfied that her ideas had worked. She continued on around the cave wall to the front part, underneath the entrance. She discovered more framed images carved into the wall, carved line drawings of faces. This really intrigued her.

The central figures were of a beautiful woman and man. There wasn't much extraordinary about their features, except something akin to perfection. The woman had long hair pushed back from her face; a small braid on either side encircled her head like a band. The man had graceful features, long flowing hair unrestrained, and no beard or facial hair—Annie could only describe him as angelic and dazzling.

On the other side of the woman's image were three smaller images, another man and two girls. As with the two larger images of faces and hair, there was no clothing to use for reference. The man's face was handsome, perhaps not quite so much as the larger one, but with some similarity of features. The girls' faces were pretty and seemed young. One appeared to be African, with curly hair and a small upturned nose. The other had high cheekbones and a flatter nose than the man, giving the impression of a Native American.

Annie quickly made sketches and began to worry that her half hour was almost up. She had no way of carrying a watch and would have to approach Missy or Billy and make some sound or splash so they'd know when she was ready. She wanted to stay, but she didn't want to go much over half an hour. They might get worried and one of them might try coming in to rescue her. Her secret would be exposed.

She folded all the rest of the rubbings and notes and stashed them in her pocket. She did want to investigate that glow, though, if only for a quick peek. She flew timidly over toward the tunnel. As she peeked into the tunnel, however, she froze.

Just inside the tunnel entrance stood the source of the silvery-white glow: a tall man. An exquisitely enchanting tall man. He was most beautiful sight she'd ever seen, and the most frightening. His essence was like that of crystal, bright, yet cool at the same time, pure silvery-white with no murkiness, like the guardian angels she'd glimpsed, yet he looked human. Unable to move, she slowly began to sink, as she was slightly heavier than air.

The man said something Annie didn't understand, but his voice was very pleasant and he bowed gallantly.

Annie had never seen someone actually bow in earnestness before—it seemed somehow from a different time.

The movement of the figure and the sensation that she was sinking made her snap out of her momentary paralysis. She screamed and immediately flew toward the opening, panicking that she wouldn't be able to find the opening fast enough.

Was this a demon? A ghost? Was he after her? Was he angry that she'd intruded?

She somehow found the small light patch that came from the opening and immediately pressed her body into the wall. She did it too quickly, however, and bounced back out, momentarily stunned.

She found herself lying on the ledge of the entryway. Quickly sitting up, she glanced around, only to find the man hovering just behind her. She inhaled sharply, ready to scream again.

He raised his hands in a pleading motion. He said something again that she didn't understand, though she registered his soothing tone.

He began to speak in English now, still using the same soothing voice. "Please, young maiden. Do not be frightened. I will not harm you. If you try to do that again, you may hurt yourself. I am Aaan. I am not a ghost or demon. Please, do not go."

As he spoke, Annie backed slowly away, keeping her eyes on his. She was curious and momentarily tempted to listen to him and stay with this compelling creature that was begging her to stay.

But her fear won; she was spooked and wanted to be out in the sunlight. "I gotta go," she said.

Slowly backing into the wall, her heart pounding, she departed through the rock, losing sight of him and emerging out into the sunlight.

Outside, she calmed down, relieved he hadn't followed her out. She looked around and saw Billy and Missy chatting quietly, their feet dangling in the water at the pool's edge. She was sure that her half hour had long passed and quickly went over to a spot just in front of them and splashed the water to get their attention.

Billy looked at the spot where she'd splashed. "That you, Annie? You ready?"

She tried to answer him, but wasn't sure if he could tell it was her. But he must've heard because he said, "Okay, then, come on over to the zappin' spot."

She was zapped back to normal. "How was it?" Missy asked eagerly.

Not wanting to spoil their fun, Annie forced herself to giggle and said that it was as awesome as yesterday and that she hoped she hadn't gone much over her half hour.

"It was fine," they said in unison. She was sure they wouldn't complain if she had been gone two hours.

Annie felt she had to mention she'd seen an apparition, maybe an angel or some type of spirit. "He seemed good and not evil, though," she said, and pointed in the general direction of the cave. She conveniently failed to mention that he was inside it.

Billy and Missy glanced upward in that direction. "I guess there're a lot of things all around us, if we could only see 'em," said Billy. "I don't know, maybe it's best just to leave 'em alone. They don't bother us an' we don't bother them." Missy nodded. They gave each other a small peck on the lips, obviously still glowing from their adventure together.

As Annie walked toward the road, she glanced back to see Missy and Billy, his arm draped lovingly over her shoulders, her arm around his waist, strolling slowly toward the trailer. *I sure hope I didn't bring anything evil on that sweet couple,* she thought. She thought about the angelic man in the cave. Should she have warned them more forcefully about him? Then again, he hadn't really seemed harmful and didn't try to chase or catch her. She walked back to Mamaw's with her thoughts racing, anxious to be alone to look at her rubbings and try to make sense of all this.

CHAPTER 5

# The Tongue of Angels

K aye and Red were scheduled to arrive on Friday to visit with Mamaw for an evening and then drive Annie back to Maryland on Saturday. Annie felt a little smug as she cooked a large dinner of garden vegetables, fried apples, and fresh biscuits. She knew her biscuits would be flaky and yummy. Mamaw had overseen several attempts that summer until she perfected the moisture content of the dough and the number of times she kneaded it. Her mom would be especially pleased. Annie felt she'd learned a lot this summer from her grandmother and would be a little sad to leave.

"Annie, I think I heard a car. Do you see them?" Mamaw called.

Annie looked out the kitchen window over the sink. "Yep, it's them all right. Looks like Red's drivin' — wonder if she got her license this summer?" Annie heard the dropped "g" in her voice and thought for an instant that she sounded very much like Missy. She wondered if she'd picked up some of the mountain accent. Her mouth pulled into a sideways grin at the thought.

It felt good to see her mom and sister and Annie enjoyed the embraces and compliments. She felt proud when her mom observed how well Mamaw stood and how she walked without any assistance now, knowing that she had helped. Her mom even proclaimed during dinner that Annie's biscuits were smoother and lighter than her own, which Annie considered quite a compliment since she knew her mom dearly loved a good biscuit.

After dinner, Annie did the dishes and cleaned the kitchen, not without some grumbling, however, as she'd expected Red to pitch in, given that she had cooked. But Red had driven most of the ten-hour drive and her mom really wanted to visit with Mamaw for the short time she'd be there. So Annie gave in, demanding only that Red stay to help clear the table and put the leftovers away. Despite the slight resentment that Red didn't offer to do the dishes, Annie was still glad to see her, and once alone in the kitchen, began to relate bits and pieces of her story.

Red listened with some interest but also seemed somewhat distracted. When Annie told her she'd made a friend, she responded, "That's nice," and when she mentioned that she'd smoked cigarettes, Red responded, "Uh-huh."

Annie was beginning to wonder if Red had heard anything she said. So she told her about using the STAG control to go into the cave and finding sculptures and carvings. Red said, "Wow." But Annie wasn't sure she really felt the amazement.

"And I saw a ghost, or demon, or something, in the cave," Annie said, watching her sister.

"Ah," Red said. Annie felt a flash of irritation until Red suddenly seemed to snap to attention and register what she'd said. "You saw what?"

Now, Annie knew she had her attention. She summarized the whole escapade and once again told Red about the cave and its resident. Red was rapt with attention this time. "Oh my gosh, Annie. Take me there. I want to see this," she demanded. "Do you think it's a ghost? Or a demon?"

"I don't know, Red. I mean, he didn't *seem* evil, not at all like those things you told me about that were in Roy," Annie said. "I guess if I had to call him something, I'd say 'ghost,' but I really don't know. I'd love to get your opinion. The only time we'd have, though, is if we slip out after Mom and Mamaw are asleep, 'cause Mom wants to leave first thing in the morning."

"Okay, let's do it. Let's go tonight," Red said.

Annie thought it felt good to share her secret with the one person she could really trust not to exploit it and was anxious to show Red the cave.

Annie and Red pretended to go to bed in the same bed they'd always shared during visits to Mamaw's, offering no hint that they would be going out later. They talked a little more and exchanged iPods, each wanting the other to appreciate newly downloaded tunes they'd collected over the summer. Annie lay back on the bed, fully dressed, earbuds in place, to relax for a while and wait for her mother and grandmother to cease talking together in the living room and turn in.

Unfortunately, the next thing she knew, the sun was peeping through the curtains and Red was sound asleep beside her. Disappointment washed over her. She slammed her fist on the bed at the realization that she'd lost her one opportunity to show Red the cave before driving away.

On the drive home, with the subject of exploring the cave a moot point for now, Annie tried to refocus her attention on Red to extract from her the reason she'd been so distracted the day before. She knew it undoubtedly had something to do with Erik and was curious to know the latest.

But there was very little opportunity to talk to Red without their mother hearing everything, and their mother wanted to hear all about Annie's first full summer away from home. She asked many questions and Annie found herself talking a lot about gardening and cooking.

Red gave her a look that told her that she was back in the modern world now and that those activities weren't cool.

Nonetheless, it did feel a little good to reassure her mom that the experience had been good for her, and for her grandmother, as well, she thought. She told her a little about her friend, Missy, and about their visits to the Swan Hole, but, of course, mentioned nothing about the STAG control or cigarettes.

All their talk about the country launched her mom into a discourse of trivia about who had married who in that hollow, or *holler,* as it was said in the local dialect. She knew a lot about Billy and Missy's families, and Annie knew if she'd been interested enough to listen, she'd have learned their pedigrees all the way back to the 1700s. Annie kept one earbud in so she could listen to her music and yet still respond to her mom without appearing rude. Her mom also retold all the tales she knew about the Swan Hole—at this Annie perked up and removed the earbud. As her mom talked about the Swan boy drowning there, Annie wondered if what she'd seen was his ghost. She'd try to see if she could find anything on Google as soon as she got back home. And she'd pin down Red and force her to reveal what was so distracting her. Annie noted that Red stared out the window, dreamily and perhaps with some angst, all the time she wasn't busy driving. Something was definitely on her mind.

They arrived home just in time for dinner, which consisted of a pizza from their now-favorite local restaurant. Annie's father had clearly missed her a lot and asked a gazillion questions. She answered all, leaving out nothing but the STAG control, the cave, the ghost, and the cigarettes. He looked bronzed by the sun from a summer of bicycling and swimming and his beard had grown at least an inch. Was he ever going to cut it again? They saved a couple of slices of pizza for Erik, who was to arrive a little later.

"Red, what's up with Erik?" Annie asked her sister the moment they had a second alone together. "I'd have thought he'd be here waiting for you to get back. You two seemed joined at the hip when I left." Annie hoped that the newness hadn't worn off and that her sister wasn't headed toward heart-break. *Nah, not Erik,* she thought. *If anyone's smitten, it's him.*

"That's what I've been trying to tell you. Here, come up to my room for a minute," she said. Just then, Erik arrived, and she pointed him in the direction of the pizza. "Back in a minute, Erik."

"Take your time, Sonia. It's great to have you back." At this he made an adorable kissy motion toward her.

Red blew a kiss back and glowed. *Okay, at least that's settled,* thought Annie. *No trouble there.*

When they got to Red's room and the door was closed securely behind them, she turned to Annie. "Can you keep a secret? I mean, it's not really going to stay a secret, but it is for now."

"You two gonna elope?"

"No, no, nothing like that. I still have to go to college." Red rolled her eyes.

"You're not ..."

"Oh my gosh, no." Red glowered. "Just listen."

Red sat on the bed and motioned for Annie to sit next to her. "You remember that Erik's dad got kidnapped when he was working in Iraq in 2004? He was declared dead some time later, but no evidence was ever found of his death."

"Yes," Annie answered warily.

"Well, Erik wants to go find him. He wants to use a STAG control to infiltrate the radical groups still there and look for him. It could take weeks or months." Red sounded somewhat alarmed.

"So? Red, you can't be mad at him for that—you'd do the same thing. So would I," Annie said rationally. She knew it'd be difficult for Red to part with him now that they'd become so close, but this was the right thing to do.

"Of course I'm not mad about him going. Don't be silly." She made an exasperated face. "I'm mad because he won't take me with him."

"Ooohhh." Annie nodded her head thoughtfully.

"I mean, I know it's a long time for me to miss school, but how am I going to focus with him in danger? And we can't forget—that horrid cult's still out there somewhere. Still wanting to get their hands on the stones," she said. "He will definitely be in danger."

Annie tried to soothe her sister. "Not really, Red, not if he's transformed. I mean, what can they do, put him in a bottle like a genie? I don't even think they could do that. He'd slip right out. Though, I don't know, maybe if the bottle were kryptonite or something …"

Red rolled her eyes. "I know all that. And yes, I know I'm being emotional. But Annie, the genie thing's in Saudi Arabia—wrong country." The tension now broken, both girls laughed.

"Red, you're in high school. You'd probably get sent to a foster home if Mom and Dad let you go into a war zone, trying to rescue someone who was kidnapped almost ten years ago."

"I know." Red sighed. "Erik says he's looking forward to my joining him at Georgetown next year and doesn't want me to have to repeat my senior year. And I guess he's right."

"Exactly."

"You know what, Annie? I missed you." Red hugged her warmly and Annie finally felt better about Red.

"Well, you better get downstairs before this man you want to spend every minute with thinks you don't love him anymore. Or, worse yet, becomes best friends with Dad and starts bicycling all the time." She cackled at this, feeling mischievous.

"Annie, don't even suggest that." Red laughed too.

"Oh, yeah, Red. I need a favor," Annie said, remembering. "Can you please tell Erik about the cave and ghost, and then somehow, can the three of us go off somewhere alone so I can ask him questions? But you're absolutely not, under any circumstances, to tell him I have a STAG control."

"Yeah, he'd flip if he knew you had a STAG control. Only a few people know Uncle Alistair has them. I'm pretty sure Uncle

Alistair returned the stones as quickly as possible because he didn't want anyone coming to collect them and finding the STAG controls. If he or Erik knew you'd used one with two strangers, I'm pretty sure they'd be furious."

"I know, but I trust Missy and Billy," Annie said. "And I do want to talk to Erik about the ghost thing. He might have some insight. After all, your ghost turned out to be something else. What if this one's something else? I hope he's not a demon. He looked—well, handsome."

"Oh, no, Annie. Not you too. What is it with this family? All the girls fall for ghosts." They both laughed.

Downstairs, Annie found her mom and dad engrossed in a movie. They tried to interest her in joining them since it was a romantic comedy and Annie usually loved those. But Annie assured them that what she really wanted was to go out for some pleasant air now that the day had cooled. Annie caught Red's eye and made a silent entreaty; Red quickly caught on and said she and Erik were thinking of a walk on the towpath and perhaps Annie would like to join them.

"We were?" asked Erik innocently, to which he received a nudge to the ribs. "Oh, right." He smiled and quickly stood to stretch his legs. "Can't get enough of that pleasant night air."

Annie noted that her mom and dad weren't listening to anything but their movie, and so the threesome sauntered outside.

"Did you tell him?" Annie asked Red.

"Tell me what?" asked Erik.

"No, just when do you think I had an opportunity?" Red said, rolling her eyes.

Annie took a breath and recounted her story to Erik about finding the cave and seeing the apparition. She conveniently left off the part about the opening being small and that she'd used a STAG control to enter the cave. She described the sculptures and writing and tried to describe the apparition as best she could without giving away that she had been in a transformed state. "So what do you think of the apparition? Do you think

65

it was a ghost? Or do you think it was a demon? Or maybe a good angel?"

Erik took a long slow breath, thinking before answering. "Okay, the apparition. I know that you aren't going to like my answer very much, but I simply don't know. I mean, the angels I saw were either guarding other people or zooming to and fro, carrying messages to the man upstairs or to some higher angel, I assumed. I tried to talk to them but they scurried away every time. It seemed there must've been some rule they followed, like they were forbidden from talking to me. Maybe they have to complete a special task or something before they can communicate with us. Or maybe it was because I looked like something they didn't like. I just don't know."

He took another thoughtful breath. "I did see demons, though. And Red saw them, too." He glanced to Red, who nodded. "But I didn't learn anything from them, other than they exist, and that if they have a toehold inside of someone, they seem to swarm them like parasites. Except the one in Lorenzo. Maybe because it had been there longer and seemed to have an established territory, or maybe he was a more powerful demon. Tell me, Annie, did your apparition have a particular color? And was he murky or clear? You probably couldn't see these attributes too well without being transformed, but could you describe the apparition in more detail?"

"Sure. He was silvery-white and yes, he was crystal clear. He was really kinda, well, beautiful. And as I told you, he'd evidently spent a lot of time making beautiful sculptures. So I think he's good."

"Well, I have to agree. If he's clear, he's good, at least that's my interpretation from watching and studying what I could see. I'm surprised, though, that you could see him that well. But if he had a white light, then he's likely angelic, I think. The guardian angels had a whitish light." He again looked to Red for confirmation.

"That's right, Annie. I saw guardian angels, too. They were a beautiful silvery-white. Everything about them was beautiful—their flowing movements, their peaceful focus on the ones they were protecting. Does that sound like him?"

"It does. I think I knew it all along. I'm pretty sure he was an angel."

"Did he have a kind of, well ... undefined flowing aspect, rather than feet?" Red asked.

Annie thought back. "I don't know. I think I had the impression he had feet. I didn't notice a flowing aspect. Does that mean he was a ghost?" She looked at Erik imploringly, wishing he knew more and wanting him to give her more information about this beautiful being.

He shook his head regretfully. "Annie, I didn't see a ghost while I was transformed, or any other time. At least, I didn't recognize one if I did. I saw lots of energy of various hues and clarities. It seemed to emanate from all things, both living and non-living, but I didn't see a ghost. Does that mean they don't exist? Certainly not. If my experience has taught me anything, it's that we have to have an open mind and that it's possible to believe in the unbelievable, in things I'd previously discounted without proper investigation. Lots of people have reported seeing ghosts, though, in all eras of history, so I suppose they probably do exist, at least in some places at some times."

Later, in her room, Annie's mind was whirling. She needed time to process and reflect before she could even think of going to bed. She took a slow bath, all the while thinking of the cave and her discussion with Red and Erik.

She knew she still had more questions than answers. She toweled off, enjoying the feel of her huge fluffy body sheet as she buffed her skin to a pink glow. Annie thought about Mamaw and how her towels had been more practical, probably because that's what small farm life demanded. The richness of the existence was more about things that money couldn't buy—like the beauty of fog lifting each morning from the river valley and the peach-and-golden hues of rising sunrays.

And the smells. *Wow*. She knew that in the back of her mind she'd always loved river smells—that was one thing about living at Uncle Alistair's that she loved, too. But on her mamaw's farm, the earthy smells had been just as rich as the Potomac River valley, but more varied. She'd never before spent so much time with her hands actually in the soil. The richness of the organic scent of dirt was something she'd never before acknowledged to herself, but it was a sense of home—like some ancient ancestral yearning.

Thinking of dirt and mud brought her thoughts around to the cave again. As she brushed her teeth, she wondered what to make of the elaborate decorations in the cave. It had been like an artist's lair. *Why? Why create all that art if no one can see it? Had there really been a proper opening at one time? Did the Native Americans, or someone even earlier, come to enjoy the art?* She felt goose bumps on her bare arms.

Had it been part of a larger palace at one time? This didn't seem likely because the art seemed to actually be built *from* the cave. But then, all those ruins from ancient Egypt and Jerusalem seemed to always be underground. This had always puzzled her—why did everything sink into the ground? Did it actually sink or did dirt blow over it, burying it deeper and deeper over time? That really only made sense in a desert climate, where the sands blew around. Her head swam. This was too much to think about—it required hours on Google to figure out and she was too tired tonight.

But again, her mind came back around to the apparition. It was starting to feel surreal, like a dream or her imagination. She shook her head slowly. *Did I actually see that?* Funny how one's mind played tricks, she thought, making her wonder if she'd been mistaken. But she knew there had been no mistake. She had seen him. An angelic being. She knew from both her ghost transformation and from talking to Erik and Red that angels do for sure exist. Heck, even Roy's demon possession proved that. So why did she doubt this being? Was it because he'd tried to make contact with her? The guardian angels she'd seen had shied away, and even in her normal state, she never saw them but knew they were there, like so many things in the natural world. But this being had tried to talk to her. What did that mean?

She knew the only avenue she had, barring another ten-hour drive back to Tennessee, was to decipher the text from her etchings. Perhaps that would reveal his story. Who knew? Maybe her ghost or angel or whatever-he-was could help them with this nasty cult that was after the stones. Wouldn't that be nice—an ethereal champion. She had to believe he was good. In fact, she decided she would not think about him in any other way. She just wouldn't.

With that pleasant thought, she crawled under the covers and drifted off to sleep.

The next day, Annie went with her mom and Red to an early church service. She knew from Red that her mom had begun attending Reverend Joan's church regularly all summer, partly to show appreciation for the priest's help during the demon crisis with Roy and Lorenzo last winter.

Reverend Joan gave her a hearty handshake and Annie wondered if she might be able to provide some insight about her angel. On the spur of the moment, she asked, "Reverend Joan, if I had a question about spiritual things, could I ask you by email, or how should I contact you?"

"Absolutely. Any time, Anya. My email address and phone number are both on the webpage. Email is always a safer bet, but if it's a crisis, I have a pager."

"Okay, thanks—no crisis, just researching something."

Annie was beginning to think about how to research the etchings. She'd heard the phrase "tongues of angels," in the past and wondered if that meant angels had a separate language.

If this apparition was an angel, he might speak a different language. She decided to research online before emailing the priest. Annie's online search revealed several Biblical references to "tongues of angels," and seemed to be linked by some with the phrase "speaking in tongues," or "glossolalia," something practiced today by a few religious groups. *Hmmm, no mention of Episcopalians, so Reverend Joan might not know about it.* Still, the priest did have degrees in theology, so perhaps she should still ask. But how to ask without giving too much away? Perhaps she could carefully word it in such a way that might make her assume it was a school paper. That meant she'd need to wait until school started to send it, but as luck would have it this was only too close—tomorrow, in fact. She drafted the message but didn't yet send it, simply saying she was doing research on glossolalia and wondered if she knew anyone who spoke the language and if it had a written form that she knew of. *There, that should do it.*

The next day at school was somewhat uplifting since she was no longer a freshman. She found Nyah and some others that she knew from the year before and was glad to discover she and Nyah had two classes together after lunch. They both talked very fast, relating their summer adventures. She, of course, left out anything to do with the STAG control, but did boldly, and somewhat braggingly, mention that she had smoked a few cigarettes.

"Girl, you didn't. No way. You know what that stuff does to you, don't you? Bad breath. Lung cancer," Nyah chastised.

"I know. I didn't really like it and don't plan on ever doing it again. I just did it to make a new girl like me."

At Nyah's shocked expression, she quickly added, "I don't mean that I did it to fit in or be popular. I'm not that lame. It's just that, I met this girl and we spent a lot of time together this summer and exchanged secrets and that was hers, and I didn't want to appear judgmental."

"Okay, I guess that's a little better. At least your heart was in the right place. Just don't do it anymore." Nyah wagged her finger at Annie.

"Agreed."

"Now, just what was *your* secret?" Nyah teased.

*Uh-oh.* Annie didn't want to tell anyone else about the STAG control. She thought quickly and came up with an idea. "I'll show you my secret if you want to walk home with me after school. I found some ancient writing on a cave wall."

"Ooooh. Sounds mysterious. All right, I'm game."

After school, the same gang from last year walked home together, plus Nyah; she also lived near the school but not in the same direction, and so it was a rare treat getting to have her with them.

Upon their arrival home, Red went straight to her room, no doubt to shower and change before Erik came over. Annie grabbed two cold glasses of juice from the kitchen and started to grab a bag of chips, but remembering the wholesomeness of the farm, grabbed two apples instead, then took Nyah to her room to show her the etchings.

Nyah looked carefully at the etchings, her eyes wide. "This is really something. You found this in a cave? And no one else knows about it?"

"Do you recognize the language?" Annie asked.

Nyah shook her head.

Annie hesitated, then said, "I know this is gonna sound crazy, but what if it's in angel tongue?"

Nyah looked at her as though she had two heads. "Why would you think that? Wouldn't you think it was Cherokee or some other tribe?"

Annie paused again, then decided she had to confess her secret. "I'll come clean. I saw something in the cave," she confided, and watched for Nyah's reaction.

"What do you mean? Like a ghost or something? Girl, you're giving me goose bumps." Nyah seemed cautiously interested.

"I don't know, Nyah. It was like a glow—a human-like form. I just saw it for an instant." Annie was downplaying it since she knew how incredulous it sounded.

"And you think it was an angel? And that it wrote this?" Nyah sounded doubtful.

"I don't know." Annie wrinkled her brow in an exasperated expression. "I just thought it might be something related to the apparition. I just wish I knew what language this is. I feel like I could figure out if this was a ghost, angel, or … demon, if I could read this."

"A demon?" Nyah dropped the etching. "Maybe you should just burn it. You don't want to mess with that stuff, Annie."

"I don't really think it was a demon, Nyah," Annie said. "I just didn't get that feeling. It seemed good." Annie felt strangely defensive of the apparition and didn't want to think that others were scared of it.

"Angel tongue," Nyah repeated. "The only thing I know about is from my aunt. She belongs to a church where they do something called 'speaking in tongues.' My parents think it's silly—you know they're both doctors at N.I.H. and don't go in for a lot of religious stuff. But I don't know, my aunt doesn't seem like someone who would lie. Or even exaggerate … well, maybe she'd exaggerate. But she says it's something they do with the help of the Holy Spirit. They have a service where they pray for the spirit to give them utterance. Some people start talking in a strange language and others interpret what they're saying."

"What kinds of things do they usually say?" Annie was curious.

"Gosh, I don't know, Annie, she hasn't really gone into a lot of detail but I get the impression it was mostly worshipful stuff. Like, once somebody said the translation was, 'I will send showers of blessings.' And once it was something about being thankful."

"Do they ever have anything written down?" Annie wasn't feeling very hopeful that this was going to be easy to crack.

"I don't think so, Annie. I guess there's a story about a hand writing on the wall once and I think that might've been in the angel tongue, but I don't know for sure." Nyah was trying to be helpful.

"Does your aunt live around here?" Annie asked.

"No, she lives in Kentucky with my grandmother. I saw her this summer. I could call her, I guess, if you want me to ask her about it."

"I wonder if there's a church around here that speaks in tongues. You and I could go and ask questions," Annie urged.

"What're you trying to get me into?" Nyah laughed. "You and me at a service where they're speaking in tongues? I don't think so."

"Awe, come on. It'll be fun. It'll be a new adventure. We can tell my mom we're doing research and ask her to drive us next Sunday. Pleeeease, Nyah. I'll owe you a huge favor if you go with me," Annie pleaded.

Nyah expelled a puff of air in resignation. "All right. But you owe me big time. Like chemistry homework for a month."

The next weekend was Labor Day weekend, a weekend that normally included a Greene family camping trip. This year, however, both Red and Annie had begged out of it, both playing the too-busy-with-school card. Annie knew Red didn't want to be away from Erik for a whole three-day weekend and he'd already stated that he was too busy with his research on his father's disappearance to come along. No one questioned that. So Annie's parents decided to skip the trip, this year proclaiming that without their girls, camping didn't really appeal to them as much as other projects they each had underway.

So that Sunday morning, Annie sent her email off to Reverend Joan, then got her mom to drop off Nyah and her at a large, modern mega-church that Annie had found on the

Internet. It advertised speaking in tongues. They followed a stream of other people from the parking lot, who seemed to be converging on a wide set of doors. Upon entering, they were greeted by a well-dressed woman with an expensive-looking precision haircut.

Annie attempted to present the image that they weren't newcomers, but seasoned members of the congregation, by saying 'hi' but not slowing down to chat. She pulled Nyah along with her. Nyah seemed to be on the same page.

Annie could see the crowd moving toward a large room, somewhat like an auditorium, with many rows of folding chairs and a huge movie screen over the stage. On the stage was a band playing modern gospel music.

Nyah nudged Annie just as a man in a gray suit walked onto the stage. Annie looked over and Nyah pointed to a bulletin board with notices and announcements. Under the heading *Schedule of Fall Classes*, Annie spotted a class on glossolalia. It would take place Thursday evenings at seven. Beneath it were both a phone number and email address. *Bingo.* This was exactly what she was looking for.

They sat through the service, but the class turned out to be their only lead. Annie grumbled to Nyah as they emerged into the sunlight an hour later, "I can't believe no one spoke in tongues today."

"Yeah, I think my aunt said it's usually at certain services. But at least you have an email address," Nyah pointed out. "Isn't that your mom's car?"

Annie, too, had seen her mom's yellow smart car. Annie sighed at how easily it could be spotted in the huge parking lot amongst hundreds of cars, even though she recalled that it had been she who urged her mom to buy the car. It seemed fun at the time and after all, it was cool to be green. She caught Nyah's eye and had the feeling she was thinking similar thoughts.

That afternoon, Annie worked feverishly to turn the text from her etching into a format that could be emailed. She tried scanning it in Uncle Alistair's study but it didn't scan very satisfactorily. She then photographed it, but found the image came out too dark. She collected a couple of study lamps and brought them into her room. She found a flat piece of glass used to protect a small table to hold the paper flat.

She asked her dad if she could borrow his tripod and good camera. He hesitatingly obliged after lecturing her about only cleaning the lens with lens paper. She agreed. Luckily, he didn't ask what she wanted to photograph, probably assuming it was something related to school.

She locked herself in her room, cleared her desk, and placed the first wax-paper-etching on the desk, covered by the glass. She tried different lenses, distances, and light settings, and eventually loaded the best pictures onto her computer. She was pleased with the result. Even though she wouldn't be able to convert the etchings to text as she might've done from a scanned image, at least, not with any software she had, she could clearly see the letters and even zoom in if needed. She cropped the best photos and made a document.

Then she wrote an email to the person teaching the glossolalia class and asked if the class taught anything on written glossolalia and if this example text might be glossolalia. She sent this off, then decided to check her inbox, which she hadn't done in a few days, and was excited to find a message from Reverend Joan.

But she was disappointed to find that the priest didn't think glossolalia typically had a written form, though she agreed to see if she could find out any more. Perhaps, the priest suggested, it would be helpful for Annie to send her an example of the text in question and she could pass it around? Annie smiled at the perfect timing and sent her a photo of the text.

Lorenzo ran his hand exasperatedly through his hair—still thick, but much shorter than before. It really didn't register that he was doing this; it was just his latest compulsion. It felt so good to touch it now that it was neatly trimmed and always clean—and since he was determined to control all his other compulsions, he had to do something. He'd worked so hard to pull himself out of the pit of hell, and now this. Now his baby brother was falling for the same trap—*Damn them!*

Reeling with emotion, he took a sip from the aluminum can of cherry soda that he'd been holding in both hands, fighting an urge to crush the can for emphasis, while his kid brother—much too young to be drinking—took a long drink from the wine bottle resting between his knees as he slouched in a faded armchair, followed by a long draw from a joint.

"Antonio, I do know how you feel," Lorenzo said slowly and carefully, "but I've been there and I know the truth about these people. They are liars. They will make a demon possess you and you will lose everything. You don't know what they will do to you."

The young man laughed, and then coughed a few times, choking on the smoke that billowed from his mouth and nose. "*Porca miseria. Vecchio.* You worry too much. A thousand euros for just two days work. Where else am I going to get that kind of money?"

"But how happy will you be when you land in prison, eh?" Lorenzo looked grim. "A pretty boy like you wouldn't last a day in prison before becoming *ragazzo* to some bald one-hun-dred-fifty-kilo guy."

"I can take care of myself," Antonio scoffed.

Lorenzo looked at the aluminum can he now swirled and then continued, "But you cannot trust this cult. I, too, thought it was the cool thing to do at your age—it made me feel tough. Invincible. But look at what I became. I was their tool to use any way they wanted. I had no freedom—none. They made me take a demon into myself, Antonio." He beat his chest with one fist for emphasis. "A *demon*. Do you know how that felt?" He was panting now, his ire rising.

"You were hallucinating, *Vecchio*. From all the drugs you took. I do not believe in demons. You were just weak. And crazy. You still are."

"And what is it they want you to do in London to earn such euros?"

Antonio, obviously giddy from the wine and the irresistible power he presently welded to irritate his brother, had a loose tongue. "That's the best part. We get to kidnap someone. Some old man. It is going to be so funny to see his face when he realizes we have him." Antonio's laughter seemed forced and mirthless, as if trying to sound like he knew what he was doing and wanted to convince his brother that he actually wanted to do it.

But Lorenzo suspected the worst. As much as he didn't want to admit it to himself, he believed his baby brother had already gone through the initiation ceremony, and was already possessed by his own demon—or demons.

## CHAPTER 6

# The Magic of Google

The next day, Annie was delighted to see email messages from both the glossolalia instructor and Reverend Joan. She was stupefied, however, upon reading them. They both said the same thing: the text from the engravings was Latin. *Latin?*

The glossolalia instructor went on to expound on what Reverend Joan had said earlier, that glossolalia wasn't a real language, in the sense that it couldn't be taught the way French or Spanish can be taught. Instead, it was considered a spiritual gift that involved a certain type of meditative technique, which *could* be taught. Dates and times for upcoming classes were listed and he encouraged Annie to sign up.

Annie felt so foolish for not recognizing on her own that the text was Latin. She looked over the photos and her face reddened as she realized just how close the alphabet was to the modern one; if it'd been truly ancient, there wouldn't have been any recognizable letters. But between the fancy penman-ship and the setting where she found it, her imagination had made it seem more different than it was, she realized. *Angel tongue—yeah, right.*

Her self-chastisement turned into a thrill of hope, however, once she realized that it should be easy to translate Latin text. There were undoubtedly multiple programs that she could download this very evening to begin translating. She'd have the text translated if not by tonight, then very soon. All in all, she was overjoyed.

She looked at the beautiful handwriting, probably carved into wet mud with a sharp instrument and allowed to dry. It was very artistic in its form; the middle plaque looked like a poem with a regular pattern. She began typing text from the first plaque into a Word document.

*Ego sum Aaan, natus ex Ila et Daanak. Terra mater virgo, et pater esset una et angelus caelestis qui rem detestabilem hoc interdicuntur. Nisi pater neque mater, frater Zaak non abstulit illa mihi diluvii terram. Iratus perniciem dolorem adsumptis viribus cuius nomen non obscure scribam. Patre meo vidi numquam matrem, fratrem Iam bis. Spero illa terra requievit in pace. Quoniam dimidia Angeli non conveniunt cum matrem meam vitae, placerat sed adhuc spe, quod ego ad aridam, quod nescio an aliquid prius negotium. Frater meus adhuc nescio.*

*Quia prima infantia reincarnated sum amores saepe suis. Singulis ligula videtur fieri, et hoc minus proprie. Quoties novus ineo Incarnatione oblitus fuero usque meam praeteritam vitam. Et secundum numerum incarnationis tabulis cogitationes meas ad utrumque.*

She immediately ran it through a translation program and turned up some phrases that were recognizable, but didn't make any sense. The first few lines translated:

> *Aaan I am born of the Ila and Daanak. The land of the virgin mother, and the father did a detestable thing, this would be one and the angel of Heaven, who is forbidden. Unless the mother nor the father, the brother of Zaak and she to me did not take away the flood of the earth.*

Even in her feverish excitement, Annie realized it would take a while to clean up the text to a point of understandability. Still, she allowed herself to squeal with delight. *Angels. Detestable thing. Wow, this is awesome!* Her feet did a happy-dance even while she sat. She vowed not to give up until every word made sense. Now she might actually learn something about him.

She spent the rest of the day working on it, then a lot of time in the evenings the rest of the week. Luckily, Thursday was Rosh Hashanah, a no-school day in Montgomery County, which had a large Jewish population, so she spent all morning working on it. She showed it to no one, not even Red, until she felt it was ready. Then, that afternoon, she felt it might not be perfect, but she'd smoothed it out as much as she could. With a sense of satisfaction, she called Nyah.

"Nyah, I did it!" She was so excited she could barely talk. In a rush, she explained about translating the Latin prose into English.

"Slow down, girl," Nyah said, laughing. "Okay, read it to me—unless, of course, it's going to be your little secret."

"No, of course not. Okay, here's what it says," and Annie began to read the translation:

*I am Aaan, born of Ila and Daanak. My mother was an Earth maiden and my father a celestial angel and their union displeased the one who matters, this being forbidden. My father could not save my mother, my brother, Zaak, or me from a great flood that swept the land. In his grief he became angry to his destruction, joining the dark forces of the one whose name I shall not write. I have seen my father once and my brother twice since that time, but never my mother. I hope she is resting in the land of peace. Because I am half-angel, I did not share the same after-life as my dear mother, but still live in hope that someday I too will go to that land, but think I must first do something though I know not the task. I do not know if my brother is there yet.*

*I have been reincarnated many times since my first childhood with my loving family. It seems to happen about every five centuries, but this is not exact. Each time I enter a new incarnation, I forget my past until that life is over. On this tablet is the list of my incarnations and my thoughts on the purpose of each.*

- *First, I was a priest and worked very hard to carve stones for Stonehenge, but lacked the tools of the original builders who were known only in legend, and so the work was grueling.*
*In this life, I learned to meditate and connect with the white light from the creator.*

- *Next, I was a son of Abraham, not of Sarah but of Hagar. I was a prince of the Qedarites in the land of Sinai.*

82

*I learned courage and fortitude. This I used many times.*

- *I was then a son of Abraham, through Sarah, of the tribe of Aaron. I was a priest in the court of Solomon and served in his temple, of which beauty was and is unsurpassed.*
  *I learned prudence, justice, and other forms of wisdom from his teachings and the great value of worship through ceremony.*

- *I was a Kambojan trader and attained much wealth from horse-trading. I traveled to see Lao-tzu, Buddha, and Confucius.*
  *I learned faith by learning to meditate and connect with the creator and learned more wisdom.*

- *I was a Roman soldier's boy and watched the crucifixion of Jesu of Nazareth. I wanted to help him but did not. I had great sorrow because I did not help him. His sacrifice changed the universe. This I feel.*
  *I learned that great love and sacrifice can bring newness.*

- *I was then a monk, crippled of body, living on the Iberian Peninsula, spending all my days fasting, meditating, and writing about Jesu.*
  *I learned humility, temperance, and restraint and was glad to write of this great love.*

- *I was then female for two lives, first a Slavic girl, captured by Viking raiders and sold into slavery in a cold desert land, where I was made to toil and bear children that I was never allowed to keep. I loved no*

*one but only hated. I used temperance and restraint every day, for I had nothing.*
*I learned that all are precious and feel pain and misery. I do not know why I should hate after having before learned of the existence of such great love.*

- *Then I was once again a slave girl, born in Africa, in a jungle paradise on the Zaire River, having a sister named Zyou, whom I loved dearly. We gathered fruits and lived in harmony with the earth. We had many animal friends. This was the most joyous time of my existence. We loved to laugh and sing. I was captured and sold to the Portuguese in my maidenhood and taken to a cursed island sugar plantation. I did not survive long there and was immeasurably glad that Zyou escaped and still lived free in our homeland. In that life, I learned to love another even though my own life was wretched; I had already learned that cruelty was wrong. I am not sure why I had to be a slave twice. Perhaps it was because I failed to learn the first time to love despite pain.*

- *Then, I was born a vile creature trapping innocent animals, first in Siberia and then in America, where my greed brought me. I caused much suffering.*
*I learned how cruel one can be if one does not choose that which is good. I did finally choose good. I stopped trapping with metal traps and gave myself to help the native people defend against the cruel invaders. I was given Inolah to wed but she did not love me. She bore a daughter to me whom I called Seya. I loved Seya more than anyone since my own dear mother and my sister, Zyou. Inolah died on a forced march from Cherokee land to a loathsome hot land to the west. I could not save Inolah, who wished*

*to go with her people, but I rescued Seya. I hid her in this cave and she later took a husband and stayed in this valley. After that life, I stayed in this cave and watched over her until her death. I learned that justice and compassion are precious and without them, one is a truly cruel and vile creature, even after knowing of great love.*

*In nine lifetimes, I have loved only five others: my dear mother and brother, Jesu, my sister, and my daughter. If asked to name one more, it would be my father, though I did not know him well. If there are more lessons to learn, I think it is to love people more. I should have loved someone in each lifetime.*

*After Seya was buried, I stayed in this cave and spent many days creating art, trying to recall the beauty that I had seen in the world through sculpture. Then, I decided to remain here and sleep, being tired of struggling.*

Annie stopped reading. Nyah was silent for a few seconds. "Nyah, say something." Annie couldn't wait to hear what her friend thought.

"I'm just trying to digest it. I mean, it's beautiful—and really sad. It's like this poor soul's seen a lot of misery."

"Aaan. That's his name. Sounds like an angel name, doesn't it?" Annie said. "Come to think of it, I think that's what he said that day in the cave."

"Annie, you promise me you're not pulling my leg?"

"Nyah, you know me. Does that sound like me?"

"Well, I've got to admit, I do think you think you saw something. I mean, if this is for real, then this is huge. Didn't he say his father was an angel—a real angel?"

"Yeah, but you know I told you before—I saw angels when I was transformed. They are absolutely real."

"I know, I know. It's just taking me a minute. I mean, I always believed in them, I guess, but in a distant sort of way. Like, I might see one when I die. But to think that my best friend has actually seen one ... Annie, I don't know what to say." Nyah's voice was full of emotion.

"I know, Nyah. I've been feeling the same shock for a few months now. But remember, he's *half*-angel. And you know, from reading the translation, that seems to have been his problem. It's like he couldn't move onto the afterlife where his mother went, but he wasn't a full angel, either, and so he kept reincarnating—living, then dying, then reincarnating every five hundred years or so. It's so sad, Nyah."

"It is sad, but it sounded like he was advancing," Nyah said slowly. "I didn't catch all you said as you were reading, but it sounded as though he was kind of like advancing spiritually. Like, wasn't that the seven deadly sins or something he was working his way through?"

"It was," Annie said, realizing. "And he does seem good, doesn't he? Not evil. I mean, at first when I saw him in the cave, it was like I was drawn to him. I didn't get a feeling of evil at all."

"I don't know, Annie," Nyah said, her voice full of doubt. "I thought he sounded good, too. But being *drawn* to him? That almost sounds like he's a vampire or something."

"Oh no, Nyah. It was nothing like that. It wasn't like an evil thing compelling me," Annie said. "It was more like I was meeting a really nice person, but one that was really sad and didn't want me to leave."

After they hung up, she found Red in her room, chuckling over some photos on her computer that Annie assumed Erik had sent. The pics were mostly of Red on a hike, hamming it up for the camera. Annie nudged her. "Just a sec," Red said, without even glancing in her direction. *Boy, is Red totally gaga over this guy. And irritating.*

"Red," she said loudly. "Check this out."

Red seemed to catch the note of excitement in her voice and turned to Annie with mock-annoyance in her demeanor for disrupting her. Annie knew that in reality she had her big sis wrapped around her little finger.

Annie spread the page with the printed translation on Red's desk in front of her and stood back with a hint of smugness at her accomplishment.

Red scanned over the page. "What? You need help with literature? I didn't realize you were even taking it this semester." Red began turning back to her computer.

"Not exactly. Red. This was on the wall of ... *the cave*." Annie pronounced the last two works loudly and with special emphasis.

"What cave?" Red asked, her eyes already back on the computer.

"*The* cave." *Come on, Red, can you be so dense? Get your mind off Erik for just a minute.*

Annie watched as cognition began to take shape. Red's mouth made an "O" but no sound came. She looked down at the pages and began to read carefully. "Did you translate this? How? I thought it was in some unknown language."

Annie tried not to look sheepish. "Turned out to be Latin," she said dryly.

Red guffawed. "How did you not recognize Latin?"

"Hey, wait a minute. You didn't either," Annie pointed out. "All I really knew was that it wasn't Spanish or French, and it didn't have Chinese or Arabic lettering. And I guess I'd have recognized German ... maybe."

"So what you're telling me is that these words were on a cave behind the waterfall at the Swan Hole and you translated them and this is what they said?" Red was obviously catching the excitement now.

"Yes, that's exactly what I'm telling you. And that apparition I saw may be this Aaan."

Annie paced impatiently while Red read through the whole document. When she finished, she looked up at Annie, her eyes wide. "Wow. He's a half-angel from before the flood?"

Annie simply looked at her sister and nodded her head, the meaning sinking deep and the knowledge too enormous for speech.

"Annie, you gotta tell Uncle Alistair. He knows more about this kind of thing than anyone we know."

Annie made a face. "Red, are you crazy? If I tell him, I'd have to tell him I have his STAG control. And he wouldn't only be mad at me, but he'd definitely take it back."

"So? You weren't going to keep it, were you? It's not yours."

"N-No," Annie said sheepishly, then relented at the sight of her sister's stern face. "Oh, Red, of course I wasn't going to keep it forever. But, yes, for a while longer. How do you think I'll ever get a chance to see Aaan again?"

"Aaan?" Red said somewhat teasingly. "So you and he are on a first-name basis now? No, wait, he probably wouldn't call it first name. His writing seems to indicate that he's a bit behind the times. Now, let's see, Latin has been a dead language for how many centuries? And yet this is still his language of choice, apparently. So he probably wouldn't want you to call him by his given name until you two were married. Unless … oh, right. I guess angels only have one name, so I guess you have to call him by his given name, in which case—"

Annie abruptly cut off Red's words, socking her with a pillow to the back of the head.

"Why, you little …" Red sprang from her desk chair and grabbed another pillow in self-defense.

Ten minutes later, Annie and her sister were lying face-up across the bed. Annie was still giggling, trying to catch her breath. When she was able to stop laughing, the closeness to her sister felt so good that on the spur of the moment she decided to open up. "Red, you know what you said the other day about both of us falling for ghosts?"

"Yeah."

"Well, yours turned out to not be one, and so has mine. I mean, isn't a half-angel better than a ghost? He does reincarnate sometimes," Annie said in serious contemplation. "Of course, even if he did right this minute, he'd be a baby and I'd be fifteen years older."

"Yeah. Tough breaks, huh?"

"Maybe it's not a family thing, though, maybe it's a stones thing. Transformations were involved in both cases. In your case, Erik was transformed and then transformed you. And in my case, I transformed myself and went somewhere others can't go and saw him. I guess it's just that the transformations open doors to being able to see other forms of existence."

"I guess so. We really are living in a kind of fairy tale," Red said. "We're seeing things others haven't had an opportunity to see."

"And we have a tool that no one else has ever had. Well, I guess some have had the stones, but we don't know if they really knew how to use them. I mean, Erik and Uncle Alistair still don't know how to use the third stone, right?"

"That's right. But I'll bet they'll figure it out soon."

"You can certainly see why Uncle Alistair wants to keep it out of the wrong hands. But I'm glad Erik's going to try and use it to find his father. Wouldn't it be awesome if he could rescue him?"

"It certainly would," Red said, but a shadow crossed her face. "But what if his dad's dead? Erik's so into this now that he's totally obsessed with finding him. I don't know what'll happen if he doesn't." Annie watched a tear run slowly down Red's cheek to the bed.

"Red, give him more credit than that. I mean, look how he endured a whole year being cut off from everyone. Erik's strong. He came through that just fine and he'll be okay. Maybe it'll be easier for him to accept that his dad's dead if he finds it out for sure, don't you think?"

Red looked over at her and smiled. "Yeah, I guess so. Thanks, Annie. You may be an annoying little sister but I guess I'm glad you're MY little sister. But don't expect me to own up to that in front of anyone."

Back in her room, Annie read through the translations again. This was big. She was giddy with excitement to learn more about this unique being. Just what *was* he? Had she really made contact with a half-angel? Did this mean he had superhuman powers? Was he perhaps … dangerous? She had goose bumps as she closed her bedroom door behind her, dreaming of Aaan.

Antonio fell backwards into his armchair, reeling from the blow to his jaw. He thought at first his jaw had been knocked out of place, but it clicked and he was able to move it again. Pietro's angry deep voice was still smooth, showing no emotion, not at all fitting with the action of a moment ago. "Antonio, we need your brother. If we still had him, we'd probably have the stones by now," Pietro said.

Antonio used his sleeve to wipe a trickle of blood from the side of his mouth—his teeth had cut the inside of his cheek. The handsome man in the expensive gray coat turned and approached him with chilling slowness. He stopped in front of Antonio and gently straightened Antonio's collar, then slapped his face. Antonio didn't make a noise, just cowered. *What he gotten himself into?*

"Not quite your brother, are you?" Pietro chuckled mirthlessly. "Antonio, I dislike using corrective measures, so please, bring your brother back to us. Our distinguished leader is very angry with recent events and will not tolerate failure to capture the professor—understood?" He frowned to himself.

Antonio nodded, hoping he'd leave. This whole thing didn't seem fun anymore. What if he and the other guys failed? They'd probably kill them. He felt like crying and at the same time felt something laughing inside him—enjoying his pain. How he wished he'd listened to his brother. How he wished his mother was alive to hold him. He felt his eyes begin to water.

Pietro snatched up his umbrella and ambled toward the door. He glanced at his watch as he opened the door. "Don't be late. The three of you should be on the road by eight p.m. And do not fail." He stood in the doorway, both eyebrows raised, awaiting Antonio's agreement.

"I understand." Antonio was able to force this much out without actually crying, though his voice threatened to break. Finally, the door closed behind Pietro, and Antonio was able to breathe.

# PART TWO:

## Erik's Quest

Quote from <u>Ascent to Mt. Carmel</u> (Sixteenth Century):

*To come to the pleasure you have not, you must go by a way in which you enjoy not.*

*To come to the knowledge you have not, you must go by a way in which you know not.*

*To come to the possession you have not, you must go by a way in which you possess not.*

*To come to be what you are not, you must go by a way in which you are not.*[2]

CHAPTER 7

# Red's Apprehension

R ed was worried about her relationship with Erik. He was so obsessed with his quest to find his father that he barely paid attention to her. It was hard not to feel taken for granted lately. She liked to think she was a bigger person than to worry about something so petty, but she felt a distance forming between them and it worried her. She knew he was preoccupied with trying to find out everything he could about his father's last movements before his disappearance, and she supported that. But she wished he'd at least let her be a part of it all.

She'd been trying to work on a digital art project for school and as much as she loved art, she felt a strong need to think right now. Sighing, she took her pocket calendar out of the desk drawer and started thinking about all that had transpired in the past few months.

She couldn't believe it had been over eight months since Erik and Uncle Alistair came home. She smiled each time she thought of that day. She guessed it was still the best day of her life. To see the joy on all the faces of her family and friends who knew Erik and Uncle Alistair had been amazing. But the joy hadn't been shared with the outside world for a while. Her family had learned to keep a lot of secrets, not the least of which was the matter of Roy and Lorenzo and their demon-possessions. After the exorcisms, Roy and Lorenzo had completed a thorough psychiatric exam. Roy had returned to his normal life and Lorenzo had returned home to Italy, profusely grateful for the help in extricating himself from the spiritual servitude to which he'd been victim since a teen. From what Erik had told her, she didn't think Lorenzo would ever go back to the cult.

The whole time, Erik and Uncle Alistair had kept the fact that they were alive a secret from all but a few people, knowing it would create a stir and attract unwanted attention while they were working on sending back the stones and helping Roy and Lorenzo. It felt like ages until Uncle Alistair returned to the university, telling people he'd hit his head on a rock when his canoe capsized and had temporary amnesia.

But Erik had to wait the longest before revealing that he was alive. After all, it would have been suspicious for both of them to return at the same time. So he "arrived" back into society at the end of spring semester, saying he'd been doing research in Central America and that he'd told Uncle Alistair he was going. Anticipating the question of why his mother hadn't known, he said they'd had a fight over some girlfriend she'd disapproved of and that was why he hadn't communicated with her. Red had thought it was a flimsy story; no one who knew Erik or his mother would ever believe they would behave this way—no, Erik would cross Heaven and Earth for his mother or his father. Of this, there could be no doubt.

"Whatcha doin'?" Annie entered the room unannounced and sounded like she was still in a good mood from her success on the translations.

"Oh, just feeling sorry for myself, I guess," Red said with a sigh. "I was just remembering the hectic time we had when

Uncle Alistair and Erik first came home and all the stories that had to be concocted when they made their debuts back into society. You know, Annie, at first I thought the whole thing was over and there would be smooth sailing ahead. Boy, was I naive." She sighed. "Once all that was over, I thought we'd live happily ever after. And that was true for the first part of the summer. We were inseparable and our relationship was ..."

"T-M-I," Annie said, pretending to put fingers in her ears.

"No, nothing like that—well, not nothing, but you know what I mean. We're taking it pretty slow. I mean, we both live with our parents," she said. "But things were coming along great before he received his epiphany."

"What epiphany?" Annie asked.

"The epiphany that he could use the stones to find out what happened to his dad," she said with a sigh. "That's what changed his focus from us, to him looking for his dad. That *ah-ha* moment when he realized a STAG control could be used to break someone out of prison." She shook her head. "It was actually me who came up with the idea. We'd been having a stroll on the towpath and he mentioned something about his dad's disappearance. I said, 'It's too bad he didn't have a STAG control.' I thought Erik would have a cow. In fact, he grabbed my hand and we ran all the way back to the house and into Uncle Alistair's study."

"Well, it does seem like a good idea," Annie pointed out.

"*Brilliant*, was what Erik called it." Red did enjoy that memory.

"What did Uncle Alistair say?" asked Annie.

"He seemed to think it a good idea, but, of course, he warned Erik that chances were slim that his father was still alive. It's been ten years," Red said. "But I don't think I've ever seen Erik with such excitement and determination to follow through on something. I actually admire that about him. And he said that even if his father is dead, he wants to find out for sure so his mom can have closure."

"So why can't you help? What's he been doing since then?"

"That's just it," Red stood and paced, frustration coursing through her. "He won't tell me exactly. He's just absent and preoccupied when he's here. We still have our dates and walks and I know he still cares for me. But it's kinda like the honeymoon's over before it started. I think he's a fascinating person and I know he thinks I am. But he's on a quest and I'm not part of it."

"What do you think he's doing when he's not here?"

Red knew she had to tell someone and knew she could trust Annie more than anyone, so she decided to come clean. "Annie, I've overheard him talking with Uncle Alistair a few times and picked up enough to suspect that he's using a STAG control to view top-secret information, probably at the Pentagon. I asked him about it and he refused to tell me anything on the grounds that it might endanger me or cause legal trouble later."

Annie's eyes grew wide. "Red, that's *huge*. I can see where you're worried sick. He probably isn't in danger if he's using a transformation, but he could really get in trouble if he got caught." She hugged her sister. "Why didn't you tell me?"

Red sighed. "I wanted to, but you had your own thing going with trying to figure out the cave etchings. I thought about trying to distract myself from being mad at Erik by helping you with your cave quest, being a good big sister and all, but you had Nyah."

"Red, of course I want your help with the cave quest. And he has a name. It's Aaan," she said. "Actually, Missy and I keep in contact and I got an email from her today. She told me an odd story that may have something to do with Aaan. It seems that something happened only days after we left. Some old friends of Billy's were producing crystal meth and approached him to try to talk him into joining them. They tried to tempt him with the usual stuff about easy money and what else was he going to do to make enough money for his family in such a remote place, blah blah blah." Annie shook her head. "And

Red, you won't believe this, but Missy's pregnant. She's not much older than me."

Red whistled. "Is she stressed out about it?"

"No. We're getting off topic. She's happy about it, but she was worried that Billy might actually succumb to the temptation to help with the expenses of a new baby," she said. "Well, he turned down the offer, but then things weren't quite as simple as that. One of Billy's so-called 'friends' had evidently put forth his name to some stranger involved in underground drug trafficking. And even worse, the friend had sold the idea of the legendary hidden cave at the Swan Hole as being the perfect storage place for drugs."

"Oh, my gosh, Annie. That'd be awful." Red stared at her, her face serious.

"Missy said Billy tried to laugh off the idea of a cave as just an old wives tale and Billy even took those guys to the Swan Hole one evening to prove there was no cave. Well, Missy didn't know all the details of what happened down there, but she told me she heard footsteps running in a panic away from the Swan Hole. She said those guys jumped into their car and churned up road dust as they got the heck out of that holler. Billy had been very pale, like he'd seen a ghost, she said. But he said everything was fine."

"Wow," Red said. "What do you think he saw?"

"I don't know," Annie said. "But she told me he sat up all night with his shotgun and then within a week asked her to come look at a new place with him. It ended up being one of the small houses over the hill from the Swan Hole. He claimed he wanted to move because the place was much nicer, with air conditioning and a room that could be converted to a nursery and because she'd be closer to other people during her pregnancy, but Missy is sure it's to get her away from the Swan Hole."

"Do you think this Aaan did something to scare those guys off?" Red asked.

"Of course. What else?" Annie said. "I knew he was good. I think he guards the cave."

Red shared Annie's exuberance and both laughed. "Annie, I'm in awe of your half-angel—he almost certainly saved Missy and Billy from those guys. But don't you wonder what they saw?"

"Whatever it was, it worked. I don't think they'll be back. Just wish it hadn't scared Billy away. He seemed nice."

"At least they're still nearby. And sounds like a move up for them."

"At least we can stay in touch," Annie said. "I just wish Aaan had a cell phone so I could call and congratulate him."

Red laughed but after Annie left the room she thought more about the idea of Aaan having a cell phone in the cave. It created a brain chain that made her wonder if a cell phone could be transformed by the stones and go on Erik's quest with him. She kind of doubted it since Erik's metal key had dissolved when he'd first been transformed. A cell phone would have metal parts, too, though she didn't know all the particulars of how the stones affected all the elements. She didn't think Erik fully understood that either. But she vowed to give the idea more thought.

Over the next week, with school now underway, Red tried to immerse herself in her studies. She really wanted to get into Georgetown. It hurt her feelings somewhat that Erik kept saying she could go to any school she chose and he'd visit her as often as possible. He'd be faithfully hers, he said, but didn't want to hold her back. She'd squelched that somewhat by saying what she really wanted to do was accompany him on his search for his father, pointing out that she already knew the ropes about being transformed.

He'd quickly countered with an argument that she'd miss too much schoolwork and needed to keep up her grades if she wanted to get into Georgetown. Okay, that was something, at least. Though, to be honest, she really would love to have such an adventure—her desire to go with him hadn't been based solely on togetherness.

Still, Red thought about having a serious discussion with Erik to let her wants be known. After all, he needed to know how much togetherness she expected. Wasn't open communication what relationships were built on? She considered the relationships to which she was privy. Okay, there was her mom and dad. Did they have open communication? She had to admit she didn't know.

She considered the other relationships she knew. There were Roy and Xenia. Somehow they'd weathered the demon possession evil-Roy period just fine, which she couldn't fathom, but they had done it. But somehow she didn't see herself as able to be as quiet and long-suffering as Xenia. There were Daniel and Rachel—they seemed to have a good relationship, one of mutual respect, but then, those two were joined at the hip. They had the same interests and had been together forever, she thought. She and Erik just weren't like that.

Her brain-chain leapt to famous fictional couples—which of these could give her some guidance? Angel and Tess? Definitely not. Alec and Tess? Even less so. Not Romeo and Juliet, either, though somehow she liked the commitment and passion. She had to admit to herself that she craved more of that kind of passion from Erik these days—he'd shown that before getting obsessed with saving his father. Erik and she were more like Rochester and Jane, only the roles were reversed—she, like Rochester, wanted to throw caution to the wind and just be together.

Red's chain of thought came back around to real people and she wondered if there'd been some spark between her Uncle Alistair and Ms. Catsworthy. Red could tell that Ms. Catsworthy had been a real beauty. Even in her old age, her bright eyes, strong chin, and cute nose were pretty, and when she smiled, her whole countenance seemed to glow. And Red loved the person she was—an altogether beautiful person. Was her uncle crazy for not marrying her? Was one of them gay?

When Red had asked her about Uncle Alistair last Christmas, Ms. Catsworthy had given her an evasive answer. It'd seemed that they got started on the wrong foot and no one wanted to rock the boat—at least, that was what Red took from her answer. Did this mean that passion hadn't progressed? This really did seem to imply that either one or both were gay or in love with someone else. Her uncle had mentioned a sister of Ms. Catsworthy—was this the elephant in the room? Had he been in love with her sister after all this time, even though they'd only been kids when the girl was killed? Red mulled the situation over, her inner matchmaker humming. Perhaps she could do something to assist their courtship.

The next Saturday morning, Ms. Catsworthy invited the family for morning tea. The other members of her family had been occupied with various activities and projects, so Red went alone, looking forward to having Ms. Catsworthy all to herself. She could talk with her for hours about her art collection alone, even without relationship issues to discuss. She'd felt close to her ever since the day Ms. Catsworthy had taken charge of Roy when he'd threatened to attack her during his possessed period. Encouraged by the easy compatibility she felt, she decided to broach the subject of why Ms. Catsworthy and Uncle Alistair had never hooked up.

She began by sharing her own frustrations with Erik with a vague idea of establishing a mutually supporting conversation. She stated that she felt like Rochester in *Jane Eyre*, and then realized she needed to explain. "I just want to throw caution to the wind and be together always. Like, no matter the circumstance. But I don't think Erik's as excited about me as before. I know deep down that searching for his father's the most important thing to him right now and I know that this is as it should be. I just feel so selfish even noticing that we aren't spending much time together, with his father possibly sick or injured in prison somewhere. But it still seems like we're drifting ..."

Ms. Catsworthy, who had been attentive as she sipped her tea, at that moment looked up in such a way that told Red they weren't alone. Red's face turned scarlet as she slowly peered around to see Erik and his mom standing in the doorway. She tried to recall exactly what her words had been right before they walked in. She silently chastised herself for not realizing Ms. Catsworthy may have invited others or that her close friends might enter without knocking.

"Erik. Mrs. Wolfeningen. How nice to see you." She so hoped her voice sounded convincing as she rose to kiss them.

Erik gave her a peck on the lips and paused for a moment to give her a sad look. What was he trying to convey? Sadness that they were drifting apart? Sadness that he just couldn't do any better right now because of his dad? She wasn't sure.

He sat on a seat adjoining hers and reached over to take her hand. Her head was so full of embarrassment to be caught talking about him that she didn't hear what was being said by Ms. Catsworthy and Minah. She sensed he was in the same boat as they sipped their tea.

As soon as one might reasonably leave without being impolite, he stood. "Mom, Ms. Catsworthy, would you please excuse Red and me? We haven't spent much time together lately and I hoped that she'd take a short hike with me on the towpath while you have a leisurely tea."

"By all means. The day is beautiful and it would be a sin for two lovebirds not to take advantage of this golden morning," Ms. Catsworthy said.

Once outside, Red felt that she had to address what she'd said, "Erik—" she began, but at the same moment he'd also begun with "Sonia—" They stopped and tried again. Red decided to plow through and not be timid and so took over the conversation.

"Erik, sweetie, I'm sorry you heard me complaining to Ms. Catsworthy. I feel guilty for feeling abandoned, but somehow I can't seem to help it. It's as though I only just found you and you seem to already be moving away from me."

"Sonia—" He paused. "Let's wait until we get on the tow-path so we can have privacy, okay?"

It took only moments to go down the path to the towpath— that fateful path where she'd first beheld her Viking ghost. It still made her stomach flutter.

As soon as they were on the towpath, Erik looked up and down the path to ensure they were alone. Then he took her face in his hands and gave her the hungriest, longest kiss she'd ever known. He pulled her to him, their bodies pressed together, and devoured her lips again.

After a few minutes, he pulled back a fraction of an inch and asked, "Okay, now do you still think I'm losing interest?"

"I'm not sure, let me tell you in a few more minutes." Red pulled his face back to hers by a handhold on the neck of his T-shirt.

After some time, they pulled apart again and Erik looked seriously into her eyes.

"Sonia, I love you," he said seriously. "I will love you until the day I die. No other woman has even come close, or ever will. I know I've been preoccupied, but Red, that's my *dad* out there."

Red felt a rush of guilt. "I'm sorry to make you feel bad for being preoccupied. Your caring nature is why I love you so much. You know, I do love you too. And it's not just some high-school crush. I love who you are and I love that you're such a hero. I even love how you talk to the animals. And you have to be the hottest guy I've ever seen and I feel so lucky that you love me." Red's eyes moistened and Erik devoured her mouth once more.

As they walked back, Erik said, "I wish I could involve you more in my search for my dad, but I just don't know how. I'm using a transformed state most of the time for the research and will be using a transformation when I finally go looking for him."

That reminded Red of her thought about transforming a cell phone. "I've been thinking about something Annie said. Have you tried to transform a cell phone? I know your key disintegrated, but think about it—if you had a cell phone with you, you could communicate with the outside world, or with me. You could let someone know if there was danger and you could take pictures. And you could—"

"A cell phone can also be traced," Erik broke in gently. "Don't forget that. For most of this mission, I can't afford to be traceable. Still, I like the idea. There could definitely be some times when it would be priceless to have a cell. I had been thinking about trying to figure out what made the key dissolve. It might have been only one element and if we identified it, using the stones could be much simpler by just avoiding materials that contain that element. That was part of our long-term research goals. We may need to step up that part of the research. I'd also already been thinking about experimenting on remote controls to see if I could transform one to take with me so that I could travel in the ghost transformation but carry a couple of STAG controls with me. That way, I could rescue my father with much less risk to him." He squeezed her hand. "You know, Sonia, I'm glad we had this conversation. I don't know what I'd do without you. Heck, without you, I'd still be a ghost. I should have kept you more involved all along."

She squeezed back. "I'm glad, too. I've decided that even when someone else has important work to do, it's good to remind them that their loved ones are still there by their side. I just wish I'd been more open earlier and hadn't wasted so much time fretting."

CHAPTER 8

# Mission Launched

I n late October, Erik told Red that he felt he had as much
information as he was going to get and was ready to set off
to find his dad. Red knew he was going into one of the most
dangerous places on Earth for an American. He would fly in a
plane to Damascus, though he wouldn't buy a ticket. According
to the plan, he didn't want to be traceable, so he'd fly there
using the ghost transformation.

He and Uncle Alistair had spent long hours working on the
plan and perhaps one of the biggest challenges had been how
to take along the necessary equipment. That difficulty had been
solved when they'd made the discovery that tin was the sub-
stance that had made the key dissociate into thin air. The key
had been made from antique bronze, a mixture of copper and
tin, and tin didn't survive the transformation intact. But other
metals seemed to be okay. Once they'd made that discovery,
Red helped collect equipment, including remote controls and
an old cell phone that did not rely on tin to function. Erik was

able to transform objects he would need and carry them with him in a small leather pouch tied to his leather loincloth.

The other great discovery had been finding out that STAG controls and cell phones actually worked from either transformed state. Erik would be carrying two STAG controls with him at all times because he had to use one to transform the other, then transform himself, and back again. It was a leapfrog process he would have to go through each time he went in or out of a transformed state, but it worked.

Red knew she was going to miss him but felt part of the whole process now. She was especially glad that Erik would have a cell phone, even though he'd have to keep it powered off most of the time to avoid being traced. He promised to call whenever he could but Red knew this would not be often since he'd have to remove himself from wherever he was working to keep the important locations safe.

The first call came from Damascus the day after he left. Red was thrilled to hear from him.

"Miss you already, Sonia."

"I miss you too, Erik," she said, relieved to hear he had arrived safely. "Where do you go from there?"

"I don't want to be too specific just in case anyone's monitoring this call, but I'll do a combination of hitchhiking and fly-swimming into Iraq, to the area around Baghdad where I suspect he might be."

"It's a good thing you're so good at traveling that way."

"Yep, I've had plenty of practice." Erik laughed quietly.

"So are you transformed right now? Are we talking from different dimensions?" Red asked, trying to picture him.

"That we are. Cool, huh?"

"Very cool. So how far is it and how long do you think it'll take you?"

"It's a little more than 450 miles and will likely take a few days unless I get a good breeze if I fly. Of course, sometimes it'll be faster to hop into a moving vehicle when it's going in the right direction," he said. "If I think I'm getting close, I may not be able to call for a couple of weeks—I guess it could even be a month. Who knows? But I will try to call every couple of weeks. Just remember that you don't need to worry at all about me, okay?"

*As if.* "Just be safe and find him. I love you, Erik," she said. "Don't take any silly risks to call. Call when you can. I'll be fine."

"I love you, too, so much."

She braced herself for a long wait before his next call, but less than a week went by and Erik called again to say he'd arrived in Baghdad and was ready to really get started on his search.

"Getting to Baghdad was a lot harder than the first leg of the trip when all I had to do was hop a plain to Damascus," he said. "You know, the road from Damascus to Baghdad was a major trade route from antiquity, but even with the 2011 troop withdrawal, bus service hasn't recommenced. I'm sure glad I packed a map and compass and a small Arabic/English dictionary."

Red smiled. "Yeah, I know. Remember, I laminated the pages for you so they wouldn't disintegrate."

"I remember. Don't know what I'd have done without all your help, Sonia," he said. "I'm ready to check out each and every square meter of Baghdad systematically if I have to. I'm going to find something."

"I know you will, Erik," she said. "What about fun things? Have you gotten to do any sightseeing or seen anything unusual or interesting?"

"You mean like our first beautiful moonlit flight? Actually, yeah, I did notice a really beautiful desert view yesterday. I was in a military vehicle that was moving at a good clip but I hadn't been able to see out of it to make sure I didn't bypass where I wanted to go. I pushed straight up through the roof and flew upwards to get my bearings. And I did have to stop and take a moment to enjoy the desert. It had a different kind of beauty that somehow made the sky seem bluer. I've always been partial to heavy vegetation, especially cool mossy woodlands, but this was beautiful."

"Like the towpath?" Red asked sweetly.

"Yes, like the towpath. *Our* towpath. Wish I were there now. But the desert was pretty. I promise to show you sometime."

Red heard a strange noise in the background. "Do I hear geese in the background? It can't be. Aren't you in a desert?"

"Yes, you do. Isn't it crazy? The number of birds here has really surprised me. I guess they're mostly migrating through, since I didn't see very much for them to eat or much water. I guess there may be a few lizards and insects for food. I saw a huge flock when I was hovering in the air yesterday. But just as I was wishing I'd brought a bird book to identify some of them, I spotted a cargo van speeding in the right direction. I had to be quick to grab the rack on top."

"That sounds like a good thing."

"It was, but what was really great was that once inside, there were crates with Arabic writing. I wasn't surprised to find that it translated to 'automatic guns,' since there were two very serious-looking M-4 rifles lying in the floor between the driver and passenger. I know enough about guns to know they were manufactured in the U.S. So these had likely been taken from American soldiers. Don't you see?" Erik's voice sounded oddly excited.

Red struggled to see where Erik was going with this. "So, they might have some prisoners of war? Is that what you're thinking?"

"That's exactly what I'm thinking. It turned out to be a really promising hook-up. The best lead I've had yet. I decided to listen for any words spoken frequently and see if I could catch anything that might be important. I heard a few names—Anwar, Mubarak, Rabit—the last one seemed to be the driver's name and I thought it'd be easy to remember. I heard Al-Queda mentioned a couple of times and another name that sounded like Al-Ansar. So I decided to ride all the way to their destination to see what I could learn."

"Erik, if you weren't in the ghost transformation, I'd be really scared for you. Sounds like you're really in the thick of it now. I've got goose bumps just listening to this. I'm writing this down in case you disappear or something," she said. "But Erik—don't."

"I won't. But let me tell the rest quickly 'cause I should probably hang up soon. So I watched carefully as we passed two intersections with roads that lead off in the wrong direction, one at a town called Rutba and the other further along that wasn't named on my map, but I gauged the distance. Both times, luckily the vehicle stayed on the road to Baghdad. Eventually, after nine or ten hours, I could tell we were coming into Baghdad by the sudden increase in traffic and the number of buildings. I tried really hard to remember turns and landmarks. We turned off the main road into Ramadi and skirted around the south side toward Habbaniyah Lake. But instead of going back into the desert again, these guys pulled off into a parking lot of what appeared to be an abandoned school. At first, I thought it was abandoned because I didn't see any school buses, but then I noticed there were several jeeps and military vehicles.

"So these guys pulled around back and down a ramp to a loading dock. Then two uniformed men came out. They had their faces mostly hidden by cloth wound around their faces with openings for their eyes, and they were wearing automatic weapons. Well, to cut to the chase, they unloaded the crates of guns. I checked my map to see if this was one of the sites I'd marked as possible locations to investigate. *Yes.* There, it was."

Red listened hard, her heart hammering in her chest.

"I haven't gone in yet," he said. "I think now the real work is about to begin so I figured I would pop out into the desert a ways and touch base with you before starting a systematic search of that facility. So that's what I'm doing now," he said. "Wish me luck?"

"Good luck," she said. "Be safe."

Two weeks went by, with no word from Erik. Only the pressure to keep her grades up so she could get into Georgetown kept her sane. A part of her believed Erik was safe but she also knew it wasn't absolute. She knew that if he needed to transform back to normal for any reason he'd be vulnerable. And she didn't know if he'd be able to survive fire or an explosion in a transformed state.

Finally, to her tremendous relief, he called. She thought he sounded different this time. Like he'd seen too much.

"What did you find out?" she asked eagerly.

"I looked in every room, storage closet, and bathroom in that building and every automobile in the parking lot, but there were no leads on my father," he said. "I really regret not having the foresight to learn Arabic when I was stuck in the transformed state for a year, but it never occurred to me. I've been trying to gather as much information as I can just through tone of voice and physical gestures, but it's hard."

"Have you seen anything promising?"

"What haven't I seen? After checking that facility, I checked every location on my list and saw people in these places from all walks of life. Everything from the idle rich to the most innocent child to zealots who would do anything to accomplish their goals—and plenty of characters I wouldn't want to meet untransformed. I saw bullies and those bullied. I saw frightened people, Sonia, lots of frightened people. Most of the young soldiers and insurgents seemed frightened, many civilians and prisoners … and some seemed to have given up all hope and no longer cared. I saw prisoners locked in rooms, most with bars on the windows, and some handcuffed to rings secured to walls."

Red heard him hesitate.

Erik went on somberly, "Sonia, I won't give you much detail, but I have gotten sick a couple of times watching prisoners being interrogated. Luckily, no one's gotten into any of the really hideous forms of torture I saw evidence of, though I did see three executions." Red was pretty sure she heard his voice break. "Needless to say, it fired up my resolve to work faster."

"Erik, I know what you're thinking. That you might have saved those people, but just think, if you find your dad, he might have information to help find others—to stop this madness," she urged. "Just please promise me you'll stay transformed and not take any risks. You're piloting a tool that could save a lot of lives, but not if it falls into the wrong hands."

"I know, Sonia. Thanks for the pep talk. I needed it."

"Where are you going to look next?"

"I think I may have a real lead this time. So again, it may take a while for me to get back to you. I figured out that a hotel that had been transformed into a military facility was important and checked it out. I might even describe it as a central location for several groups. One particular wing has all the windows barred and armed guards positioned at every post. I searched through all the prisoners but didn't see Dad," he said. "You know, Sonia, I've begun to worry that I might not recognize him if he looks really different. A lot of the prisoners I've seen have been pretty emaciated, or worse ..." Red noticed that Erik let the last part of that sentence drift away, and she wasn't completely sure she'd heard him right.

"But I saw prisoners come and go a lot from that hotel. It seems to be a place where prisoners are sorted and maybe even exchanged. I started following some of them to their destinations and have picked up a few leads —one in particular. It just happened earlier today. I saw a skinny teen being beaten, but what really got my attention was that a man came in and started

113

interrogating him in English, accusing him of being a spy and calling him *Thomas*—I think he got that from his dogtag.

"I don't know if it was because of the English or if it was just something about the kid, but I really felt sorry for him. The questioning and beating went on for half an hour, but it seemed like hours. The only way I knew the length of time was that there was one of those plain black-and-white clocks on the wall at the back of the room, the same clock that hung in almost every classroom I've ever been in. It just struck me as odd that something so innocent was part of something so vile. I just needed to help that kid."

"So what happened?" Red was almost afraid to ask.

"He passed out and I ended up doing a mind-meld with him to offer him some comfort. And I promised to try to help him. I thought about zapping him and bringing him with me but then the cat would've been out of the bag that something odd was going on and I didn't want to lose the element of secrecy. And I decided I needed to watch what happens to him. If he's American, they may take him to wherever they've got American prisoners held. I feel a little guilty, like I'm using him as a guinea pig."

"Oh, Erik. I know it must've been hard to leave him. But I do think you're right. This may be the break you've been looking for. Could you read anything useful in his mind when you mind-melded?"

"Not really. He was unconscious. I detected a vague stress dream at first, one of running down dark corridors, but luckily, the pleasant thoughts I forced into his brain seemed to help ease this agitation and his dream became better—walking on a beach. But that did give me a new idea. I tried mind-melding with the guards to see if I could recognize the face of my dad. But the thing about mind-melding is that unless they're actively thinking of something, it doesn't really help. I can bring in new thoughts or read whatever they're thinking, but it isn't perfect and I can't really search their memory banks. And I have to be really careful to not think of something I don't want them to know. Still, that tool might come in handy at some point. I intend to leave no stone unturned to find Dad."

"You'll find him if he's alive," Red said. "I know you will."

"Thanks."

"So what did they do with the teen?"

"That's just it, Sonia. They put him into a cargo van and left the facility and I'm riding with them. They've stopped right now to gas up and eat and so I took the opportunity to call you since we're between locations, but I need to go soon to make sure I don't miss the van when it pulls out."

"Erik, don't let it get to you. You're my Viking ghost, after all."

Red hung up with a sense of foreboding. She wanted to talk to Uncle Alistair about all this but knew she'd have to wait because he was traveling to London for a speaking engagement. The one bright spot was that he'd taken Ms. Catsworthy with him. At least the two of them were together and hopefully having a memorable trip.

# CHAPTER 9

# *Into the Mouth of Hell*

E rik hovered in the back of the cargo van as the guards drove
the skinny teen, Thomas, deep into the desert. He felt he'd
made a promise to this young man and so kept on hyper-alert,
afraid they were taking him to the crematorium. He already had
a STAG control out, ready to zap Thomas to the same state as
himself the moment it looked like they might be going there.
But they didn't make the turn-off, at least, not the same one
they'd made just days before when they'd murdered another
man. They kept driving, going south for over an hour before
turning into an isolated fenced compound jutting up from the
desert. Armed guards approached and exchanged words before
opening the gate. The van lurched forward.

He decided to put away the STAG control for now. He'd
watch and listen first to see what was going on in this facility.
They parked near the main entrance, disembarked, and removed
the gurney containing Thomas. Erik was pleased to see that
they covered him with a rough army blanket and strapped him

117

in before moving him—this was perhaps a good sign that they did not plan to kill him.

The prisoner was wheeled through wide automatic doors that swung open after one of the men typed a code into a keypad. *Hmmm, modern facility.* They stopped at a reception desk and spoke to a young man dressed in military fatigues. They left Thomas strapped to the gurney, and walked back out the wide doors, where they got into the van.

Erik stayed behind, both to protect this young man and because this new facility seemed more promising than the one he just left.

Presently, two men came for the gurney and wheeled it onto an elevator. Erik followed them up to the second floor and down a corridor he was now sure was part of a modern hospital wing. They turned into one of the rooms, which resembled a surgery, with many types of equipment and tubing. After about fifteen minutes, someone dressed in a lab coat, possibly a doctor, entered, followed by a younger, white-coated man. He used a tiny light beam to peer into each of Thomas's eyes, listened to his heart and lungs, palpitated his ribs and lower back, and wrote on a chart. He cleaned and bandaged the young man's wounds. The young man slept through it all. Erik began to wonder if the guards had drugged him.

The doctor spoke to the two men who had rolled in the gurney, apparently giving some type of orders. They strapped him down again. The doctor gave the man a shot in the arm, producing an immediate reaction from the man, who gasped and awoke. As he looked around in terror, he seemed to realize he was strapped in and that fighting the restraints would be hopeless. His eyes rolled around, taking in the men present and obviously wondering what they were going to do with him. The doctor reached into a bottom drawer of the cabinet, took out an orange jumpsuit and tossed it onto the gurney. He said something else to the two gurney drivers and left the room, followed by his assistant.

Erik trailed after the two men as they wheeled Thomas back onto the elevator. They bypassed the ground floor, however, and emerged onto a dank, basement-level hallway. They rolled the man down an aisle between two rows of jail cells. Midway down the hallway, they stopped and spoke to a guard, who quickly snapped into action and unlocked one of the cells. The man was taken inside, unbuckled, and deposited onto the lower bunk of a typical jail-cell bunk bed. The two then left, taking the gurney with them. Erik felt hopeful; this appeared to be a long-term holding facility.

Erik began his reconnaissance with some degree of cautious enthusiasm. He inspected each cell in turn. His hope increased upon realizing these didn't appear to be Iraqi prisoners. They were from a much larger gene pool, possibly from the great Melting Pot of America, he thought, as his heart began to race. Here was one red-headed man, five black men, three with Asian features, one possibly a Pacific-Islander, and several men of mixed race. There were twenty cells in all, but only one end of the cellblock seemed to be in use. Erik counted seventeen prisoners so far, including Thomas, the only one without a cellmate in the ten cells on this end of the block.

There was only one more cell to check. Something about it felt surreal. He felt he was approaching something important as he crept forward and peered in. Here he saw a skinny, bearded middle-aged man sitting on the lower bunk, reading a battered novel.

*Yes.* He answered the question he'd asked himself earlier. *Yes, I'd recognize you anywhere, Dad.* He knew he'd have felt tears stream down his cheeks if that were possible to cry in this state.

He quickly went to him to do a mind-meld. He didn't want to have his father feel despair for even one more moment. He wanted his father to know Erik was here. His father slowly

119

put down the book and looked into the air as though trying to remember something. Erik sent his love to him as forcefully as he could and tried to communicate a sense of comfort that everything would be okay.

Erik then tried to extract information. He implanted images of the guard in an attempt to get his father to think of their schedule. He received an image of a guard member bringing a dinner cart with paper plates of food. Soon afterward, Erik heard the cart approaching. The guard slid a plate of beans and rice onto an opening in the bars, where there was a small platform for passing food to prisoners. The guard kept going down the row, leaving a plate for the new prisoner, and then two plates at each of the remaining cells with dual-occupancy.

Erik stepped back to observe his dad, his face having regained the sadness he'd seen earlier—or perhaps it was tiredness. He didn't seem to feel very well. Perhaps this was why he was alone in the cell. He slowly ambled over to his plate and picked it up, then filled a tumbler with water at the small dirty sink. He sat on the edge of his bed again and picked at his food. Erik decided to use this time to develop a detailed plan.

He searched first for the best way out. His original plan had been to use the ghost transformation on his dad and just yank him through the walls like he'd done with Red last winter when he feared Roy and Lorenzo would harm her. But now he also wanted to rescue Thomas. He was entertaining the idea that perhaps he should shrink them. He could place them in a box on some tissue so they wouldn't get injured by the jostling.

All of a sudden, he felt his jaw drop as he was broadsided by an idea. If he were going to miniaturize them and place them in a box, why couldn't he do that to *all* the prisoners?

He paused for a minute to let this sink in. He was pretty certain these prisoners weren't here because of crimes they'd committed, but were prisoners of war, maybe not even official prisoners of the Iraqi army, but of more radical groups. He suspected they were being held as bargaining chips. He'd been somewhat pleased that Thomas had been attended to by a doctor, but then again, his father certainly didn't look well.

He made a decision. He had to rescue all the prisoners in this block. He'd miniaturize them, place them in a box, take them to the American Embassy in Damascus, and then return them to their normal state during the night so they could get help and go back home.

But how could he explain what was going to happen to them? Or keep them from accidentally alerting one of the guards to the plan? The only answer was to do this secretly and let people assume they'd been drugged. Or perhaps he'd blindfold them. But first he had to figure out the escape route.

He wasn't thrilled about being underground. This complicated any escape plan. He thought his options were elevator, stairs, or vent system. The elevator was problematic—he'd need a guard to come down the elevator so he could somehow get the miniaturized prisoners onboard and ride back up, but if a guard came down the elevator, he'd be certain to see the prisoners were gone. He considered mind-melding with a guard to try to suggest that the prisoners were still in their cells. *Too risky.*

He looked for a stairwell and found one at each end, but both were locked tight and the doors didn't even have keyholes to escape through, even if he made the prisoners really small. So perhaps it did need to be the vent system. Of course, in a miniaturized state, he knew a vent system might be treacherous. *Enough of this—why guess? I can just ask my dad.* He felt a thrill of excitement when he decided to let him in on the whole thing.

He'd keep the other prisoners in the dark about the transformations, but his dad needed to know and Erik knew he could be trusted with the information.

He positioned himself near his father and waited for the guard to come and collect the trash from dinner. Another guard sat at a desk near the elevator but Erik thought it likely that he was posted there and wouldn't come down the hallway for a while.

As soon as he heard the elevator door close, he zapped his dad with the STAG control on the ghost transformation setting. He firmly grasped his confused father's hand and whisked him upward through the roof and out into the starry night.

He flew over to an empty spot in the parking lot and landed. He turned to look into his father's face and saw astonishment and confusion. "Erik?" his father said.

"Please don't be afraid," Erik said. "I know this all seems very strange and I'm going to explain it to you."

"Am I dead?" His father's voice was feeble as he looked around, drinking in the outside world. Erik knew he was seeing the essence of all things glowing in the night.

"It's more like a top-secret scientific thing I've been working on in grad school," Erik said. "I've transformed you into an alternate state."

His father looked down. "Why the hell am I naked?"

Erik grinned. "That's because you were wearing cotton and it doesn't transform well. Here, take my clothing." Erik removed his leather loincloth and awkwardly tried to help put it on his dad, but his dad snatched it and did most of it himself.

"Okay, now I know I'm dreaming. My son's dressing me in a leather loincloth."

"Oh, Dad, I can't believe it's really you." Erik lost it for a moment, throwing his arms around his father. They embraced, both laughing and weeping.

Erik heard his dad laugh, too, and then make soft choking sobs as he clung to him. "I don't really know what's happening, but Erik, you're here and that's all that matters. I'll do whatever you say. Just, if this is a dream, don't let me wake up from it."

"Okay, then Dad, please listen carefully. We're outside of the prison and could leave right now," Erik said. "But I saw another young man tortured and I'd like to go back in and save him."

"Absolutely," his father said at once. "If you have the means to free any or all of those poor fellow prisoners, please do. I'll help."

Erik smiled. "Let me ask you a few questions. First, how often does a guard patrol the corridor and look inside each cell?"

"Mostly only at mealtime and medication time. Someone will come once more tonight to deliver meds."

"Will he have a cart, like a dinner cart?"

"Yes."

Do you know if there are strong tranquilizers somewhere and could you find and recognize them?"

"Yes, no, and no. I've never been allowed to see where the medicines are kept and I'm sure the labels would be in Arabic, which I can read for the most part, but don't know well enough to be safe with the names of drugs."

Erik thought for a moment. "Tell me this. Would all the prisoners trust you enough to do as you said? No questions asked? You could let them know an escape was being planned."

"Yes—well, probably. All except the new prisoner. Him, I don't know."

"I can spring them without their cooperation, but it'd be very nice to have it," Erik said. "Plus, I don't want anyone having a heart attack on me when I transform them. But that's only if it works out. There may not be an opportunity to even let them know anything about it until it's over."

"So you're going to do this to all of them?" His dad made a gesture toward his own body.

"No, that'd be too hard. I'm afraid I couldn't handle more than one in this state at a time and that'd take too long. I'll have to miniaturize them," he said. His dad looked surprised, but Erik didn't have time to explain. "Plus, and this is a very important plus—they aren't to know anything about the transformation part. We'll somehow have to convince them they were drugged and imagined the whole part about being transformed. It'd be helpful to actually drug them, but I don't want to risk giving something fatal to someone, so that option may be out."

"Agreed." His dad seemed to be sharing the responsibility for the decision-making. Erik was pleased to see that his spirit hadn't been broken after ten years as a prisoner of war.

"So how does this sound? We go back inside before the meds are distributed. Do you have another orange jumpsuit?"

"Yes."

"Okay, you'll need to put that on, but wear the leather loincloth underneath, because I'll be transforming you back to this state."

"What about you, son? What're you going to wear?" His concern was touching, especially given all he'd endured, Erik thought.

"Not a problem, Dad. I'll eventually find something I can use, but the others are going to be transformed in another way, so they won't see me anyway. You see, I have a device that can minimize them, so I can just pop them into a box and carry them out without anyone's knowledge. I'll look for something common, like a matchbox, in the trash. That way, they'll be in the dark and hopefully won't see me or figure out what happened." He worried for a moment about keeping the transformation secret. "Boy, it sure would be nice to have them tranquilized."

"I could throw a fit and have them tranquilize me," his father suggested. "Then you can watch to see where they get the tranquilizer."

"That's a great idea, but no, I don't want to risk having someone harm you. I couldn't bear it if something happened to you now that we're so close to getting you out of this hellhole." Erik's voice broke slightly.

Erik's father patted him on the back. "It's going to be all right."

They mapped out a rough plan then went back the way they'd come, down through the roof and into the cell. Erik loathed having to do it, but he transformed his dad back to a normal state. He almost wept at how vulnerable he looked, locked in a cell wearing a loincloth. It killed him to watch his father, Viggo Wolfeningen, once a giant to him but now an emaciated victim, behave like a well-seasoned prisoner of war. But his father seemed to be taking it all in stride and focusing on the tasks ahead. He took another orange jumpsuit from a wooden peg on the wall and stepped into it. He then sat on the edge of his bed and picked up the old tattered paperback novel, just as Erik had found him.

Erik didn't have long to wait before the guard with the cart of meds stepped off the elevator. The guard placed a tiny paper cup containing pills on the small platform inside the opening where dinner had been placed. He moved on down the line to Thomas's cell. He placed a similar paper cup on his platform and called to Thomas. Thomas seemed to be asleep and didn't respond. The guard said something under his breath and called to the man seated at the desk. The man grudgingly got up, walked over to the cell, and used one of the keys from a large cluster on his belt to open the cell door. The first man took the pill cup from the platform, walked over the sleeping prisoner, and tried to shake him awake. After some effort, Thomas's eyes opened, and, seemingly caught in some torture-induced nightmare, launched into a panicked state and began screaming and trying to push the guard away. The guard retreated. The other guard re-locked the cell door and the first went to the elevator, leaving his cart in front of Thomas's cell. Erik followed him.

He went to the floor above, down a corridor, and turned into a locked medicine closet. *Success,* Erik thought. Erik watched as he pulled out a drawer filled with disposable syringes and plucked a bottle from a shelf. He filled the syringe and left. Erik made a careful note of the exact location of the bottle and followed the guard back down.

The guard re-entered the young man's cell, assisted by the other guard. Thomas was still highly agitated and seemed confused but unable to fight off the two guards as one held his arms and the other force-fed him something from the paper cup and then delivered the tranquilizer shot. Within moments, he was fast asleep once more.

The guard finished delivering meds to the prisoners and left. Erik tried speaking to his father by a whisper. His father's hearing must've deteriorated and this didn't seem to work. He thought about trying to mind-meld, but decided to just go for it and transform to a normal state just for a few minutes to communicate with his dad. He appeared behind the bunk beds, crouching down to make himself less likely to be noticed if there were cameras.

His dad started but evidently grasped what was happening fast enough to not make any noise. He looked around cautiously, and seeming to assure himself there were no onlookers, slid quickly over to Erik. "Yes, son?"

"Dad, the plan has changed. I know where the tranquilizer's stored. I'll simply wait until lights out and everyone's asleep, give everyone a shot of tranquilizer, miniaturize them, and place them in the box. I'll then come for you, transform you to the state you were in before, and you'll exit through the roof while I transfer the box to the elevator and then watch for a way to get it out of the building. I'll probably need to hide it in something or on someone that's leaving the building. That's the weakest link in my plan," he said. "You may have to wait some time. Probably until a guard goes off duty and I can hide the box on him. Are you up for this?"

"Absolutely. I haven't had this much fun since ... well, never mind, not in a long time. But I feel bad leaving you behind," his father said. "What if you get caught? Shouldn't I stay and help you?"

"Dad, for one thing, I can't possibly get caught in this state. I'd feel better having you safely out of the way. And neither of us will really be in any danger—only the others will be vulnerable. The minimized state is almost as vulnerable as the normal state. Molecules can't just pass through like they can in the state we'll be in. But I think the danger is low enough that they'll be more likely to survive the escape than being left here."

"I wholeheartedly agree, son. But since I won't be in any danger, perhaps I'd be of some help to you. I'd really rather go with you."

"Okay, Dad. I could never talk you out of an idea once you had your stubborn cap set."

"That's not true. Remember the time—" but he stopped abruptly. Erik had heard it too—a sound from the guard at the desk. *Whoops.* Were they talking too loud? Had they been overheard? Erik immediately transformed himself and saw his dad resume his customary pose. The guard slowly walked down the corridor, peeking into each cell, and then ambled back to his desk, sat back down, and propped his feet up.

Erik watched his dad for a moment, trying to drink in all he'd missed in the years he'd thought he was lost forever, fighting overwhelming emotions to keep his head clear. He watched him go over to his tiny sink and begin to wash his face.

Erik decided it was time to go in search of an adequate box. He ghosted through the ceiling and onto the main floor. He hadn't seen any trash containers near the cells and thought this more promising. If there were sixteen people, each approximately three quarters of an inch tall, a matchbox wouldn't be adequate. But he needed it to be as small as possible to allow more options for hiding it. If he did three zaps, rather than two, he'd be able to fit them easily into a matchbox, but he wasn't confident of being able to pick them up without causing damage to someone that small. Plus, he worried that things like static electricity might be serious concerns to a being that small.

No, he wouldn't experiment on these prisoners. He'd find a box that worked. Perhaps he'd find something in the medicine closet. He needed to get the syringes there, anyway, and he'd pick up some cotton balls to cushion the box.

He decided things would go faster if he transformed back to his normal state once in the medicine closet. He did so and began his search.

He looked into the trashcan in the corner of the tiny room and found a couple of boxes, but neither was what he was looking for. Finally, after a few minutes of searching in the cabinets, he found one adequate for his purpose. He emptied its contents into the trashcan, filled the bottom with cotton balls, and then thought better of that. To get the materials into the cell area, he'd need to transform them using the ghost transformation and he wasn't sure if cotton balls would transform well. He knew cotton fabric didn't, but that was because the strands were held together by friction; he didn't think that was the case with cotton balls.

Best to test it first. He took out his STAG control and tested one. He zapped it back, and to his delight, it was intact. Just then, he heard footsteps approaching. He quickly put the box and cotton balls into a cabinet and zapped himself into invisibility.

He waited a few minutes for the footsteps to move past the medicine closet. He transformed back to normal and resumed his work.

He decided he'd better test a syringe to make sure the metal would transform well. The syringe disappeared and reappeared intact, as well. He counted out enough syringes with a couple extra in case someone needed two shots or some other contingency occurred. Perhaps he'd have to tranquilize a guard. He'd never given a person a shot before, but he'd watched the guard deliver it into the man's shoulder, which seemed easy enough. He found the bottle the guard had used, filled each syringe, recapped each, and placed them into a plastic tray atop a paper towel. He wasn't sure the paper towel was sterile, but he thought it more likely to be sterile than the plastic tray.

Next he lined the small box with cotton balls and placed the lid on top. He searched for a roll of tape in case he needed it to secure the lid and perhaps even tape it to something for transport. He found a roll of white medical tape. That would do. He needed to connect all the objects to himself for the transformation, and since he had no pockets, found a plastic bag to carry his stash.

He transformed himself with his bag using the ghost transformation and then pushed himself down through the floor and back to his father's cellblock.

Lights were already out. He looked at the guard with his feet propped up on his desk and was relieved to find him sound asleep, his head thrown back. He pitied the man once the discovery was made that the prisoners had escaped. To be safe, he decided to use one of the extra syringes and gave the man a shot of tranquilizer.

He methodically went from cell to cell, leaving Thomas and his father for last, deciding up front to enter each cell, check to make sure both prisoners were asleep, then transform himself back to normal before tranquilizing and collecting the prisoners in that cell to ensure he didn't drop someone by letting them slip through his ghostly fingers in the transformed state. Once he'd decided this, he felt a little less nervous.

He took care not to contaminate the clean syringes with the dirty ones. Who knew, some of these men might have AIDS or hepatitis. But he also didn't want to leave any evidence behind that might reveal any clues about the operation, so he carefully stashed them in the plastic bag.

Once he'd tranquilized first one and then the other cellmate, he double-zapped each with the STAG control set to minimization. After each person was zapped, he gently swept him into his hand using the other gloved hand, being careful to not bruise or allow the person to fall to the floor, which would likely be fatal. He gently laid each one in the box before zapping the next.

Finally, he made his way to the end of the row opposite his father. He was afraid to transform the box into an invisible state. A combined transformation—a minimization followed by a ghost transformation—hadn't been tested, and he wouldn't expose the prisoners to the risk, though it certainly would've made it easier to sneak them out of the building.

He was sure his father was lying awake, listening for him. He ghosted across the corridor, scooting the box full of minimized prisoners, and began going up the row toward his father. To his dismay, the prisoner in the top bunk in the first cell in that row was awake and staring at the ceiling. He wondered what the man had made of the scooting sounds of the box and hoped he'd thought it was mice. He decided to skip that cell; he'd come back to it.

He continued up the row. No one else was awake. To his relief, when he went back to that cell, that prisoner was asleep.

He now went to Thomas's cell. He didn't know how long the tranquilizer would work and anguished for a moment over whether he should give him another dose or not. On one hand, he was already tranquilized and might sleep for the rest of the night. On the other, the prisoner had been so panicked and had possibly been having a psychotic episode, so if he did awaken and find himself trapped in a box with the other prisoners, he might harm them, or worse, give away their location. A person in a minimized state could still be heard.

He decided that for the good of all, he must take the chance and give him another dose; after all, it had already been several hours since the guard had tranquilized him.

Now all the prisoners were minimized and in the box. Erik taped the box with only one strand of tape for now, in case he needed to open it quickly.

He scooted the box in front of his dad's cell and entered, not bothering to transform to a natural state, and saw that his father was awake and smiling. He zapped him into a ghost state. Immediately the two embraced.

"Good to see you, son."

"Good to see you, Dad. Are you ready to boogey?"

"Hey, I've been ready for ten years."

"The guard outside is tranquilized."

"Great idea."

The two left the cell and approached the elevator, Erik scooting the box along the floor. His dad caught on fast and began to help. On reaching the elevator, Erik pressed the button to call it to the basement and scooted the box inside.

As the elevator ascended to the main floor, Erik pushed the box up to the elevator ceiling and kept it suspended there. This was difficult to maintain and took both Erik and his dad working together, using all the force they could muster, pushing upward with first one hand and then another as the first hand slipped slowly upward into the box, the molecules of their hands too far apart and small to provide a solid surface.

The door opened. They saw the guard at the entryway counter glance up expectantly. Seeing no one get off the elevator, he arose from his chair and walked around the end of the counter to the open elevator doors. Looking inside, he arched an eyebrow and then shrugged.

As he turned his back on them, Erik moved quickly to make the box fly out of the elevator to land gently on the soft dirt inside a nearby planter.

As the man reseated himself, Erik made the box slowly move to the floor, then across the space until it was underneath the front of his counter and hidden from his sight. Erik was relieved that the floor here was highly polished and the scooting of the box made very little sound. With the box hidden from view now, Erik was able to scoot it all the way around the counter until it rested just beside the automatic doors to the main entrance of the building.

Suddenly, he heard the sound of a door close in one of the corridors leading off the main entryway. A uniformed, well-decorated man came through the foyer, nodded to the guard, and then noticed the box.

Erik panicked, thinking he might try to pick it up as trash—or worse, look inside. Thinking fast, he quickly positioned himself to mind-meld with the man and suggested an urgent need to urinate. The man quickly changed his course and disappeared down another corridor.

Knowing that the man would likely return soon and might remember the box, Erik considered tranquilizing the guard and opening the doors to escape. But to his great relief, the doors swung open and three uniformed men entered. Erik waited until they'd cleared the doorway and then he and his dad pushed the little box outside as fast as they could while the three men stopped at the desk to talk to the attendant.

Once outside, Erik quickly pushed the box away from the main walkway and around the side of the building. They tucked it behind a raised curb so it was hidden from sight from almost any angle.

He caught his dad's eye and they high-fived. The moment was sweet but brief; they needed to be at a much safer distance. They were out of earshot, however, and could risk speaking.

"I need to find a big bird, like a crow or a duck," Erik said.

"Son, I don't know if you've noticed, but we're in a desert."

Erik allowed himself to chuckle slightly. "There's a lake nearby. I did a little research and there are some crows here, though a different species from back home."

"Son, why are we talking about birds? I hesitate to question anything you're planning, since it's obvious a lot's changed since I've been away, but please humor me. Why do we need a bird?"

"Because you and I can fly out of here and a bird can carry the box taped to its back."

"And what makes you think it'll fly in the right direction?"

"Dad, you know what I did with that man who was getting ready to pick up the box?"

"No, son, I haven't a clue. I saw you ... I don't know, it looked like you went inside him. And then he almost ran down the hall."

"Yes, I mind-melded with him and implanted the suggestion that he needed desperately to urinate."

His dad laughed heartily at this statement. "Okay, so you're telling me that you're going to mind-meld with a bird?"

"Yep, done it lots of times. That's, um, kinda how I courted my girlfriend."

"Son, when we get home, you and I need to have a long talk. I may've been imprisoned for ten years, but I still know a thing or two about how to court a female. And since I've been away, it appears that your training has gone awry."

Erik laughed, too. "Okay, since I don't hear any birds right now, I think the best thing to do is to scoot the box out to the road and catch a passing car going in the direction away from Baghdad. Then, once we're a safe distance away, perhaps we can spot a promising bird and be on our way."

"Okay, I guess you know what you're doing."

They scooted the box out to the road and waited. Erik flew upward briefly to see if he could spot a car coming and caught sight of some headlights in the distance. "Looks like one's coming in the right direction now. It should be here in a few minutes. I'll mind-meld with the driver and suggest something to make him stop. I'll have to buy enough time to tape the box securely onto the fender."

Erik flew toward the approaching vehicle, leaving his dad to guard the box. He pushed through the roof and into a position to mind-meld with the driver. Luckily, the driver was alone in the car. As they approached the prison, Erik implanted a suggestion that there might be a flat tire. The man still seemed hesitant to stop in front of the prison, likely not wanting to arouse any interest in himself by whatever group was running the facility.

He stopped anyway, pulling just past the glow of the street-light illuminating the entryway. He got out of the car and walked around to inspect the tires, leaving the door ajar. Erik took the opportunity to make that man discover a sudden need to urinate, since it had worked so well on the other man. While the man was doing that, he and his dad placed the box on the floorboard of the car behind the driver and the two of them climbed into the back seat. "Dad, there's a pouch attached to your loincloth and inside it is a map of this area. Would you please take it out?"

"Certainly, son."

Erik noticed gratefully that the driver was listening to music so any possibility of their whispery voices being overheard was very low. He began to study the map. "We're traveling south on this road, I think," Erik pointed. "I don't think we should go back into Baghdad—just too complicated. I was thinking of trying to find a goose or crane somewhere around this lake." He pointed to Razazza Lake. "We can tape the box to its back and then I'll instruct it to fly north to connect with the road. That way, we could bypass Baghdad. The only problem is that we need to get them to Damascus before the tranquilizer wears off."

"Are you out of your mind?" his dad asked incredulously.

"What?" Erik shot back, feeling a hint of his old rebellious-teen self awaken.

"Son, do you know how easy it is to spot a game bird flying across the desert? Do you know how many men have guns in this country?"

"Oh ... right," Erik saw the logic. "What do you suggest?"

"First of all, why Damascus? Shouldn't we just go to the nearest American embassy?"

"Okay, but I wasn't sure how safe an embassy inside Iraq might be. What if they can't get you out of the country once you're in the embassy? I want to have you safely outside of Iraq before un-transforming you."

"Son, you worry too much. Okay, let's look at the map. America has embassies in Baghdad, Basrah, Erbil, and Kirkuk." He pointed to each location.

"Are you sure they still exist?"

His dad paused thoughtfully. "Okay, guess I have to give you that one." He scowled playfully at Erik and they both laughed. Erik took a moment to savor how good it felt that they could so easily drift back into old forms of teasing before pressing on.

"Hey, I wouldn't even mind going to the embassy in Baghdad," His father said.

"Dad, that's where you disappeared."

"No, I was always safe inside the embassy. I got nabbed going to my apartment," he said. "No, I think we're on a good track. Let's see what this guy does and play it by ear. But just so you'll know, if we're dropped off at the embassy in Basrah, we'll likely be taken back to the Baghdad embassy for processing anyway. So don't get your knickers in a bunch if that happens. It's perfectly okay, son. They know what they're doing."

Erik breathed a long slow breath of surrender. "Okay, Dad, it's your ballgame now."

# CHAPTER 10

## *Flying the Coop*

As it turned out, to Erik's relief, the driver did go in the right direction, stopping in Nasiriyah to refuel and use the toilet. Upon pulling back onto the road, the car was suddenly awash with lights and a siren gave one short note. The man pulled over to the side of the road.

Erik watched with some anxiety as two armed military men walked up to either side of the car, their weapons drawn. The man rolled down his window and exchanged a few sentences with the man standing outside the driver's window. The man outside his window seemed to be barking questions. The driver submissively, and somewhat nervously, answered them.

The man then gave a command and the driver pulled a lever to pop open the trunk. The man walked around behind the car and jabbed his bayonet into the trunk a few times while his partner held a flashlight. Erik soundlessly scooted the little box under the driver's seat, mostly out of sight.

The one with the flashlight walked forward from the back of the car and began shining the beam all around the backseat. Erik felt a moment of panic when the light beam stopped on the visible end of the box. Time seemed to stop, and then the light beam moved off. The man shined the light around the front floor board on both sides, had the man open the glove box, looked briefly in there, and then had the man pop the hood latch. The man shined his light around the engine. Erik guessed that the disappearance of the prisoners was now known to the captors, but was a little puzzled with how these men thought they could hide prisoners in the engine compartment or glove box, but he guessed an automobile might be modified in some way to hide escapees inside in creative ways. He looked at his dad's face and saw a calm vacancy that he suspected had been practiced many times, kind of a shutting down until the bad part was over.

After a few minutes, to Erik's great relief, the men left and the driver continued on his way to Basrah. Once inside the city, the driver turned into a driveway in a somewhat modern-looking housing complex, with multiple terraces and small palm-treed yards. He shut off the engine and took out a battered suitcase from the trunk, then walked with a tired, dragging gait up to the front door. Erik noted the luggage had been scarred from the bayonet. As soon as the man disappeared into the house, his father turned to him.

"Okay, now how're we going to get this box out of the car? Can you open a door in this state?"

"Shouldn't be a problem." The man had locked the doors, but Erik was able to push up the lock button and carefully open the door. After a few minutes, the box was out on the driveway beside the car.

"Which direction, Captain?" he asked his father.

Erik watched his dad first look at the sky and then point. "I'm pretty sure it's west of us and possibly slightly north. It's pretty much in the center of the city. We probably need to walk out to the last street we left. I don't think this one's big enough to have a bus route."

They began pushing the box down the street, but Erik's dad pointed out that it was a little bumpy and might awaken the prisoners. Since it was still dark, Erik decided to take a chance at carrying the box. This worked much better. "You know Dad, fly-swimming is much faster than a bus anyway. I think I could fly with this box, with a little help—you know like we did when I first transformed you?"

"I thought I'd either died or was having a really weird dream."

"One of us could pull the other upward and the other carry the box. It's easy to pull someone along with you when you fly. I think it'd be slow going if one tried to just use their legs for a kicking motion without being pulled along, though. But with teamwork, I think it'd work."

"Okay, I'm game."

Erik turned the box over to his father, who focused most of his concentration on keeping the box suspended. Erik grabbed his upper arm and began flying upward, using one hand to "swim" while kicking his feet. Once they were airborne he spotted what appeared to be the center of the city and flew in that direction.

It wasn't long before his dad shouted, "I think it's that building there, the brown one with the two pointy towers. I was there once and I'm pretty sure that's it."

"Excellent," Erik exclaimed, veering in the direction of the brown building with the pointy towers. In just minutes, they landed on a very small, grassy lawn in front of the building. The building was quite pretty, a brown stucco with ornately carved trim around the roof, reflected in the design of the shutters. Some nicely kept shrubs and one palm tree on each side of the walkway appeared to be the work of a professional lawn company, or even a groundskeeper. He couldn't help but smile at the placard next to the front door written in both English and Arabic: "American Embassy."

"This is it, Dad." He felt himself beginning to tear up and remembered that tears wouldn't be produced in this transformed state.

"Son." His dad looked him in the eyes and said with much feeling, "No father was ever more proud of a son than I am of you. I've never given you enough credit, but you know something? You're a brilliant man. You've successfully pulled something off that neither myself nor anyone else would've ever dreamed. Now, it may take a couple of weeks to process me through, so please give my love to your mother in the meantime."

"I think I'll wait and let you tell her yourself. If I tell her, she might not be able to show appropriate astonishment when the authorities tell her. And Dad, I cannot emphasize enough that the transformations are top secret. We've had some trouble from a group already that would like to obtain these capabilities for nefarious purposes. Just imagine what it would mean if these were in the hands of crooks or terrorists?" Erik said. "So, now when we go inside, here's what I need to do. I'm going to find an empty room, zap us back to normal, lie all the prisoners out on the floor, zap them to normal size, and then give you a small injection of the same tranquilizer I gave them. That way, you'll be just like all the others in case they do a blood test. And the storyline is that none of you know who tranquilized you and sprang you from prison. Okay?"

"Sounds like a brilliant plan, son."

He hugged his father. "Now, *bon voyage*. I'll hang around and watch over you until I know the right people have you, so don't worry."

"I'm not worried. *Bon voyage*, yourself."

Once inside, Erik saw his dad move quickly to the door and begin his lookout duty. Erik gently peeled the tape from the box and inspected the contents. The men had definitely shifted; some were lying atop others, many arms and legs sprawled out. He picked up the cotton padding in one hand and, using his fingers, very gently teased each man off the cotton, rolling them onto the carpeted floor. He laid them with as much space as he was able, given the length of the room, allowing at least a foot between each. He found the tiny orange jumpsuit he'd packed for his dad in the cotton packing so he'd have clothes to wear once Erik transformed him.

Then he took one of the STAG controls and zapped each man back to normal size. No one awoke, he was relieved to see. He next went to his dad. "Hey, Dad, time now to get dressed for your grand performance. I'll watch the door while you dress."

His dad quickly dressed. As he came toward the door, Erik put a finger to his mouth in a shushing gesture and pointed to the end of the line of prisoners. His dad nodded and quickly laid down beside the last person in the row. Eric wasted no time injecting him with a small amount of tranquilizer. The two exchanged a meaningful glance and then his dad closed his eyes.

Eric did the stepwise process of zapping one STAG control, then himself, and then the other, as fast as his fingers could work. The last STAG control disappeared a millisecond before the door opened and a maid flipped on the light and screamed an ear-splitting scream at the unexpected sight of eighteen men asleep on the floor.

Erik smiled to himself as he pressed upward through the ceiling and roof. He hovered overhead for some time, watching and listening. After a few minutes, American military vehicles began arriving. The building became heavily guarded in a very short time. Eventually, a military helicopter landed behind the building and he watched as a suited man was rushed inside between two military escorts. He assumed this was the ambassador. That helicopter flew away and another arrived, this time carrying a decorated American military figure. This surprised Erik somewhat since he thought all American troops had been removed. Perhaps he was some type of embassy personnel.

As he hovered over the embassy, he couldn't help but notice the sun rising over the Shatt-Al-Arab waterway. He looked

141

all around and was saddened by evidence of years of war, but was glad to see that many reconstructions were underway. He was awed by the beauty of the contrast between the earthy colors of the desert with the glorious sunrise striped across the waterway. He remembered that some people thought the Garden of Eden had been just north of Basrah, near where the Tigris and Euphrates converged to form the Shatt-Al-Arab. At this moment it seemed very believable. There was something ancient and mysterious about this land.

As Erik looked again at the embassy, he noted that several ambulances had arrived. He decided to fly down and listen to see if this meant the prisoners were being transferred somewhere. He quickly eased into the room where the prisoners had been left. Things had changed drastically. Most of the prisoners were still in the room. Now each man was lying on his own gurney. Some had an IV attached to an arm, delivering rehydration fluid, or so Erik assumed. It appeared that one prisoner at a time was being moved to another room, probably for a thorough examination. Photographers were also on the scene. He saw his dad lying on a gurney, still asleep. But some of the prisoners were waking. A couple of prisoners were answering questions. He saw a man being interviewed in front of a camera. The man, possibly the ambassador, said that the men had been prisoners of war and the details of their escape weren't being released at this time. The men would be thoroughly examined by medical personnel and would be flown to an undisclosed military base in America beginning tomorrow.

Erik was overjoyed. It all wouldn't take so long to process after all. It made sense, though, since America's military presence had been withdrawn, that most of the investigation and medical examinations would take place in an American military facility.

Erik's original intent had been to fly back as soon as he knew his dad was secure and to await his dad's official return. But he decided to just wait and fly back with his dad. He thought about calling Sonia, but realized that now with all the mystery surrounding how the prisoners got out, security would be on high alert. If he tried to call from Iraq to Sonia's cell phone, it might link her to this and he really didn't want to risk having someone snoop around and discover the research they were doing. So he decided to wait until he got back and surprise her.

He didn't have long to wait. His father was on the first medical helicopter out that evening, along with three other rescued prisoners. It seemed they were the oldest of the prisoners. They stopped only briefly to refuel once. Erik couldn't believe his luck when they were taken to Bethesda Naval Hospital in Maryland, not far from home.

Antonio sat in the passenger's seat of the van, sweat trickling down his back, despite the rain and almost freezing temperatures outside. *Dannazione.* Why were they being stopped at the border on their way into Italy, when they had breezed right through into France and then Switzerland? He pulled a drag from his cigarette and blew out thick smoke, hoping to disguise the alcohol smell on his breath. He felt a bottle against his heel and pushed it surreptitiously further under his seat, hoping the cap was on tight, but even now he could smell the alcohol wafting upward.

The driver was outside, speaking with the guard, who was pulling his flashlight from his belt. A groan sounded from the back and then he heard scuffling and smelled ether again. His heart began to pound and he pushed the fingers of his right hand into his pocket far enough to feel the solid edge of the switchblade. He grasped it between his thumb and forefinger and slowly began to draw it out, unsure what to do, but the thing inside urged him to act, no matter what danger it might bring to him. He knew if the van got searched, he and the others would take the guard. He looked down the line of kiosks in the road — it was the middle of the night, but about half looked occupied. They'd have to do this fast.

To his relief, he saw the guard snatch a bill from the driver's hand and pocket both it and the flashlight. His friend jumped back into the driver's seat and fired up the motor as the guard waved them forward, not looking in their direction, but straight ahead, as if he'd already dismissed them.

Antonio heard another groan, followed by a grunt. He was tired of this whole business and the alcohol loosened his tongue. "Stop kicking him. He's an old man. Pietro will have your *palle* if you kill him," he said with some heat, though a perpetually present inner urge made him want to go pound the old man himself.

# PART THREE:

# Kidnapped by the Cult

*Quote from <u>Lilith</u>:*

*"Her bodily eyes stood wide open, as if gazing into the heart of horror essential—her own indestructible evil. Her right hand also was now clenched—upon existent Nothing—her inheritance. But with God all things are possible: He can save even the rich."* [3]

CHAPTER 11

# *Back to Mamaw's*

Things hadn't been this tense since Uncle Alistair's earlier disappearance, Annie thought, as she, Red, and her mother drove to Tennessee for Thanksgiving. She sat next to her mom in the car to allow her distraught sister the privacy of the back seat. Red was napping. Annie wore earbuds and stared out the window. But there was no sound coming from the earbuds; they were a prop to allow Annie some space to think.

The week before, she'd agreed to watch Ms. Catsworthy's two Himalayans, Snagglepus and Fluffmuffin, while Uncle Alistair and Ms. Catsworthy were in London. She hadn't realized that Uncle Alistair was an internationally recognized expert on the works of C.S. Lewis until he'd announced to the family that he was an invited speaker at a ceremony at Poets' Corner in Westminster Abbey. Annie thought that he and Ms. Catsworthy had seemed more excited about the trip than she'd ever seen them. She smiled to herself, thinking how much she liked to see her uncle and Ms. Catsworthy together. They were obviously sweet on each other. What was the deal there? She knew her whole family wondered, but all were too polite to ask. She'd been the only one home last Saturday night when the phone rang. Ms. Catsworthy's voice had sounded so different until she figured out that she'd obviously been crying. "Annie, love, something dreadful has happened to poor Alistair. I just know it."

"Where are you? I thought you were in England," Annie said.

"Yes, we are—or at least, I am." Annie heard her sniffle and pause for a moment. "Your uncle and I have been staying with old friends here in Chelsea and visiting several other families. You know, we both used to live here and have many dear friends. You should have seen your uncle's speech. I was so proud of dear Alistair." Annie heard more sniffles.

"That's great Ms. Catsworthy. Uncle Alistair's a good speaker," Annie felt that was a lame thing to say but hadn't been able to think of anything else. "What happened to Uncle Alistair?"

"Earlier today, or I guess it's yesterday now, he decided to do a bit of shopping—said he'd be gone a couple of hours. I'm coming down with a cold, and stayed in to rest up for the evening and didn't accompany him. Oh, why did I let him out of my sight?" Ms. Catsworthy's words were hard to decipher and dissolved into an episode of sobbing. "Alistair never came back. At first I thought he likely ran into some old friends and was having drinks at a pub. But then a gentleman from Scotland Yard called to say that his cell phone had been found at the bottom of the escalator at Chelsea Station!" Ms. Catsworthy said and sobbed again.

"Oh, Ms. Catsworthy," Annie said. "I'm sure he's fine and this is just some misunderstanding."

"I'm embarrassed to admit that I fainted dead away upon learning this news and was taken to hospital by my friends. But I've been back here for over an hour and have been calling all our friends to see if anyone knows anything."

"What do you want me to do, Ms. Catsworthy? Do you want us to fly over there?"

"I don't think so just yet. The detective said we should all stay put and wait to see if a kidnapper calls. My friends here are insisting that I stay with them so I can be nearby when he's found and can hear firsthand any new leads in the case. And I think the same goes for your dear family. I think you should stay there in case anyone calls."

The whole family had been sick with worry and grief ever since—Uncle Alistair had been back with them such a short time before disappearing again. Annie had heard her dad on the phone, trying to reassure Ms. Catsworthy that Uncle Alistair had always turned up before and knew quite well how to take care of himself. But Annie felt that in the back of everyone's minds, they were worried this was something entirely different. She didn't think there was any real doubt that he had, in fact, been kidnapped.

Annie was glad her parents kept their plan to drive down to Tennessee the day before Thanksgiving. They'd planned on spending Thanksgiving Day with Mamaw and driving back on Friday. At first, after the news about Uncle Alistair, her mom and dad had suggested canceling the trip, but her dad convinced her mom that she and the girls should go as planned. He argued that there was nothing they could do but wait and he'd stay in Potomac by the phone in case Scotland Yard found anything. Her mom had been hesitant but Annie knew her own little nudges had helped close the deal—she felt a little guilty for feigning a greater concern than she actually felt in not disappointing Mamaw.

Red had almost messed things up by beginning to protest, though. Annie knew Red worried about Erik's safety, fearing something sinister had happened to both men—something to do with the stones and maybe even the cult. Erik hadn't called in over a week and Red said that he had been in a really dangerous place the last time she talked to him. But Annie really didn't share her sister's concern about Erik. *He has a STAG control, for goodness sake. How could anyone capture him? If the demons could capture him from the ethereal realm, wouldn't they have done it last year?* Still, it would be helpful if Erik would just call Red.

Annie wasn't used to seeing Red so stressed out. She hoped she was right about him not being in danger, since he had the STAG controls. It wasn't like he hadn't gone this long before without calling. She guessed Red must be thinking that the danger was greater now that something had obviously happened to Uncle Alistair. But what was the deal with the two of them—Erik and Uncle Alistair? Were they destined to always disappear? Her sister had gone through a lot to transform Erik and now he seemed to be lost again. She felt protective of Red, even though she kept finding herself acting just the opposite. In fact, Annie felt a little guilty about how she'd handled the situation.

But she had a secret plan: She was going to enlist help from Aaan. After all, he was half angel. Who better to help with a cult that seemed to be run by one or more demons?

She truly was worried sick about her uncle, though she told herself there was still hope. But she had to act. It was up to her. She was the only one who could help right now because she had access to a half-angel and he obviously had supernatural powers. At least, she hoped her plan would work.

As she gazed out the window at the world going by in a blur, she thought of Aaan. *Aaan, what a beautiful, angelic name.* He could help. She just knew it. From reading his writings, she knew that he was basically good. He'd lamented loses, cared for others, and grown wise.

She sighed and suppressed a tear, thinking of how he had written about the spiritual attributes he thought he had attained while trying to be good enough to go to Heaven. She didn't really understand how that all worked—she'd always had a vague belief in Heaven, but the particulars seemed to be hotly debated by people who seemed to know more about it than she. But what she felt inside was that the whole universe would be unfair if such a good being as Aaan were abandoned to an eternity alone in a cave. A tear escaped and trickled down her cheek. She was glad it was on the side away from her mom—she really, really didn't feel like talking right now.

She knew what she needed to do. She wouldn't run away from Aaan. She'd go back to him and talk to him this time. She had the excuse of asking for his help and she dearly hoped he actually could help her uncle. But even apart from that, she wanted to see him again. She wanted to ask him questions. To tell him he didn't need to be alone. She'd be his friend. And she just knew it would work.

They arrived at Mamaw's shortly before bedtime. After hugs and kisses to Mamaw, Annie signaled to Red the need for a side chat and Red picked up the hint. The two called first-dibs on taking showers and retired while their mom and grandmother sat up and visited. "What's up?" Red asked once they were alone in the bedroom.

Annie lost no time in showing Red that she had brought the STAG control. She only needed Red to zap her and then zap her back in a couple of hours. They just needed to agree on a time. She wouldn't risk falling asleep like she did last summer. She was on a mission.

"Not so fast, young lady." Red's big-sister instincts seemed to be kicking in. "I'm not about to lose another relative this week. I'm going with you or there'll be no zapping."

Annie exhaled exasperatedly. "Fine, but that means we can't do it until tomorrow, unless you want to walk down a dark country road at midnight. Remember, Missy and Billy got a house up on the hill and moved. So there won't be a soul—well, not a body—" Annie cleared her throat "—anywhere nearby. If you stayed here, I could see by the glow of everything. You know what I mean."

Red nodded suspiciously.

Annie went on. "But walking down the road untransformed would be terrifying to do now—and what if they heard us going out? How would we get out? I don't think these window screens would come out without a lot of noise, and if we use the door, we'd have to pass by Mom and Mamaw sitting in the kitchen. So that means we have to wait until tomorrow, and how're we going to explain why we're gone for an hour or two?"

"First of all, while we're on the subject of terrifying, the thought of my little sister going out in the middle of the night to visit a ghost—whom, by the way, I've never met— in a cave … that's not terrifying? And second, there's no problem with leaving for a couple of hours, especially if we get out early— we always go for walks and runs down the road whenever we visit Mamaw. And third, I'm curious—I want to come too."

"Fine." Annie surrendered. She had to admit that it would be nice having Red along.

With her excitement over seeing Aaan again, Annie feared that sleep would evade her, but after a hot shower, she was out like a light.

The next morning, she awoke to the aroma of freshly baked biscuits. She didn't want to wait until Red awoke on her own, so she shook her shoulder, telling her that Mamaw had made breakfast and she should get up.

Mamaw's biscuits and fried apples were amazing. She had also made some delicious-smelling sausage, but Annie kept to her vegetarianism and filled up on biscuits and apples. She was amazed at how easy it was for Red and her to slip out of the house by just saying they were going to get some exercise and would be gone a couple of hours. She sensed that her mom and grandma wanted to have some time to chat privately while they worked in the kitchen preparing Thanksgiving dinner. Neither uncle nor cousins were joining them this year, which was disappointing, but also made it much easier to visit Aaan. If their cousins had been there, they'd have certainly wanted to

accompany them on their country walk, as was their tradition
when they all converged at Mamaw's.

As Annie and Red walked down the country road, Annie
felt engulfed in the smells of fall—fallen leaves, a muddy
scent from rain during the night, and that special vegetative
aroma she couldn't quite identify; it just smelled like the farm.
A few pumpkins still lay in a field as she and Red passed, and
a random corn stalk sprouted here and there, but mostly everything was well past harvest. A few birds still sang, but most had
either flown south or assumed quieter winter behavior. Morning
mist rose from the creek that followed along the road. The day
was overcast and the feeling of fall made Annie wish Buddy
were here. After all, he was a hound; he'd love to hunt in these
woods right now. She loved the dampness of the day. She often
wondered how some people could say they loved blue sunny
skies. Not her. There was something about the damp, muddy,
ferny, mossy-ness of this place that was irresistible to her. She
was so immersed in this marveling that she almost forgot about
Red walking alongside her. That was nice, too, she decided.
They had a bond and were comfortable with silence.

As they turned off the road onto the path leading to the
Swan Hole, Red took out her cell phone and began snapping
pictures, exclaiming that she'd forgotten how beautiful this
place was. Annie grew more and more impatient to see Aaan
with each step that brought them closer. *What if he isn't here
anymore? What if he reincarnated into a little baby somewhere?* She made herself stop thinking like this. All she could
do was try to find him.

They passed the travel trailer that just weeks before had
been occupied by Missy and Billy. Red asked, "Is this where
your friends lived?"

"Yeah, but they moved. They ended up buying a house over
that hill."

"Who owns this land?"

"I don't know. Billy's dad bought them this place, but I guess they sold it when they moved."

"I sure hope whoever bought this piece of land doesn't mess up the Swan Hole. I mean, it's partly on Mamaw's land, but they could probably do a lot of damage if they built something here. I guess they could even level the falls if they wanted. Though I don't know why anyone would." Red looked around speculatively.

"I know, it makes me sick to think of it. I wish I owned it. I'd never let anything happen to it," Annie mused absentmindedly. Red agreed.

They arrived at the Swan Hole. "Okay, Annie, so how much time do you need, or do you want to signal me in some way?" Red asked.

"Let's start with half an hour." Annie drew a circle in the mud on the edge of the water with a stick, much like she'd done with Missy and Billy last summer. "In half an hour, I'll be back here where you zap me to disappear, okay? If I want to transform back earlier, I'll splash three times and then stand in the circle?"

"Okay, got it."

There was a snap as Red zapped Annie. Annie had forgotten just how beautiful the world was when she was in this transformation. Everything glowed. She looked down into the water of the Swan Hole and saw glowing forms, probably fish that seemed to be many, many feet down. This pool really was deep. She saw Red relax and sit on the ground with her back against a tree, waiting to rescue her if needed. She was oddly touched and felt warm toward her sister. She knew that despite their occasional bickering, either would do anything to help the other.

She took a deep, slow breath, steadied her nerves, and thought of Uncle Alistair. Yes, she'd do this. She ghosted toward the tiny entrance she and Missy had used when miniaturized. She pressed her face into the moss-covered stone around the entrance. At first, she felt like a tiny panic attack might ensue, but she thought of the beautiful mind in the cave and all the artwork he'd done, all alone in there, and kept slowly pushing into the cave. She opened her eyes and her head and shoulders were inside the cave, her legs still outside. She pulled both arms into the cave so she had her hands free from the rock formation. Just at that moment she detected a small movement and looked toward the lounger-shaped stone.

There he was. He was lying on his back on the stone slab and he'd just raised his head to peer at her. "Tiny Bold Maiden," he said with hopeful surprise. "You've come back."

"Y-yes." Annie's heart was beating wildly; she wasn't sure if in fear or awe. He slowly sat up, moving with the grace of a large cat. Annie felt that his every movement was seductive. She'd never felt that way before and wondered if he was something like a male siren. *No,* she told herself, *he's good. I know. I read his epitaph, or whatever you call it.* "My name is Anya," she said. She didn't know why she gave her formal name. "I need your help."

"Anya. Such a lovely name. And I am Aaan. It is rather an old-fashioned name."

"No, it's a great name. Kind of ... angelic ... and powerful." Annie thought she detected a movement of his head that indicated shyness when she said that. It touched her and made her more confident to proceed.

Aaan ventured, "You, too, are half-angel?" He seemed almost afraid to know the answer.

"Only human," she said. "Or, at least I think I'm only human. I don't know of anything else." Annie felt clumsy and glanced at his face; he looked disappointed. *He thinks I'm half-angel, too, because of the transformation.*

"Then you are a ghost?" He looked puzzled. "I'm sorry to be impertinent. But how did you come through the rock if you are human?"

"Oh, that. I have this way of kind of transforming. I mean, it's a long story. You see, last summer, I copied your writing over there on the wall." She pointed, then felt awkward. *As if he doesn't know where his own writing is!* "I translated it and read it. It was beautiful." She all at once felt very shy, wondering if this was too personal to be saying to him.

"I am honored," he said, bowing his head slightly. Annie thought it was the most gallant thing she had ever seen. "Please, come in and sit with me so that we may speak at length. Or, if you are afraid, I could come out and we could visit outside."

"Outside would be good." She was grateful for his thoughtfulness. She backed out of the cave entrance and waited outside.

He came through the same spot where she'd emerged. He seemed to be awakening and greeting a new day. He stretched and looked first up to the sky and then around at the world. "So it is autumn now." He stopped abruptly, spotting Red sitting by the tree. "Another maiden, but not the same as the one who accompanied you last summer."

"That's my sister, Sonia." Red was listening to her iPod and sketching, apparently oblivious to their conversation.

"Another lovely name and maiden."

"She's a pain in the—" then, remembering her awe at this angelic vision, she collected herself. "I mean, I guess she's okay for a sister."

"So Anya, would you like to have a private audience or would you like to include your sister?"

"Well, she can't—I mean, only one of us at a time can—private audience, please," she blurted out.

"Very good. I know of a lovely spot. Here, take my hand."

She placed her hand in his. The touch was both electrifying and warm. His hand seemed so much larger than hers. Even with his ethereal form and herself in this transformed state, she could feel his hand as though it were flesh and blood. She wondered momentarily at this. Before she had time to linger long on the thought, she felt herself whisked upward. She looked up at Aaan, who was gracefully soaring, nothing like the awkward movements she'd made in her own feeble attempts at flying last summer. She felt the wind, and since most of the molecules were of a different scale, the wind not only felt silky gliding over her face, but the silkiness could also be felt gliding through her entire body. There was such a cool, frosty euphoria, even though she couldn't really feel temperature; it was more like a quality of damp-coolness.

She ventured a look downward into the Swan Hole and was awed once again at the beautiful colors swimming around way, way down below the water's surface—how far? It seemed like many tens of feet. She made a mental note to ask Aaan about that.

As he changed direction to head slightly southeast toward the ridge top, he moved with a flourish, reminding Annie of a ballet dancer. She was twirled around gracefully as they spun and then headed off toward the ridge top. He laughed and she couldn't help but giggle as well, though at first she'd gasped at the sudden change of direction. Then, Aaan once again twirled her and somehow the swirling finale culminated with his carrying her in his arms. He looked down, smiled, and gently sat her upon a smooth stone outcropping that capped the ridge top. She was surprised at the playfulness in his actions. She smiled shyly up at him and then looked around. The stone looked polished on top and appeared to be white quartz with a translucent icy glow. "This is beautiful," she remarked and ran her hand over the smooth surface.

"Yes, this is my favorite place to sit and think," replied Aaan.

"I didn't know there was white quartz on this side of the Smokies—I thought it was all on the North Carolina side."

"Ah, a young geologist. Yes, Tiny Bold Maiden—um, Anya, if I may be so bold. May I call you Anya?"

"Sure." Annie shrugged, not sure how to act under such obviously well cultivated manners. "Though my sister and parents call me Annie. But I like having you call me Anya."

"Anya it is." One corner of his mouth rose slightly. "Well, Anya, there are white quartz outcroppings on both sides of the Smokies, but most are covered with lichens and appear grey. I keep this one polished just for aesthetics, though I have not spent much time up here in many decades, until you awakened me last summer. Since then, I have been here quite often to think and meditate. But—" he looked seriously into her eyes. "That isn't what we came here to discuss. You said you needed my help, and you shall have it. It is yours for the asking. Please tell me, Anya, what you desire."

Annie gulped. His voice sounded so seductive. She struggled to find her voice. "No, I … don't … *desire* anything … I mean—" *Oh, gosh.* What had she gotten herself into? What if he was something else? She didn't want to be like poor Roy, possessed. Then, she found her own boldness. *No.* She'd read his writings, he wanted to be good—he *was* good. "I need help for my uncle and for Red's boyfriend, Erik."

Annie eyed Aaan as he considered for a moment. "Go on. Are they in some type of trouble?"

"Yes, but first I should tell you that I already knew you were half-angel even before you said something about it today." She looked into his face to see how he reacted to this. She sighed. "It's kind of a long story."

"Please, Anya, take your time. Believe me. I have all the time you could possibly need." He sighed and Annie caught a note of sadness.

"Okay, here goes," she said. She told him about Roy's possession by demons, the cult, Erik's quest to find his father, and finally about Uncle Alistair's disappearance in London. "My family thinks he's been captured by this cult of demons. I think it's in Italy."

Aaan continued to nod. "I see. And you need my help finding him? Battling with demons?"

"Yes, I guess that's what I'm saying. I thought that since you're kind of like … a demon. I mean, I know that you're good and all, or want to be ... " Annie felt horrified at how this sounded. "I mean, please, no. I don't think you're a demon."

"It's okay, it's okay," Aaan said soothingly. "I can see where one could certainly think that. You see, Anya, the difference between an angel and a demon is all about choosing sides—they are the same creatures, or, at least, they start out that way. It's kind of like whether you are a Whig or Tory ..." Then, seeming to realize this was an outdated example, he tried again. "I mean, on which side you are on—like being Union or Confederate." He watched her face.

"I know what Whigs and Tories are." Annie didn't want him to think her not well educated.

"Excellent, a well-read young lady." *Is he flirting?* Annie blushed slightly.

"And no, I am not a demon. At least, I certainly hope not. I have tried for many centuries to grow spiritually so that I might be allowed to join the blessed land where my mother, sister, and daughter went. I think you probably call it Heaven. It has different names in different cultures.

"You see, I have come to think the reason that crossing angels and humans has been forbidden is because they each have such different destinations. I have not been able to fulfill the journeys for either completely—at least, not so far. I usually exist in this state but reincarnate into a different human life sometimes. This happens approximately every five hundred years, but it is not exact. I never know when to expect that I will find myself back in this state and realize that I just lived another human life.

"But that story is for a different time. So you wish for me to first find your uncle and then exorcise any demons that might have found a toehold? You do know, by the way, that a demon cannot possess anyone unless invited, don't you?"

"Yes. I mean, I've heard that. But couldn't the demons capture him and torture him?"

"Well, they could certainly manipulate other humans into doing that. I will need more information, though."

Annie suddenly remembered the time and became agitated. "Oh my gosh, do you know how long we've been up here? I'm supposed to be back with my sister in half an hour!"

Upon landing in Maryland, Erik knew his part was over. He watched the rescued prisoners being loaded into waiting ambulances. It was time to go home and let Sonia and his mom know he was okay.

He knew this part would be difficult because he'd have to withhold the fact that he'd found his dad. He didn't want to compromise the mission's success by having something slip when the military officials informed his mom that his dad was alive. Any suspicion of his involvement would certainly raise questions, given that he'd only just emerged from all the questioning about his and Alistair's disappearance last year.

Erik didn't bother with a bus, needing some fresh air to clear his head, and he wanted to enjoy the morning light. It was now getting to be well into the morning, but he had no idea of the date. He knew his search had taken weeks, but he hadn't bothered to keep up with the time, focusing one hundred percent of his attention on his quest.

He felt lucky to be conveniently transported to within fifteen miles of home. It felt good to see familiar sights, the Beltway, the Bethesda Country Club, Cabin John Park. Soon he found himself dropping down through the roof of Alistair's house to surprise Sonia. Even with his hyper-driven focus over the past few weeks, she'd always been hovering somewhere in his mind. He was just realizing how much he missed her.

The house seemed silent, except for Buddy's tail thumping lazily on the carpet as he acknowledged Erik's entrance. "Hey, Bud-ster," he said in his airy ghost whisper. He assumed it must be the middle of the week and everyone was at work or school. A nearby thump as paws landed on the wooden floor from some nearby perch told him that one of the cats had also sensed his entrance. Ghosting by the kitchen counter, he saw a copy of the *Washington Post* strewn on the counter. Peering at the date, he was shocked to see that it was almost Thanksgiving. The paper was dated Wednesday, November 27. Erik was beginning to be psyched. Tomorrow would be Thanksgiving. Hopefully, his mother would be informed by then that his dad was found. He began to envision the celebration they'd have.

At that moment, he heard footsteps on the stairs. *Must be Ms. Greene working at home today,* he thought. But it turned out to be Mr. Greene. Mr. Greene seemed deep in his own thoughts. Erik thought about transforming and saying hello, but decided that since Sonia wasn't here, he'd let his mom know he was okay first before returning.

He flew to his mother's house, not expecting to catch her at home. Feeling impish, he thought about popping over to her office and surprising her there, or better yet, popping over to the high school and surprising Sonia as she got out for the day. But as he neared his mother's house, he noted that her car was in the driveway. This was a nice surprise—she was home after all. He didn't want to scare her by just appearing inside, but on the other hand, it was broad daylight and he couldn't very well transform in the front yard and knock. He decided to go to his bedroom. He smiled to think that now that his dad would be coming home, he'd be finally free to fly the coop. He thought of Sonia and their future together. He knew his love for her would last a lifetime but he had been trying to take things slow for her sake. She was still so young and he didn't want her to feel tied down. She could take all the time she needed and even if she chose someone else, he'd love her still and support whatever made her happy. But damn, maybe he was being too responsible. Maybe he should pay more attention to passion. He just knew that right now, with the burden of his dad off his shoulders, he couldn't wait to see her.

As he ghosted through the roof and down into his bedroom, he heard voices in the house—sounded like at least two women. Probably his mom had a friend over—maybe Roy's mom. He quickly transformed, changed into some jeans and a T-shirt, and thought about a shower but decided that he'd better greet his mom first before she freaked out. As he descended the stairs, he called out, "Mom, I'm home. It's Erik."

He heard a gasp from the living room and his mom rushed out, embracing him with relieved sobs. "Shhh. It's okay, Mom. I'm okay. I didn't mean to scare you like that. I just didn't—"

Ms. Oglethorp peeped around the corner shyly and greeted him between sobs of her own. "Ms. Oglethorp. Hi. Great to see you. How's Roy?"

"Oh, Erik, I was so worried about you." His mom held him so tight that he almost couldn't breathe and struggled to control her sobs.

"Gosh, I'm so sorry, Mom. It's just that I couldn't give away my location by phoning. I thought you knew that this could take a few weeks. But Sonia knew I was okay. Didn't she tell you?"

"Oh, Erik, of course she did, but she hadn't heard from you in a week or so."

"I'm here now, safe and sound. And really, there's nothing anyone could do to harm me in that state, anyway."

He looked anxiously toward Ms. Oglethorpe. She knew all about the research but he still felt like she might be a weak link and certainly didn't want to announce finding his father while she was present. Best to wait, anyway, so his mom would have a natural surprised reaction, as planned.

Still, she seemed so upset. He had no idea she'd be so worried. He wondered if something else had happened while he was away. "Mom, is everything okay?"

"Oh, Erik, you haven't heard?" Erik's heart turned over. "It's Professor Hamilton. He was kidnapped last week in London after speaking at the C.S. Lewis dedication. We think it's that cult that Lorenzo and ... Roy ... were in." She obviously didn't want to say anything too hurtful in Ms. Oglethorpe's presence. Ms. Oglethorpe spoke up. "I'm afraid that my Roy may have brought a real evil on us all when he got involved with that Italian cult. He feels so bad. He's determined now to go and find Professor Hamilton. Lorenzo is over there already, searching. I just hope we can trust him ..." She wrung her hands in despair, tears streaming down her cheeks.

Erik took a deep breath to calm down and buy time to think. "Don't worry, Ms. Oglethorpe, I'll go with Roy. Where is he now?"

"At home on his computer. He and Lorenzo are in contact and he's preparing to fly over, though I don't know the details."

"I'll go over straight away and talk to him. And Sonia—she must be worried sick with both her uncle and me missing. I could kick myself for not calling sooner. Is she in school today?"

"Erik, today is Thanksgiving. Sonia and her mom and sister drove down to Tennessee to visit her grandmother. Only her dad stayed home in case the police or kidnappers call."

"Oh, no. What a horrible time for the family." Erik's head was spinning after his whirlwind trip. "I'll call Sonia right away and then go see Roy. Mom, everything's going to be all right." He tried to give her one of those looks that told volumes. She seemed to catch the significance but Erik wasn't sure.

She smiled at him and Erik thought maybe she relaxed a little, "Erik, why don't you get cleaned up first and I'll let Sonia know you're okay. That way you can have a more relaxing chat with her."

He nodded appreciably and had a nice long shower. He considered his options and decided he really did need to talk to Roy before formulating a plan. He didn't know if Alistair had a STAG control with him on his trip. That would make all the difference in the world. With a STAG control, he'd be impossible to hold captive, but if the control was stolen ... Erik couldn't think of that.

163

As he descended the stairs, he heard a knock at the front door. There was the sound of a man's murmured voice, and then he heard his mother gasp and then shout, "Oh my God. Thank you, thank you!" and burst into sobs for the second time in an hour.

He slipped quietly onto the stairs and saw that she was hugging a uniformed naval officer. This made sense, since his dad had gone to a naval hospital. Erik stopped on the step to allow his mother to revel in her joy. He smiled and his heart filled with warmth to hear her thank the officer and invite him in.

The man declined the invitation but gave his mom a card with a phone number so she could reach her husband after ten years of silence.

He entered the room and found his mom and her friend embracing, both sobbing with joy. Perhaps he'd been too hard on Ms. Oglethorpe, he thought.

He allowed his mom to give him the good news and tried to act surprised for Ms. Oglethorpe's sake, but he suspected they both sensed the truth.

Erik offered to drive Ms. Oglethorpe home so he'd have a chance to speak with Roy and his mom could have a long and long-overdue phone conversation with her husband.

But, first, it was time for him to call Sonia.

# CHAPTER 12

## Asking For Help

S itting on the ledge next to Aaan, Annie worried about the time. "Would you like for me to take you back now? Would it frighten your sister if I appeared and spoke with both of you?" Aaan asked.

"I'm in a kind of transformed state. I don't think we can see or hear you once I'm zapped back," Annie said.

"Zapped," he repeated. "I wish to hear all about this zapping, but that will have to wait until a later time. I am angel enough to be able to 'appear,' as Biblical scholars have called it. I can appear in a form that I think both of you will find acceptable, so please, as beings greater than I have said many times in the past, 'fear not.' "

Annie was awed to think that she would be honored by an angelic appearance. She was so mesmerized by his charm that she didn't really even remember the flight back. He sat her down near Red, who was just pocketing her cell phone and was so excited about something that Annie saw her jump up and

165

do a free-spirited romping kind of dance. Annie quickly went over to the water and slapped it three times, so that it rippled and made a splashing noise. Red's head jerked in that direction and she obviously recognized the signal. She quickly fumbled in her daypack for the STAG control and approached the transformation spot where Annie was waiting and zapped her back.

Annie wasn't prepared for the humongous hug that she received from Red. Red jumped up and down, squealing as she hugged Annie. "Hey, Red, calm down. What gives?"

"Annie, Erik's okay! He's back and he found his dad!"

Annie could barely grasp what she was hearing. "That's awesome." She threw her arms around her sister to share her joy.

Red quickly pulled back to say, "Oh, but remember you can't tell anyone about Erik's role in the rescue. Erik wants it all kept top secret."

"Okay," Annie shrugged, unsure whom Red thought she was going to tell. "Does he know anything about Uncle Alistair?"

"No, I wish. But he does have a STAG control, and he's leaving straight away to look for him."

"And he just may have some help." Annie was thrilled to say this. "Red, listen carefully. I know you're excited, but I have to tell you something quickly. Aaan's going to appear and talk to us, so don't be scared, okay? He may even say the 'fear not' line. Isn't that the coolest thing?" She giggled.

Red was obviously so overcome with her own joy that it took some effort for her to grasp what Annie was saying. "You mean, your half-angel is going to materialize here? Now?" Just as she was saying this, a glow began to form over the Swan Hole and the most beautiful vision Annie had ever seen materialized, floating in mid-air. He had long, flowing, white robes. His face was also exquisite, though Annie recognized it easily from his spirit-self. His long hair and robes blew and twirled as if a breeze were blowing, though she didn't feel one. Annie was once-again awestruck. Red seemed more frightened and reflexively stepped in front of Annie, assuming a defensive tae kwon do position.

"Oh, Red, chill." Annie quickly got over the shock and felt the warm presence of her friend. She pushed Red to the side and gestured toward the apparition. "It's just Aaan. He's my friend."

"Fear not, maidens," he said with a hint of humor. "I love saying that."

"Oh, you." Annie giggled. "What's up with the windy-swirly thing?"

"You like it, Tiny Bold Maiden? I thought you might. It's just to soften the effect and make me seem more ethereal, perhaps less of a threat."

"It's cool, but you can kill it now. Just come here and talk with us."

Aaan laughed heartily. He stopped the motion and drifted down to the ground. Where his flowing robes had been, he now had feet. He still appeared transparent, but much more like a human than before. It was hard to believe he was eons old; to her, he looked just about her age.

Red was just recovering her breath. "Okay, you two. Enough of the theatrics before I have a heart attack."

Annie snickered. "Aaan said he'd help us find Uncle Alistair. But I think we should sit and discuss the whole thing so he knows what's needed."

The three sat in lotus positions on the ground. "So you think your uncle was kidnapped by a cult that houses at least one demon?" Aaan asked.

"Yes," Annie and Red said in unison. Annie said, "He's a professor and is researching some artifacts from the Vatican. We think this cult is trying to get them, and that they've kidnapped him to try and force him to tell them where those artifacts are now."

Aaan seemed to be in deep thought. After a few moments, he began, "I suspect, as I am sure do you, that the cult took him back to their lair in Italy." He hesitated a moment. "Since we do not have the location, the fastest way I can arrive to help him is by a technique that is part of my angel heritage. You see, angels can relocate almost instantaneously, by a kind of telepathic connection."

Red became animated. "Oh, I know what you mean. I saw the small angels zooming up and down when I was transformed and I wondered if they were taking messages. I mean, angels are supposed to be messengers, right?"

"Yes, I think so, but …" Aaan didn't seem certain that he fully understood what Red was describing, but seemed to want to get back to the issue at hand. "What I need, however, is to connect with him telepathically, and since I do not know him or his mind, I will need to establish a connection through someone else's thoughts."

"What do you mean?" Annie wasn't sure she liked the sound of this theory. It sounded like demon possession. She couldn't think of her angel in that way.

Aaan seemed to understand the note of concern in Annie's voice. "Anya, I am not a demon. I do not wish in any way to control your thoughts or actions. All I intend to do is listen. I will need permission for that. But you can be specific in what you agree to allow—does that sound reasonable?"

Red obviously caught the drift of this and her inner-warrior seemed to be emerging. "No way. No little sister of mine is getting possessed. If one of us has to do it, I'll do it."

Annie quickly changed her tune, pushing Red's shoulder. "No way, Red. Back off. This is my angel."

Annie noticed that Aaan politely averted his eyes as if to allow them privacy to interact.

"But what if he's really a demon?" Red whispered this as she eyed Aaan.

"Oh, don't be ridiculous. He's not a demon. He's good. At least he wants to be. And who kept your secret when you were in love with a Viking ghost?"

Aaan looked toward the girls now with a puzzled expression. Annie let it pass.

After a few minutes, Red relented, shrugging and stating that this was Annie's adventure. So Annie gave Aaan permission to listen to her thoughts. She saw Red resume her position at the base of the tree and take out her cell, probably to check for new messages from Erik. Still seated on the ground, Annie closed her eyes and thought of her uncle. She felt her hair lift ever so slightly, as if a breeze had rustled it. She wondered if Aaan had done that for effect or if it were a natural occurrence of this kind of thing.

She remained still, her eyes closed, and felt a warm sensation resembling contentment, but nothing more concrete as the minutes ticked by. Annie felt a little disappointed at not being able to read anything of his mind at the same time, but knew this had been the agreement. She tried not to think about that, but to focus on Uncle Alistair. The process seemed to take an hour, though it was probably only a few minutes.

Eventually, Annie felt her hair rustle again and opened her eyes. Aaan was seated opposite her, facing her with an angelic contented expression that she was beginning to associate with him. He took her hand in his. "Anya, thank you for honoring me by allowing our essences to connect. You are a truly beautiful being. I will always remember the beauty of your soul. And thank you for the memories of your uncle. Yes, he does seem to be an outstanding individual and one I am now happy to know and to help if I can. I think I have enough information to complete my task. I can go to him. I will comfort him if he allows and may be able to help influence the captors. I will analyze the situation and respond accordingly. I saw in your thoughts that someone named Erik is also going to look for him. I will try to watch over your uncle and await Erik's arrival. Please try not to worry. I will now take leave of you, my Tiny Bold Maiden, and you, her sister." He nodded to Red, who nodded back, seemingly stunned into silence by his beautiful manners. "Farewell, Anya, until we meet again." He kissed the hand he held and then vanished from sight.

Annie sat mesmerized for some time, staring at the hand he'd kissed. Eventually, she began to awaken from her reverie, and looking around, took some time to familiarize herself once again with her surroundings and register that he was indeed gone.

She looked at Red, who also seemed to be in shock at the rapid departure, but said, "Well, guess our mission is accomplished." She rose and dusted off her pants.

Annie felt too distracted to think. Following her sister's lead, she arose slowly, still inwardly glowing from the encounter. She looked around once again at the waterfalls, sky, ferns, mosses, the whole picture, trying to etch it into her mind. She took a deep breath and slowly exhaled. She looked at Red and nodded. She was ready.

Annie walked back to Mamaw's house in such a state of awe and contentment that both her mother and grandmother commented on how much the fresh air had given her a healthy glow. She somehow managed to help prepare the traditional meal, filling the house with amazing aromas of cinnamon and nutmeg, but she wasn't totally present.

Only as she began to awaken from her Aaan-induced stupor did she begin to wonder why she hadn't had the presence of mind to ask him if she could come along. *Stupid, stupid, stupid.* He was an angel; who knew, maybe he had some way he could've transported her along with him. The thought began to gnaw at her. As the morning wore on, it became an obsession. Why hadn't she thought of asking? Was there anything she could do about it now?

"Here, *bambino*, take this soup to the old man," the gravelly voice was slurred. The beefy hand threw in a few crackers and then reached for a bottle.

"Stop calling me that," the youth spat, but did as he was told.

170

Antonio carefully carried the tray so that neither the soup nor the plastic teacup spilled as he descended the dark damp staircase. He didn't like the guy seated at the desk watching over the prisoner. He didn't trust him and he thought he'd made a pass at him. He tried to stay away from him.

This time, the guy at the desk didn't bother Antonio. Yawning, he tossed a torn magazine aside, removed his feet from atop the desk, and walked over to unlock the metal cell door without speaking. Antonio was relieved.

Inside the cell, the old man was asleep still. His color looked bad. His mouth hung open and his lips were dry. He thought they were giving him too much ether, or whatever other drugs they were using to sedate him, but he didn't dare to mention it, remembering the beating he'd received last time he'd annoyed them.

The guard locked the cell door behind Antonio—Antonio wondered why he bothered; he didn't think this old man was going anywhere today. He'd at least try to get him to drink some water—his lips looked so dry. But his alter ego inside taunted him, giving him the urge to do something cruel to the defenseless old man instead.

# CHAPTER 13

# Once More Into the Fray

E rik had no time to think. Still glowing from the warm feeling of his role in reuniting two of the people he loved most in the world, he hadn't had time for the news to sink in about Professor Hamilton's kidnapping. Now, as he drove Ms. Oglethorpe to her house, she filled him in on all that was known of his disappearance. "Roy is convinced this is the work of the cult from Italy," she said. She seemed upset each time the cult was mentioned and he found himself spending more time soothing and reassuring her than gathering information. He wasn't totally convinced he could trust Roy one hundred percent after all that had transpired, but his sense of empathy made him reassure Roy's mom that, of course Roy was all the way back to his old self and Erik had absolutely no hard feelings. In fact, Ms. Oglethorpe confided in him that she felt Roy really wanted to make amends for the harm he had caused when he went astray with the cult. Erik assured her he'd support Roy, allowing him the opportunity to make amends, but in the back of his mind, he hoped he wouldn't regret this.

When they arrived, sure enough, Roy was immersed in gathering information on his computer. He jumped up and excitedly began telling him all he'd found out from Lorenzo. Yes, the cult was still in full swing, but no, Lorenzo hadn't been able to get the inside scoop on Alistair. It seemed Lorenzo had announced right away upon returning home that he was no longer interested in the cult, but had to be very careful to avoid suspicion that he might be working for the other side.

Erik knew he had to either trust Roy or go off on his own. He carefully watched Roy to see if he could detect any hint of the demon still lurking beneath the surface, but try as he might, he could only see the old Roy trying very hard to make amends. He made a decision to trust him. Without Roy, he didn't know where to find the cult, and researching on his own would take weeks to months, if it were even possible to find the information.

He told Roy he had a STAG control on hand they could use to infiltrate the cult headquarters. Roy seemed visibly relieved he'd be allowed access once again to the stones and that he was back on the research team. It seemed to mean a lot to him and part of Erik was glad he could help his friend. He wondered how he could've ever allowed himself to be seduced into such an evil cult.

After a brief discussion, they decided that since they were going to use the STAG control to travel, they could catch any plane they wanted. They would go straight to the airport and hop the first plane going in the right direction. Erik was sad that this wouldn't allow him time to see Sonia before leaving once again, but rescuing her uncle was top priority. After all—Erik didn't want to think about it—it was very possible Alistair was being tortured this very minute. The cult was desperate to get their hands on the stones and he knew they would not dare to attempt to enter the Vatican. Now that he had seen angels, he suspected forces invisible to the human eye heavily guarded that fortress.

Even with the flexibility of not having to book a flight, Erik felt like he had to keep hustling Roy so they could catch an overnight flight to Rome; most nonstop flights seemed to be leaving around 5:15. They had plenty of time but Roy wanted to pack a few things.

"No, Roy, we'll be traveling light—very light. In fact, you need only two things, your leather coat and a map of the area where the cult's located. And the map has to be laminated or it won't do us any good. Please tell me you've got a laminated map from your summer in Italy."

"I'm pretty sure I've got one somewhere," Roy mumbled as he ruffled through a drawer. "Mo-om," he called loudly.

Ms. Oglethorp appeared in the door and said anxiously, "Yes, Roy?"

"Do you know where my map of Italy is? I thought it was in this drawer."

"Did you check the box in the top of your closet?"

Erik rolled his eyes in disbelief that a grown man would be asking his mom for help finding something in his own bedroom. Erik remembered how Roy had once tried to help him to be smoother with the ladies, and now it looked like it was going to be his turn to help Roy break the apron strings. He wondered if this weakness in independence was why Roy had joined the cult. He'd have a talk with his old friend during the long flight, he decided.

Once they located the map, Erik explained to Ms. Oglethorpe that they were going to depart now and would be leaving from Roy's room in a transformed state. She looked worried but Erik assured her everything would be fine. Roy told her he was very excited about having an opportunity to help.

On hearing this, she readily agreed that this was for the best and told them to be safe and travel well. Erik wondered if she was beginning to get that she needed to give Roy some space. He hoped she was at least vaguely aware that her over-protectiveness may have contributed to Roy's rebellion. *Better late than never.*

They transformed and Erik showed Roy how to fly, helping him negotiate the push through the ceiling and up through the roof. The fastest way to the airport was by using their own power, so they veered west toward Dulles International Airport. Erik had to fight hard to suppress laughter at watching Roy learn to fly—Roy, who had always been so suave, was at a disadvantage in this. *It'll do him good to be humbled a little,* Erik hoped.

They found a nonstop flight. Once on board, Erik wanted to find a quiet place so he could have a heart-to-heart with his friend, but Roy, still awed by his first transformation experience, wanted to have fun with it.

*What the heck,* Erik thought, and they rode in the cockpit with the pilots.

With the roar of the plane, no one could hear their whispery voices, but they could hear each other well. Erik wondered about this aspect of the transformation and decided to spend some time later trying to figure it out. The best he'd come up with so far was that the transformed state was somehow different, more than just shrinking quarks, but when the subatomic particles snapped to the grid of this existence, all things in that state had an affinity for each other; two transformed people could hold hands, for example, whereas, if only one were transformed, the transformed hand would simply slip through the other.

One corner of his mouth pulled up as he thought of taking Sonia's hand for the first time when he transformed her in the lab. It'd been electrifying for him. Her hand had felt heavenly, just as he'd known it would.

Erik realized he was being addressed. "What was that, Roy? I'm sorry. I was off in a daydream."

"Oh, nothing, really," said Roy, leaning back against the window and peering out into the clouds. "I—well, was just offering my gratitude at being trusted again after being so stupid."

Erik looked levelly at Roy for a moment and then asked, "Want to talk about it? What happened over in Italy?"

"Confession, time, huh? Actually, yes, I'd love to get it all off my chest. Looks like this is a good opportunity since we'll be in the air for several hours."

"Have at it, friend. You know that I've already forgiven you, but it would probably be good to discuss it." Erik pressed his lips together, trying to express his regret that his friend had gone through a difficult time, and trying not to appear judgmental, or as though he was taking it too lightly.

Roy took a deep breath, leaned his head back against the window, and exhaled slowly. Then looked down into his hands, seeming to struggle with where to begin. He chuckled mildly to himself. "You were such a green kid when you first started working in the lab. I felt sorry for you—can you believe that?" he scoffed. "Then, in no time, it seemed that you and Professor Hamilton were totally immersed in this stone research and you were the star and I was the one struggling to keep up. And to top it all, Xenia seemed to be attracted to you."

"Roy, you idiot. She was trying to make you jealous by flirting with me." Erik was incredulous that Roy hadn't picked up on that.

Roy seemed to just at that moment get it. "Really?" he laughed. "I'll be damned. I guess I always had too much pride for my own good. My mom always built me up. I was her hero— the man of the house as far back as I can remember. Nothing was too good for me—and no woman good enough. I think that after Dad died, Mom felt threatened by my dating, and so, I guess I played along, imagining it was all fun and games. But with Xenia, I actually fell for her. But I didn't know the first thing about how to have a giving relationship. I just knew jealousy."

He took a moment to look out the window before continuing. "Guess you see where this is going. I wanted to show you up. I signed up for the summer course in Italy, determined to find something that would wow Professor Hamilton, well, and everyone. It had to be big. I did a lot of online searching and that's how I found Lorenzo and his group of thugs.

"Lorenzo offered me an ancient manuscript that mentioned the stones, but to get it, I had to meet with this cult and participate in an 'ancient ritual.' " Roy made a gesture indicating quotation marks. "Well, the ritual turned out to be an invitation for a demon to enter and control me. As I read the words, I knew there was something really off about it, but I was just in too deep. I'd started out with good intent, at least in the beginning. To be successful and to have a loving relationship with Xenia, heck I even wanted to help you at one time, but once the negativity entered, it was just such a slippery slope. I didn't know how to stop. The jealousy grew and along with it, anger and rage. I was out of control. It was like I was really ready to sell my soul for revenge. So I went through with the ceremony, totally ignoring that warning bell in my ear."

Roy stopped a moment and squeezed his eyes shut, the memory obviously painful. "After that, it was like I didn't really have control of myself. I mean, I could still think, sort of, but then when I went too far in a certain direction, my thoughts were reeled in toward the same old hate-filled thoughts and my intentions changed so that I actually desired to do what the cult wanted. I think I'd have killed one of you if I had the opportunity. I don't know … maybe not." He seemed to be struggling with whether he'd have been able to stop himself if the demon had compelled him to do something really awful. "I just don't know. I know that I was really mean to Xenia, but I'd like to think that I never could've really harmed her. But I just don't know." His eyes would've filled with tears if it was possible to cry in this state, Erik suspected.

"I'm sure I could've been a better friend, as well," Erik said. "I just didn't see you were suffering. I was so keyed into the research, I didn't even realize I'd displaced you as the favorite student. I'm sorry."

Roy smiled. "It's okay, kid." Erik was glad to hear his old nickname used once more.

"And I should apologize about scaring Sonia and her friends," Roy added.

Erik's attention perked up and he realized that perhaps he hadn't totally forgiven Roy after all. He retorted in a threateningly calm tone, "Roy, if you'd harmed a hair on her head, we wouldn't be sitting here having this conversation."

Roy nodded and exhaled. "Erik, I was following the cult's orders on that—trying to get inside in case the family found the key. I'm so very glad Sonia and Ms. Catsworthy were able to fend me off. That's one time I'm not ashamed to have been outdone by females both physically and by sheer command. In fact, I think maybe it was Ms. Catsworthy's matronly, commanding tone that started snapping me back. I'd really like to think that somehow, even without the rescue, I'd have—"

"Don't waste your time thinking of what might've been. Let's just be glad for what is, okay, bud? As for Professor Hamilton, I think he'll be impressed by this rescue mission, which, by the way, is your baby. I have the STAG control, but that's all. You have all the knowledge of where to search. I'm sure that before this is over, you'll have fully recovered your honor."

"I hope so," Roy said humbly.

Annie continued all that morning to come down off her Aaan-induced high and to become more obsessed with going along on the rescue. Walking into the bedroom she was sharing with her sister, she looked longingly at the STAG control, wanting desperately to zap herself into the ghost transformation and hop a flight to Rome with Erik and Roy. Red told her that Erik had said they were planning to catch a 5:15 flight. So close, but so far away. If she were in Maryland, she could simply transform herself and follow them. She so wanted—no, *needed*—to be involved in the rescue. She wanted to see what Aaan did and help him save her uncle.

A tear trickled from the corner of her eye when she remembered how much fun she'd had playing with the miniaturization transformation at her last birthday, his gift to her. It just didn't feel right preparing to feast on a huge meal when he was likely getting a knuckle sandwich for his Thanksgiving dinner. Despite herself, she rolled her eyes at the phrase "knuckle sandwich." Did she just think that? She'd been watching too many old reruns.

She'd helped make pumpkin pies and they were now in the oven baking along with the turkey. She eyed her laptop lying on the bed and a thought came to her.

An hour later, her mom called to her to say that the meal was ready. She looked at the clock—1:15. *Good, they're eating early. This just might work.* She was thankful that the biggest meal of the day in Mamaw's tradition was the mid-day meal. She called to Red, who was still in the kitchen.

Red appeared at the bedroom door and Annie quickly snatched her inside and closed the door. Red's eyebrows drew together suspiciously. "Yes?"

"Red," Annie clasped her hands together in a pleading gesture. "If you never do anything for me again, that'll be okay, but I really, really, really need your help right now."

Red nodded slowly. "Go on."

Annie now began to speak so rapidly she knew she was hard to follow, but couldn't seem to slow down. "I've been on the computer the past hour and know exactly what I need to do to help rescue Uncle Alistair. Erik and Roy are trying to catch a non-stop flight out at around 5:15 today—in about four hours, right? I researched all the flights from both National and Dulles to Rome. And the same timing is available for flights out of Atlanta, which only takes two hours to get to from Knoxville. Since I'll be traveling in the ghost transformation, I'll be able to hitchhike without being in any danger." She stopped briefly here to pat Red's shoulders, as Red's mouth was now hanging open.

Then she continued, "I can catch any number of short flights from Knoxville to Atlanta as long as I get to Knoxville by four, and with any luck, make approximately the same schedule as they will. The only problem will be that I have to eat the Thanksgiving meal first so Mom and Mamaw won't suspect anything. I need to leave here by two o'clock this afternoon. So we need to eat fast and here's what I need you to do—"

She was interrupted when Red finally caught her breath and whisper-shouted, "Are you out of your mind? First of all, you don't know your way to Knoxville and second ... well, it's just crazy. How are you going to find them? And even if you do, Erik will kill you. And he'll tell Mom and Dad and you'll be grounded for the rest of your life."

"Just calm down, Red. I've got it all figured out. I've memorized the route to Knoxville as well as the airport gates I need to find. I'm going to tell Mom and Mamaw a tiny lie—that Missy just called me and that they need me to come housesit for a few days. I'll say Billy is going to pick me up, but then I'll start walking toward his house right after I eat to save time. That's where you'll help. You'll walk down the road with me until we're out of sight, then zap me and come back and tell Mom that Billy picked me up." At the look on Red's face, she said, "Or you don't have to say anything so you don't have to lie—I know you don't like to. I don't either, but in this case it can't be helped. I'm going to tell them that Billy is so appreciative of this that they'll drive me back to Maryland on Sunday."

"N-O. No." Red folded her arms stubbornly.

"Red, you know I'm going to do it with or without your help," Annie said, just as stubbornly. "Why do you want to worry Mom when she already has so much to worry about? And need I to remind you how much I helped you and Erik out when he was a ghost?"

"Yeah, I guess so. Hey, wait a minute—you didn't help me and Erik at all." But Annie could see that Red was weakening.

Annie shrugged. "But I would've if you'd needed it." She saw her sister's folded arms relax.

A few minutes later, Annie emerged from the bedroom full of excited anticipation, with Red following. "Oh, yeah, help me find a large trash bag—I'll need something to wear."

Red nodded like a shell-shocked soldier.

By two-twenty that afternoon, Annie was invisibly flying over Route 33, wearing a black trash bag like a tunic and looking for a fast-moving ride. She'd lost five minutes finding a ride on the first part of her journey and now she was looking for a straight shot into Knoxville. She watched the truck traffic and thought that would likely be best, but then she spotted a movement coming up the highway at breakneck speed—some teen in a shiny, new, black sports car. *Yes.* That was her car. She quickly flew down and pressed through the roof before it got away.

With that kind of speed on her side, Annie had no trouble making it to Knoxville well ahead of her schedule. The hardest part was remembering which road she had to take to get to the airport. She shouldn't have worried because huge, green signs over the interstate showed the way to the airport—Alcoa Highway. She'd have tipped the driver if it were possible, but quickly shot up through the roof so she wouldn't be propelled away from her path at high speed. She mentally said goodbye to the young driver and hoped he wouldn't have an accident.

She didn't even need to bother hovering overhead to choose a car. The Interstate traffic was heavy enough that all she had to do was pop sideways into another car going onto the correct ramp. Wow. This was a lot like a video game. In fact, some day, maybe she'd make a video game like this.

The car she'd chosen was driven by a woman with two toddlers in the backseat, watching *Scooby Doo* on an overhead video screen. She smiled, remembering similar trips with her mom over the holidays, watching the exact same movie. It was the one where they were in a Western "ghost town" and she decided to move to the front passenger's seat so she wouldn't get caught up in the movie and miss the airport.

Luckily, the little family was flying as well. As the sedan pulled into the long-term lot, she popped up out of the roof and flew to the terminal.

Within an hour she was on a non-stop flight to Rome.

# CHAPTER 14

## *Angelic Advice*

Aaan had met many brilliant and creative people in his existence but not many he liked more than Anya's Uncle Alistair. He had known something of what to expect from reading Anya's mind, but once he arrived in Alistair's cell in Italy, he was amused to note that despite Alistair's bleak imprisonment, the man wasted no time fearing Aaan's manifestation at his bedside.

Rather than comforting the elderly professor as he'd expected, Aaan found himself deep in conversation about angels and their ways, as if the two were merely having tea. They were, however, keeping their voices low in case any of the captors appeared.

Aaan looked around to get his bearings; they were in an authentic Middle Ages dungeon, complete with iron clamps and bars. Thankfully, the captors had at least given the old man a cot and some type of thick, warm bed covering. He guessed they were somewhere near the Mediterranean, from the smell of the air.

Aaan listened patiently to Alistair's questions. "So my dear fellow, tell me, since you are half-angel, will they talk with you?" He gestured in a general upward direction. "Erik, my student, tells me they avoid any conversation with him, to the point of hiding from sight once they perceived that he was actually seeing them when he was transformed by the Angel Stone."

Aaan started as he realized what he was hearing. "Angel Stone? You have access to the Angel Stone?" Aaan felt dumbfounded. "And it worked on a human?"

"Y-eeees," Alistair seemed perplexed by this response. "You know of this stone?"

"I have only heard legends, but I thought the stones were lost from the world of mortals for low these many millennia. There were three, roughly called in your tongue, the Angel Stone, the Elf Stone and the Sight Stone."

"Yes, yes those are the ones, except we call the third the Star Stone. This is indeed incredible." Alistair paused a moment, presumably to let the significance sink in, then said animatedly, "Oh happy day. Please tell me all you know of these stones. I borrowed them from the Vatican for a time and have retained some stone dust and shards from the box containing them, which I still use in research. Only for good causes, of course. Do you know of the Vatican?"

"Oh, yes, I have been there many times. But of the stones, I do not know much, other than the common stories—that they arrived in a meteorite long ago in a forgotten time of antiquity, that many have died to gain their possession, that whole armies have fought to gain them, and that the greed to possess the stones has caused many to turn to evil. Yes, I know this all too well." Aaan paused, remembering rumors that his own father had succumbed to the lure of the stones' power.

Then he made a decided effort to get back on track with answering Alistair's question. "The Elf Stone makes matter smaller; the Sight Stone makes a human invisible and able to see angels and the essences of all things, and the Angel Stone makes an angel transform to a state that is a kind of place of respite, where they only see other angels without the clutter of other stimuli in the world. You see, angels have much stimuli to wade through at any given moment. Especially when they have the task of being guardian angel to a human. They constantly perceive the human's thoughts and actions, and help communicate their prayers up the chain; they also perceive the presence of other angels and demons, as well as their thoughts and intentions. To add to the complexity, they perceive the natural world and its many changes and threats, such as upcoming natural disasters, nearby speeding chariots—in your case, I suppose they are called automobiles—and they are tasked with assisting their charge to accomplish their mission in life, their calling, or destiny."

Aaan looked at Alistair and was startled by the intensity of his stare. "You have another question?"

Alistair, obviously agitated now, had a tear in his eye. He squeezed his eyes together as if to steady himself to bring up a painful subject. "Yes, sir. You see, this is an incredible opportunity for me—one I never dreamed I would have in this lifetime." Alistair continued hesitantly, "Sir, would you do me the honor of both hearing my confession and helping me to understand if there is anything I can do to right a wrong, done inadvertently to someone so dear to me?" He stopped, the tears now streaming down his cheeks.

Aaan waited a moment, then spoke. "Of course, I am happy to hear your confession, my brother. I was once a monk and have heard many confessions. I do not have a cross, or holy oil, but will improvise."

Aaan turned to Alistair and gently placed one hand on either side of Alistair's head. He used one thumb to trace the sign of a cross on Alistair's forehead; then, saying a brief blessing, dropped his hands.

"Please forgive me, for I have sinned," prayed Alistair.

"What has been your sin, my brother?" asked Aaan.

Alistair leaned his head back. "Where to begin—this may take some time."

"Take all the time you need." Aaan tried to sound soothing.

"I have never told another living soul this story. I didn't think anyone would understand. But being part angel, perhaps you can." Alistair took a long, slow breath before continuing. "When I was a mere lad of six, I had a best friend, a little girl of the same age, named Victoria. She was the sweetest and loveliest being I had ever beheld. She lived in Budapest, Hungary and her father and my father were in business together. I loved to accompany my parents to visit her several times a year. We'd go by train and I was allowed to go when it didn't interfere with school. Victoria lived in a mansion with her mother and father and baby sister. Sometimes, my parents and I stayed with them, and other times, we stayed in an apartment in town. Either way, Victoria and I spent all our time together. We had elaborate imaginary games, and since we were both now in school, we often played school. I even deigned to play dolls with her. I loved her so much that I'd have done anything she wanted."

After a moment, he resumed. "My family was Anglican and her family wasn't. I didn't know at the time that her family was Jewish and were keeping that fact a secret because of the Nazi threat—the year was 1945. Victoria was allowed to accompany me to children's classes at the church sometimes and during one such visit, our teacher taught about two things that really struck me—her, too, I think. We learned about guardian angels and we were asked to pray for all the children that had been taken away from their homes and were now frightened and perhaps even separated from their parents by the war. I saw a tear glisten in my dear friend's eye and was resolved to make her feel better. So back at home, I told her I had an idea. We'd send our own guardian angels to those poor frightened children. She was delighted. So we took a candle into the playroom. Neither of us had been allowed to light fires, but we knew how. We lit the candle from the fire burning in the fireplace, placed it on a trunk, and we both knelt before that trunk. I'll never forget the moment. I said a prayer aloud, asking God to please send my guardian angel to some child in one of those horrid camps. I can still remember the feeling of cold fear that immediately washed over my body. I knew somehow in my spirit that I had done an awful thing. I felt so alone and abandoned. My guardian angel was gone. I wanted to tell Victoria not to do it, but it was too late. I heard her finish her own version of the prayer at that moment. This made such an impression that I still carry the vivid memory even though I was only six."

Alistair stopped here and took a moment to steady himself. Aaan started to speak but Alistair continued. "Before we could even talk about what we had done, Victoria's father burst into the room and told Victoria to quickly pack an overnight bag because the family would be staying at our rental flat. Neither of us could guess why this seemed to be an awful thing, as her father had intimated. Having them as houseguests was a delight. So they came to our flat and stayed that week. I overheard the grown-ups talking about plans and it sounded like they might be coming to England with us. I was overjoyed. I began to think this might be our reward for sacrificing our own protection by sending away our guardian angels to comfort someone else.

"Then one day, I was outside on the sidewalk, I don't remember why, while everyone else was upstairs in the flat. A pretty lady in a uniform approached me. In my infinite stupidity, I thought she was a schoolteacher." Alistair became agitated. "I mean, even at six, I should've recognized a military uniform." He clenched his teeth for a moment. Aaan sat quietly and waited, thinking it best to allow him to unburden himself at his own pace.

Presently, Alistair continued, "She asked me if I knew a little girl named Victoria Varga. I was delighted to be helpful. I told her that yes, I knew her, she was my best friend, and she and her family were staying with us in our flat up there—and I even pointed to our window so she could find her. I offered to escort her up there and she declined, saying she wanted to surprise her and to please keep it a secret that she had asked about her. I said okay and went upstairs without a notion at all of the immense evil I had just brought on my best friend and her parents." Aaan watched Alistair wait for a moment, tears now streaming down his face.

"Shortly after that, four crisply dressed soldiers showed up at our door. Upon seeing the reaction of my father when he opened the door, I immediately knew something was terribly wrong and began to suspect this was my fault. The soldiers barged in and arrested Victoria's parents—and Victoria." He paused. "While they were there, pointing to papers they'd brought with them, Victoria's little sister, just a baby, started to cry. They looked at each other and at Victoria's mother, who ignored the cry. My own dear mother, I'll never forget, arose from her seat and walked into the bedroom, bringing the baby out. She then pulled up her blouse and placed the baby to her breast. The baby suckled, even though there was no milk, and fell back asleep. I saw her exchange a look and a nod with Victoria's mother and then they were gone. I watched Victoria exit my home and my life. She walked out with her mother's arm protectively clutching her, her face pressed into her mother's side. She never looked back to me and I was sure she knew it was all my fault." At that moment he seemed to lose control and wept as if his heart would break.

After allowing some time for Alistair to compose himself, Aaan spoke gently, "So the two sins you are confessing are sending away your guardian angel and then, possibly because you and your friend were not under the protection of your guardian angels, being tricked into betraying your friend by giving away her location?"

Alistair nodded, unable yet to speak.

"I see," Aaan said slowly and emphatically. "As for the first sin, perhaps you are guilty of a sin, but the sin was arrogance. You were extremely pompous in thinking you had the power to send away your guardian angel, or your friend's angel. In fact, I am sure both had a good laugh over such childlike arrogance. Of this, I am certain. I do not pretend to know all that goes on with guardian angels, having never had that task assigned to me, if indeed I could fulfill such a task, but of all I know of the breed, they are extremely dedicated to their task and would never be deterred by the misdirected wishes of a child. They hear what the heart utters, much more so than sounds from the lips. They communicate the information upward, probably to some chain of command that concludes with the one in charge of all, though, again, I have never been privy to exactly what transpires with them, or further up the chain. But of what I know of them, they would have heard your prayer and that of your little friend, and known your wishes were for comfort for those other unfortunate children, who also would have had their own guardian angels working hard. So, no, your prayers did not in any way cause Nazis to find them." Aaan spoke this last statement emphatically, each word pronounced with a pause.

Aaan watched Alistair take a deep, slow breath, his eyes closed. He knew he must be trying to rethink something that had festered for decades in his soul, as if it were only now being exposed to sunlight for the first time.

Aaan continued after a moment. "As to whether your giving of information to the Nazi constituted betrayal—the answer is no. This was a six-year-old child. The woman asking the question betrayed you by not giving you the full information of her intent before asking the question. She tricked you. Don't you see this? Would you hold a child accountable when an adult, likely demon-possessed, chose to deceive that child? I know that demon-possession was rampant in that part of the world during that time—orchestrated demonic activity. Evil

191

abounded. Frenzied cruelty abounded. You were *not* the cause." Again Aaan emphasized each word in the last statement.

Alistair wept now like a child. His soul seemed to be getting some measure of relief, melting after decades of self-loathing.

"Now, if you really want to know of the impact of the information you gave—" here Aaan hesitated, considering how much to reveal. "I can try to speak with your guardian angel and simply ask—but whether I will be answered, I cannot predict. I will likely be ignored. That is, unless I could be transformed with the Angel Stone. Then your guardian angel could not likely ignore me—it would be considered unforgivable to be ignored when in that state, I think. Of course—" he paused again, then decided to plow on. "The Angel Stone might not work on me since I am only half-angel. Would you like for me to try?"

"Oh, yes, please," Alistair's voice was a mere raspy whisper, like a drowning man getting his first breath of air.

"Do you have the stones with you now?" asked Aaan.

"No, as I mentioned, it's only a few shards and a little bit of dust I retained. This material is back in my laboratory."

"Then I could try communicating with your guardian angel without the transformation, but I doubt I would get a response."

"Very interesting. So you can see other angels all the time?"

"Yes, when I am in an in-between state. Not when I am incarnated as a human. But something you said still puzzles me and I wish to re-address the issue."

"Of course, anything," Alistair responded eagerly.

Aaan switched the topic, "You suggested that this Erik was transformed by the Angel Stone? Then he is not human? But an angel?"

"No, he *is* human," Alistair didn't seem to follow what Aaan was inferring.

"But this could not be," Aaan stated. "The Angel Stone only works on angels."

"Oh, yes, you said that, didn't you? But it definitely worked on Erik, and on my niece, Sonia, as well."

Aaan smiled. "Though it would make me very happy to think that Sonia and Anya were angels, or half-angels like myself, I suspect that it is simply a matter of mistaken identity. You see, what you described as the transformed state that Erik and Sonia experienced is exactly what the transformed state is like using the Sight Stone, or the Shining Stone, it was also called, *Lapillus Splendidus*."

"The ancient writings we found referred to one of the stones as *Lapillus Sideralis,* the Star Stone." Alistair's interest was obviously piqued.

"Ah, yes, I see. Here is what I suspect happened. The Latin term for star is *Stella*, but another term that means something like starry brightness is *Sideralis*. This term is somewhat close in meaning, as well as spelling to *Splendidus*, which means something like 'seeing something that is shining, radiant, splendid.' This is mere speculation, but I think that over time, the stones became confused and the Sight Stone became the Star Stone and was assumed to be the one that didn't work on humans. Thus, the Angel Stone became the name for the stone that allows humans to see angels. So Erik and Sonia used the Sight Stone to see angels and essences and the Angel Stone is the one that has never worked because you did not have an angel to use in your research." Aaan chuckled at the thought of angels succumbing to a human's research.

This thought didn't seem at all funny to Alistair, who had an air of excitement that began to frighten Aaan. His eyes were bright as he exclaimed feverishly, "Just think if we could harness the power…"

"No," he stated before Alistair could finish.

"But sir, think of all the good we could accomplish together," Alistair coaxed.

"Now, where have I heard that before?" Aaan said cynically. Then, feeling he had been too harsh, tried to explain. "You have no idea of what you are asking. Angels are not beings with which to trifle. Not even by me, who can at least claim half kinship. I am afraid that this is an age-old story, humans wishing to have supernatural powers that were not intended to be theirs, attempting to achieve this through angelic, or rather demonic, association, and the tables get turned, so that in the end they have lost their freedom. The one thing a human has that should never be offered to another is free will. This is a gift above all others. And so many become greedy and think they can trick an angel into submission, but it has never worked, not even once."

"Oh, dear sir, please do accept my apology," Alistair said, looking contrite. "I in no means meant to infer that you would be subservient to me—only that together, we might gain knowledge."

Aaan hesitated and then tried again, "No, please, it is I who gave offense. I did not think you were suggesting anything of the sort. It is just such a taboo topic—any collaboration between humans and angels. You see, the distinction between angel and demon is much the same as the distinction between comrade and enemy, or friend and foe. It is a mere matter of intent and loyalty. And it changes. Just as a friend can become an enemy, or an enemy a friend, an angel can fall into evil by alignment with an evil group of angels. I believe it is customary to attribute this to the leadership of one called Satan, but I think it is more complicated than that. And the reverse can happen. Some legends say an evil angel can be redeemed back into goodness."

"Fascinating," Alistair remarked. "It is just as Julian of Norwich wrote."

"Who is this Julian of Norwich?"

Alistair seemed deep in thought and took a moment to respond. "Julian of Norwich was a fourteenth-century Christian mystic who saw visions with a message of 'all shall be well.' Please forgive my awkward paraphrasing, but I believe the gist of her visions was that the sacrifice made at the crucifixion changed something throughout the universe and set a healing action in motion that would culminate eventually in all evil turned to good once more."

Aaan was now the one in deep thought. "How have I missed reading this work? I will read this at the first opportunity. I would like to know what she saw during these visions."

At the sound of approaching footsteps, Aaan made himself invisible and saw that Alistair feigned sleep. Aaan decided to stay close by and watch over his new friend. He would try to devise a plan to help him or assist when Erik arrived, but his immediate task was to bring calm and peace to Alistair and to his captors. He would try to ensure that no one acted rashly and harmed him.

CHAPTER 15

# The Catacombs

O nce off the plane, Erik and Roy didn't bother looking for a bus. Having studied the laminated street map Roy brought, they decided to make a beeline for their target area by swim-flying. The sun now fully aglow, Erik was struck by the beauty of the area—the lushness of vegetation nurtured by the soft, Mediterranean air, the ancient buildings, and even the immaculate cleanliness of the neighborhoods over which they flew. Not a scrap of paper or even stray grass clipping. *Do they sweep the streets daily here?* He'd expected the cult headquarters to be in a slum of some sort, but looking down upon the neighborhoods, he saw no slums. He was surprised when the location they sought was a beautiful palatial home with stucco turrets, fountains, and a manicured lawn. He glanced sideways at Roy, who was getting the hang of swim-flying and seemed focused and dedicated to the task. At that moment, as though Roy had read Erik's mind, he said, "The actual meeting place is underground. There's a hidden entrance to the catacombs

197

through the basement of this house." Erik nodded. *Of course, the catacombs.*

Erik and Roy pressed down through the roof, through all three floors of the house, and down into the basement.

"Hang on a minute while I remember the location of the hidden entrance," Roy said, stopping for a moment to look around. "Here," he said at last.

They passed under an arched stone doorway into a wine cellar. They didn't bother to move the racks of wine aside; they just passed through them. "Very nice bouquet. Hmmm, Giacomo Conterno Monfortino, Barolo," Erik mused, stopping to glance at the label.

"That's about four hundred US dollars a bottle," Roy said. "You can see all the ways this group could sucker one in."

Erik smiled. Roy had been a dedicated wine connoisseur for years and had taught him a lot in the early days of their acquaintance. He now looked around, feeling that he should stop and genuflect or something; this place had such a sacred feel.

"Can the demons see us in this state?" Roy asked nervously.

"Probably, though they never seemed to notice me before. I think that, like all angels, they don't realize we can see them and pretty much ignore us. Just don't look them in the eye or in any way let them know you can see them and hope for the best."

"Got it," answered Roy.

They ghosted forward into the tunnel, their movements slow. Erik felt like he was going slowly more from a heavy sense of reverence in such an ancient building than from fear of being caught.

Aaan continued to watch over Alistair, remaining alert for any threat. Most of the time Alistair had been left alone by his captors and had slept. A teenage boy who was clearly possessed had come in a few times to bring food and water, but mostly to give the old man shots. Aaan considered trying to communicate with the teen, but the demon inside the boy would have given away his presence. He decided to just watch a while longer and continue looking for an opportunity to help.

Aaan heard Alistair begin to awaken and quickly sat on the side of his small bed and took his hand. The old man looked up and smiled. Then with a speech that sounded weak and slurred, said, "So, Aaan, I suspect you came here to do more than simply chat. Where the stones are concerned, I don't want to take any chances. I could spend days, weeks chatting with you. But I am not totally convinced I can withstand torture. I think I would up to a point, but one never knows until the moment. What if they've also captured Zsofia? I don't think they have her, but I'm unsure. I don't even know how long I've been here—they keep me mostly drugged. I remember strolling along enjoying the day, my mind on choosing gifts for Zsofia and the Greenes, vaguely headed toward Harrods, but also window-shopping on the way. As I passed an alleyway, I heard my name called, glanced over, and saw a youth I thought I recognized as a young man we'd helped by holding an exorcism—Lorenzo, only it wasn't him but very like him. The young man raised his arms wide in greeting. I stepped toward him, confused and felt an arm encircle me from behind and a ghastly smelling cloth cover my nose. Then I woke up here. The youth speaks English and tried to question me once. Mostly, I've been left alone to sleep, for who knows how long. Hours? Days? Weeks? I don't relish being here when the two rough-necks come again."

Aaan thought about this and of how he could possibly be of immediate help. "Perhaps I can do a few things in my present state. But please remember that I am not a full angel. I suppose you could view me as some hybrid between a ghost and an angel. I can manipulate materials to a lesser degree than a full angel." Alistair seemed to be struggling to follow along, and Aaan realized how groggy the old man looked.

"Okay, so, what next?" Alistair asked.

Aaan responded slowly. "I am still thinking. When your niece asked me to come and help, I simply came. I found you through searching her memory banks for you and connecting to your essence. It is one angel thing I can do." Aaan smiled.

"Oh, my niece. I wondered how you knew I was here and why you chose to help me. So which was it? Sonia? Anya?"

"Anya. Well, both, but Anya and I are acquainted and she is the one who requested my assistance. Sonia was not too happy about my possessing Anya even momentarily to search for information. But Anya stubbornly stood her ground." He paused a moment, recalling the pleasant memory.

Alistair smiled and nodded in agreement. "Yes, you're certainly correct about that. Actually, they both are stubborn. Like their uncle, I guess." Alistair's eyelids were drooping but he opened them now and seemed to take a moment to indulge in his pride in his nieces.

"So that is how I can help," Aaan declared.

"Sorry, sir, I don't follow," Alistair said.

"Possession—" he paused a moment to find the best way to explain. "You see, I, or we, cannot possess anyone's essence without permission, but we do have a few little tricks, I believe you call 'temptation.' We can breathe a yearning into someone, an age-old technique used by both good and bad angels. This can be done by the good angels, those gainfully employed by Heaven—at least the hierarchy in-place, or by one of the enemies to this hierarchy, those you would call demons."

"So you could influence those holding me to allow me to go free?" Alistair rubbed his chin, seeming a little doubtful this would work.

"Yes, but a little more subtly. You see, if they are determined to keep you—let's say, to demand a ransom—they are unlikely to just let you go."

"Yes, my thoughts as well."

"However, there are a hundred smaller influences a person must encounter in the course of any day. Things like whether to overeat, how to answer a question, when to be generous or selfish with a friend, and so forth."

"Okay, I think I follow."

"So I can try to influence their actions, though to be honest, I am not very good at it." Aaan pressed his lips together in determination. "I have not tried yet because the youth in attendance is possessed and I did not want to give away my presence. Demon possession complicates matters. But perhaps I may get an opportunity to distract someone so they forget the key and leave it lying about. Then, I can bring it to you and you can escape. But there may be others joining us and it may be best to wait for them. Your niece suggested this person named Erik is looking for you."

"Ah, Erik," Alistair said hopefully, and nodded, seeming pleased.

Aaan hesitated a moment before continuing, "Now, I should look about and see how you would get out of here once out of this cell. So I will, at this time, beg your patience while I make a mental map of the escape route—agreed?"

Alistair didn't seem very reassured. "Okay, sir. I will await your return. I thank you sincerely for your help— and, please, if this should not work, please do thank my lovely nieces for their noble intentions. It's the thought that counts."

Aaan began to move away but Alistair raised his hand, apparently remembering something further he needed to say. "Oh, and sir, I do sincerely thank you for your advice and allowing me to confess. You have no idea how much you've helped this old troubled soul. If I should die today, I will rest much more peacefully than I would have done yesterday. So thank you from the bottom of my heart." Alistair brushed away a tear.

Aaan was touched by this gentle old man. He reminded him of someone he'd known before in centuries past—*who? Solomon? Perhaps. David?* Likely traits of several great leaders but he couldn't put a finger on exactly whom he was thinking of. He wanted to comfort this kind soul. "Sir, would you like to see something to take your mind off your imprisonment? I could show you Solomon's temple in its heyday."

Alistair's eyes lit up. Then he seemed to think better of it. "That reminds me of a Biblical story of one much greater than I who was shown wonderful sights by another angel—a fallen angel."

"Yes, but he was asked to worship that angel," Aaan corrected him. "That is very different. It is not bad to enjoy beauty and grandeur; it is only bad to worship them or the one offering them, as if they could be given. It perverts the whole beautiful creation that springs from a mind much vaster than anything one of us could imagine. But what I am offering is simply an exchange of mental images, so you can enjoy the beauty and hopefully receive some comfort and distraction from your situation. It is perfectly fine to decline it. It is merely an offer of comfort. And I had best not take too long about it, anyway, because I need to tend to the task of helping you escape."

Alistair looked at Aaan with a warm look of friendship. "Now that you put it that way, my friend, I will gratefully accept your gift."

Aaan smiled at Alistair and then, as he had done with Anya, moved into Alistair's thoughts. Aaan knew all he would feel physically would be his hair poofing slightly as if stirred by the wind.

Aaan enjoyed taking Alistair on a memory tour of Solomon's temple—it had been a long time since he had visited it. After the virtual tour, the old man drifted into in a deep sleep with a smile on his face. Aaan exited the cell and began looking around.

Aaan, still aglow from the pleasant temple tour, found himself in the catacombs. He was delighted; it had been far too long since he had explored them. He didn't need to worry about having to work to remember the layout; each vista had been indelibly etched into his knowledge. He reveled in the beauty of the artwork and the deep sentiments had gone into the architecture for a moment before resuming his mission.

*Yes,* Annie thought as she spotted Erik and Roy. She watched them emerge from their plane.

It was morning now. She knew she'd eventually have to let them know of her presence, but would wait as long as possible. Who knew, Erik might try to make her go back and not accompany them. She wanted to be an extra pair of eyes—not get in the way. She just needed to help—and she really hoped to see Aaan.

She cautiously began to follow them across the city and down toward a palatial building. Annie was surprised at how easy it was. Erik and Roy didn't bother to look around very much, only ahead. She guessed the last thing they expected was to be followed by any ethereal beings other than their guardian angels, certainly not an ethereal version of herself wearing a large black trash bag.

Roy seemed to know where he was going. Annie had a hard time keeping up. She watched them ghost through the roof and down into the building, following at a distance. Once in the basement, they took several turns in the underground labyrinth, moving past ancient frescos, tombs, and platforms that looked like bunk beds, some containing bones of the deceased.

Soon, they came into a large room with a series of six barred cells around the wall, three on each side, with a corridor that continued on past the room. The room had arched doorways with small ornate columns on each side. Annie had read about the catacombs and wondered if these bars had been added by the cult, enclosing alcoves that had once been used as chapels or tombs. Heavily worn and chipped frescos covered the walls between the cells and lined the inside walls of some of the cells. Annie wished she had more time to look at them. They strangely reminded her of Aaan's cave—they added a quiet reverence to the atmosphere.

Annie almost gasped when she saw Uncle Alistair, apparently asleep on a cot inside the third cell on the right. She ducked out of sight, being careful not to be seen by Erik and Roy.

Erik and Roy had also seen him and looked excitedly at each other as they approached.

*This was too easy,* Annie thought too late. Erik was just beginning to congratulate Roy when deep, maniacal laughter shattered the silence, coming from one of the cells on the opposite wall directly behind Erik and Roy.

Annie slipped back, ducking behind the edge of the entryway, peeking out to watch and react as needed.

Erik and Roy swung around to face a tall, distinguished-looking man. That he was a body-builder was obvious even from the hang of his tailored suit. His body seemed totally at ease and in control, but inside was what really made Annie's chin drop in fear and awe.

The man was obviously possessed, and not with the small, lamprey-like demons Red had described, but something very different. This demon looked more like a demi-god that glowed orange, like fire, and totally opaque in its murkiness. From what Erik had told her, murkiness signified great evil, a lack of purity and clarity. But the features of the demonic face were extremely handsome and compelling, almost seductive.

"Don't recognize me, Roy?" The laughter was now gone.

Roy gasped. "Pietro."

"Pietro. Yes. Do you know what that name means?" He looked at Roy, who slowly shook his head.

"It means 'stone.' A fitting name, don't you think? Since I've been searching for the stones for *thousands of years.*" He spat out the last few words to emphasize his frustration. "And I like to occupy a body that is healthy and robust. But now that you can really see me, rather than this silly shell of a man I wear, I would like to be called by my real name, Daanak."

Annie gasped, recognizing the name. *Aaan's father!*

Roy nodded and Daanak walked slowly around the two men, who stood frozen in shock. "Oh, I knew they—the stones, of course—were in the Vatican for the past many centuries, but getting into that fortress is impossible for one like me." He grinned very widely at this statement and Annie felt her blood run cold.

Neither Erik now Roy spoke.

Daanak eyed them and continued, "So I waited for someone else, someone … *innocent* to bring them out for me. I knew all I had to do was wait and they would eventually come to me. And here you are." At this, he reared back his head and roared with laughter.

Annie saw Erik whisper something to Roy, who was obviously affected by this, having experienced the horror of demonic possession. She only caught a few words, *"can't … allow …"*

Daanak eyed Erik scornfully and laughed. "That's right, Roy. I cannot do anything you don't allow, though I do have some very powerful tools of persuasion. I venture to suggest there is not much you would not do or say at my bidding were I to employ these powers of persuasion to their fullest." He roared maniacally once more.

Annie heard Alistair stir and suppressed a gasp.

She saw Erik's hand go to his leather pouch. She didn't think the demon could see it from his angle. She suspected he had a STAG control in the leather pouch; she wished he were close enough to touch Uncle Alistair with it. He could zap him and drag him up and away, perhaps before this thug from the spirit world could employ his powers of persuasion. But she needed to distract him first to buy some time for Erik.

Annie saw Daanak watching Erik suspiciously. She didn't think Daanak could know Erik had a STAG control, or even that such a thing existed.

Erik seemed to be trying not to look Daanak in the eye as he continued to circle the men menacingly. Both he and Roy seemed to be unable to move.

Daanak pointed at Erik's leather loincloth and laughed, then picked at Roy's leather coat. "Strangely dressed, are you not, gentlemen? Need for me to recommend an Italian tailor?"

205

He circled back to a location in front of Erik. The cell containing Alistair was at his back. Annie decided that perhaps now was the time to act, before Daanak somehow took the STAG control from Erik.

Annie took a breath to steady herself, unsure if this would work, but knowing it was now or never. She stepped out into the doorway and shouted, "Stop! Daanak, we need your help. You just have to listen. Your son—" But her words were cut off as several things happened at once. First, a rapid movement as Erik snatched the STAG control from the bag and raced into Alistair's cell. Daanak went to grab him, but a commanding male voice, as clear as a cathedral bell, sounded from behind him. "Father."

Daanak whirled around to face an apparition Annie recognized—a glowing, silvery male form with hair and robes blowing in the non-existent breeze. *Aaan!*

With Daanak distracted, Erik quickly zapped Alistair, grabbed his hand, and pulled him upward. Shouting for Roy and Annie to follow, he lost no time in exiting the cell and shooting through the ceiling.

Roy disappeared through the ceiling as well. But Annie stood mesmerized, watching Aaan and his father stare at each other, neither speaking.

A second later, Roy reappeared and grabbed Annie's hand to pull her upward.

Annie yanked her hand away. "Get off!"

"Annie, we've got to go—NOW. We're all in danger here. Annie, for goodness sake, we have to leave now to save your uncle!"

Annie knew he was right. But how could she leave Aaan to an uncertain fate? Aaan and Daanak were still in a standoff.

"Annie, Erik won't leave without you. You want to get us all killed—or worse?"

Annie had no answer to that and simply surrendered, allowing herself to be pulled through the ceiling and up, up above the town, mindlessly following, then flying quickly to one side in case they were followed by the demon. They weren't.

Each man held one of Alistair's hands. He was still very groggy. They flew-swam with one hand while kicking their feet for speed. Annie felt too much in shock to be any help in carrying Alistair. She followed robotically as they made a beeline for the airport.

Erik and Roy were obviously overjoyed when they were once again sitting in a cockpit of a non-stop flight to Washington. The pair high-fived while Alistair slept on.

Annie, however, sat in shocked silence alongside her sleeping great-uncle, holding his hand. She would have wept if her tear ducts worked in the ghost transformation.

Erik tried at first to console her and tell her that she'd saved the day, but soon gave up trying. She wanted none of that—she'd abandoned her dear friend to an uncertain fate and nothing could console her. Yes, she and Aaan *had* saved the day for Uncle Alistair and she was glad of that. But how could she live without knowing what happened to Aaan?

# PART FOUR:

# An Unexpected Event

*From a conversation between Caroline and Bingley in <u>Pride and Prejudice</u>:*

*"I should like balls infinitely better," she replied, "if they were carried on in a different manner; but there is something insufferably tedious in the usual process of such a meeting. It would surely be much more rational if conversation instead of dancing were made the order of the day."*
*"Much more rational, my dear Caroline, I dare say, but it would not be near so much like a ball."*[4]

## CHAPTER 16

# The Proposal

R ed had never been so stressed in her life as while Erik and Annie were gone. Finally, Erik called to announce that he and Roy were bringing home a beloved uncle, and her sister to boot, and they were on their way.

"No way. You've got Uncle Alistair?" Red exclaimed, relief washing over her.

"In the flesh. No, actually, in an altered state, but all here."

"Is he okay? What happened to him?"

"He's, well, probably okay. He's drugged and hasn't said more than a few mumbles yet. So we have to be prepared that he may be harmed, but he's alive and away from them at least."

"Oh, I'd like to get my hands on that cult leader."

"Be careful what you wish for. But I'd better not spend much time on the phone in case the cult has a way to track this. So please give everyone the good news for us. Roy did well— you can tell his mom. And did you know Annie was coming?"

"Let's just say that you are not to tell anyone here about Annie's participation. And please ask Roy to do the same. I'll explain the whole thing to you when you get here. Promise?"

"Okay, but you gotta dish later."

Red kept trying to surf the web to kill time, anxious to see Erik and even more anxious to know if Uncle Alistair was going to be okay. Finally, she heard a very quiet knock at her bedroom door and ran to fling it open.

Erik stood on her threshold, wearing a pair of her uncle's plain gray sweatpants and a T-shirt.

She threw her arms around his neck and he planted a kiss on her lips.

"I guess I should be getting used to this, but how does one get used to the love of their life just appearing out of nowhere?" Red felt giddy with joy at actually seeing him in the flesh.

"Me, too, Sonia. I don't think I'll ever get used to the jolt of how beautiful you are to me every time I see you," he said and kissed her again.

Forcing herself to focus on the seriousness of what had just happened, Red was almost afraid to ask. "And Uncle Alistair— any change? Where is he?"

"I think he's going to be okay. He's upstairs, sleeping off the drug. I don't know what they gave him or how long it'll take for it to be metabolized out of his system. He's been in the ghost transformation for the past twelve hours or so and I suspect the drug didn't metabolize as fast in that state. He came around a little and crawled into his bed. Annie made a beeline for her room, I think. Roy's busy making phone calls to let his mom and Xenia know he's back."

"Great work, you super-hero. What should I call you? Vikingman?"

They laughed. Red loved sharing Erik's feeling of success and held his hand as they descended the stairs to announce the new arrivals to the family.

# THE PROPOSAL

Red's parents surrounded them, both asking questions at once. Red was glad to see Erik didn't forget and betray that Annie had been involved.

Her parents seemed as alarmed as she had been to learn about Uncle Alistair's drugged sleep and rushed upstairs to examine him.

Red snuggled under Erik's arm on the sofa and hung on his every word as he told of the chilling events of the rescue. She saw Annie quietly appear and listen from across the room, pretending to be doing something on her iPod.

Erik seemed to be trying to explain that they had been miraculously saved by Annie and an angel. He was obviously having some difficulty describing Aaan's presence.

Red decided to put him out of his misery and come clean. She saw his eyebrows raise when she said, "I know, Annie and I asked Aaan to help."

Then she couldn't hold back any more and lurched forward, taking both of Annie's hands in hers. "You did it. You and Aaan saved the day."

Red saw Annie respond with a strange mixture of shyness and delight, and something else Red couldn't place. *Regret?*

"What the heck are the two of you talking about?" Erik obviously wanted in on the secret.

Red saw Annie look gravely into first Erik's eyes and then her own, sorrowful tears beginning to form. "Red will tell you the story," she said to Erik. "Just, please don't mention my participation to my parents."

Then Annie looked squarely at Red. "The demon's name was Daanak. Get it?"

Red immediately recognized the name and the enormity of the situation hit her. She saw Annie's steely constitution melt away and knew Annie was moments away from a complete emotional meltdown. "I'll explain to Erik," she said, and Annie ran out of the room.

213

"How do *you* know that name?" Erik was obviously trying to understand what he was hearing. He looked so tired and jet-lagged, she thought. Two rescue trips in a row had doubtlessly drained him.

Red looked at the door where Annie had disappeared and said, "Shall we take a stroll on the towpath?"

The fall river smells were pungent in the damp morning air. Red was elated as she walked slowly along the level path with Erik. Luckily, no other walkers or bicyclers were on the path this morning, so they had all the privacy they wished. A crow cawed overhead and Red saw Moon. She and Erik waved to him and Red laughed, wondering if he was watching over them. After a few minutes, Red spotted the crow's sleek, black partner. They both looked fat and ready for winter.

"Have you begun filling the feeder yet this fall?" Erik asked Red.

"Of course. We began a month ago when the leaves fell," Red declared cheerily.

Erik gave her shoulders a squeeze and then turned his attention to the discussion at hand. "Okay, you—dish."

Red did her best to tell a fairly succinct version of Annie's story, leaving out the cigarettes and attempting to leave out the part about the STAG control. Erik had heard parts of the story before, however, so even in his tired state, he was quick-witted enough upon hearing it again and in more detail that that little detail finally emerged.

"What in the blazes was your sister thinking?" Erik asked exasperatedly. "Annie could've ended civilization as we know it if the wrong people had seen her use it. I mean, Red, this is serious. Professor Hamilton and I are proof of how desperate some are to get their hands on the power of the stones. And think about what they'd do with it. Easily break into the Pentagon and steal secrets. Steal nuclear materials by making them so small they could be hidden in a nostril. The list is long, and believe me, I've spent a great deal of time thinking of all

THE PROPOSAL

the possibilities. Annie absolutely has to give that STAG control back to your uncle—tonight."

"Okay, okay," Red was already regretting that she'd told him—Annie was going to be so upset with her. She wondered if Annie would ever be able to see Aaan again without the STAG control. And she knew Annie must be worried sick about the impact of his finding out that his own father was a demon. *But maybe he already knew that?* She tried to recall what Annie had deciphered from the cave etchings.

Annie, alone in her room, was re-reading that portion of the translation about Daanak. *"In his grief he became angry to his destruction, joining the dark forces of the one whose name I shall not write"* Hmmm, she thought, *Aaan already knew his father was a demon.*

She cried, thinking of all Aaan had gone through. He seemed to want so badly to be good. She'd never spent much effort thinking about her soul, but this beautiful being had. She yearned for a true connection with him, this impossibly beautiful being—Aaan, her first love.

The next morning, Annie awoke to a bustling house. She learned that during the night, Ms. Catsworthy had been contacted and hopped the very next plane back from London. Uncle Alistair had slept off the drug and seemed as chipper as ever, refusing to see a doctor and saying he'd be fine and would just address the issue at his next annual physical.

If Annie could be amused in her current state, she would have found humor in the argument she overheard between her dad and his uncle. Uncle Alistair declared, "And just what, pray tell, would you have me give as the reason I ingested an unknown drug? Wild party? Frat hazing? You know I can't report the kidnapping without spilling the beans about the research."

Her dad had tried to suggest a reasonable excuse—picking up the wrong drink at a bar? Old army-buddy prank? Drinking

215

from a water puddle? He'd eventually seen his uncle's reasoning and decided to give up his attempt to have him examined. "What we need is a private doctor," he'd grumbled.

"Dad, why don't you ask Erik's mom? She's a doctor," Red suggested.

"Why didn't I think of that? Red, that's an outstanding idea. Let's have a dinner party tonight to celebrate Uncle Alistair's return, and also her husband's return—um, is he actually home yet?"

"No, but Minah can visit him. She might be able to bring him out of the hospital with her for the evening. We could ask. I think he's still under observation after being locked up for so long. And having some health things done, like root canals," Red explained.

"Why don't you call Erik and invite him and whatever members of his family are available to come for dinner? Hopefully, Dr. Wolfeningen won't mind checking over Uncle Alistair. Oh, yes, and invite Roy, too, and his girlfriend, and his mother. Ms. Catsworthy, of course will be back from London by then. Hopefully she'll arrive in time to catch a couple hours sleep before coming over," her dad said. "Anyone I left off?"

Annie was sad when she heard this. She could think of one that had been left off the list, but she had no way of reaching him, especially since she'd no doubt have to give the STAG control back. She was sure Erik would ask her about it soon; Red had confessed he'd figured it out. She climbed the stairs to her room in deep thought. Oh, of course she was happy Uncle Alistair was safe. And that Erik, Roy, and she had all made it back without harm. It seemed the stones worked miraculously even against things as horrific as kidnapping or political imprisonment by radical groups. She just wished they could help her friend.

Once again enclosed in the privacy of her room, she took a copy of the translation she'd made from the cave wall and fell backward onto her bed. She held it upward toward the ceiling and dreamily re-read it. She felt tears trickle down and drip into her hair.

The last sentence particularly touched her. *"After Seya was buried, I stayed in this cave and spent many days creating art, trying to recall the beauty I had seen in the world through sculpture. Then I decided to remain here and sleep, being tired of struggling."* This beautiful being seemed so tired and sad. He'd been through so much. He just wanted to belong somewhere. He'd felt rejected by the world of angels and couldn't seem to attain the Heaven offered to mortals. He'd been so kind to her when she requested his help and had saved them. So why wasn't he included in the celebration tonight? Why hadn't Erik or Uncle Alistair invited him?

Annie knew she was being unreasonable, but she didn't care. They didn't even know where Aaan was. What had happened to him? Maybe the demon had captured him. Maybe his father had talked him into turning evil with him. Tears streamed down her cheeks now as the thought of all the years—years? Centuries? Millennia?—he had tried to make the cut—to improve to the point that he could go to Heaven to be with his mother, to belong. And now, to possibly have it all thrown away by getting sucked into a nest of evil? Yes, she was worried sick. She had to know how he was.

Eventually, Annie was roused out of her gloom by her mother, who was determined to throw a huge dinner party in just a few hours—a holiday feast; a belated Thanksgiving traditional meal with all the trimmings. Annie learned that she'd called her favorite organic market and ordered catered platters. Her dad would transport all the food. Annie and Red would be employed in straightening the house, cleaning, and setting up the large dining room to accommodate the largest group of guests either girl had ever seen entertained in their household. In addition to all the guests her father had suggested, her parents said that to make the event truly spectacular, the girls could invite any friends who could make it. So Nyah and her parents, Tatyana and her parents, and Quinn and Wali were all on their way over.

Uncle Alistair had surprised the family by placing a few phone calls and supplying a brass band for the evening. And someone, she suspected also her uncle, had also arranged for some wait staff to serve.

As the band began setting up and the hired staff took over the food management, Annie noted she had only half an hour to shower and get ready. The warm water felt divine. That was, until it ran out. *Crap, guess everyone in the household is taking a shower tonight.* Nonetheless, she felt refreshed.

She tried to style her thick hair, but without time for it to fully dry, it wasn't much use. She didn't bother with makeup, but did decide to dress up, trying on a nice sweater and black pants (as a rule, she shunned dresses whenever she could, unless it was summer and she could wear a comfortable, light sundress; she liked those). The sweater outfit, however, didn't cut it and she ended up wearing a stretchy black skirt with black leggings and a long-sleeved knit shirt. She was sure Red would be busy spending at least half an hour applying makeup now that she had a boyfriend.

Annie started downstairs to see if Nyah had arrived yet. She was glad she was coming. It might keep her from gagging at all the togetherness she'd encounter, as almost everyone coming tonight was paired up. Even Quinn and Wali were on their way to being an item. Only Nyah, Tatyana, and herself would be lone wolves. Well, there were the band members, but with her luck they'd be paired up, too, she mused wryly.

She realized she was going overboard by letting her hopeless attitude take over. She needed to reel it in and share the joy of Uncle Alistair and Erik's dad being freed. That really was something; she was sure both had been saved a world of misery. She was glad, too, that Aaan had helped. *Whoops.* She shouldn't have allowed herself to think of him—now she had to

rally again to return her mood to at least one of pleasant watch-
fulness, an indifferent spectator of the festivities.

Annie was impressed with her uncle that evening—he
looked debonair and handsome. He wore a tux and Ms.
Catsworthy wore a formal gown. No one else dressed quite
so elaborately, but still, Annie thought she caught a hint of
enchantment in the air. This helped boost her mood. Dinner
music drifted from the ballroom as they dined.

Nyah was dressed in a pretty party dress. Annie hadn't
noticed before how pretty she was. She told her so and Nyah
seemed appreciative.

Erik's father looked as though he'd been ill. She could
tell he'd been once a handsome man, but she could see the
strain of the imprisonment. Erik had told them he was vastly
improved from the way he'd found him. Erik's mother certainly
didn't seem to notice, however; they couldn't stop gazing at
each other.

Annie envied anyone such a connection. Would she ever
find it? How could she, while she was in love with an angel,
or was he more of a ghost? A half-breed. Annie felt a sudden
pain for all he'd suffered because of his status, not belonging
fully in either world.

She was jerked from this reverie by a sound of silver on
glass, a call of attention, and she realized the music had died.

Her Uncle Alistair stood tall at the head of the table and
made a beautiful speech about the sacrifice that many men
and women made daily for our freedom, and especially wished
to honor and congratulate Viggo Wolfeningen on his outstanding service to this country and his return home. The crowd
applauded loudly and gave him a standing ovation as he bowed
and thanked his friends.

Erik's dad declined to give a lengthy speech, except to say
it was good to be home. Some chatter erupted around the room
and Annie heard some of it. She noticed no one seemed to be
mentioning Erik's role in the escape and she was pretty sure

this was because it wasn't known outside of the immediate family and research team. Nor did anyone mention Alistair's rescue, probably for the same reason. Many of the guests were likely only aware they were honoring a prisoner of war who'd been recently rescued.

As Erik's dad re-seated himself, Uncle Alistair remained standing. "And now, I wish to tell a story and a recent revelation that was shown me. And then I wish to right a wrong that has cheated the person I love most in this world out of the truth and perhaps some years of happiness."

The room became deathly quiet at these heavy words. Annie saw Uncle Alistair turn to Ms. Catsworthy and extend his hand. She thought Ms. Catsworthy seemed to be in on the secret, smiling a lovely smile first to him and then to the audience as she arose from her chair and made her way gracefully to place her hand in his and stand beside him.

Uncle Alistair pulled her hand to his lips and then clutched it to his chest as he began. "You see, dear friends, when I was but a boy, I had a playmate, my best friend, Victoria, the older sister of my dear Zsofia." They exchanged a meaningful glance.

Annie noted the peaceful quality of Ms. Catsworthy's face, like a patience wrought from a lifetime of pain.

Uncle Alistair continued, "Victoria and I were six years old, Zsofia but a baby, when the Nazis came for their family. My father and I were in Budapest at the time because he was in business with their family. I won't depress you with the details—we all know of the atrocities of that time—but what I do wish to tell is that a little boy and girl made a pact and the girl was taken by the Nazis to Auschwitz. The boy spent a lifetime thinking it was his fault she'd been captured and never forgave himself. He vowed to take care of the one remaining member of the family, little Zsofia, for the rest of his life—to serve her and defend her with all he had. But he never considered himself worthy to take her hand, as he's doing now." He kissed the hand again and Annie saw a tear trickle from Ms. Catsworthy's eye.

"Yes, the boy was me and the baby, my dear Zsofia. We've spent a lifetime looking after each other, and then, at some point, I realized I was head-over-heels in love with my young charge. But my misguided promise to care for her from a distance kept me from ever acknowledging how I felt. Until very recently, when I had a vision. An angel named Aaan came to me."

Annie gasped. Only Nyah seemed to notice. Annie saw Nyah give her a look, as if to say she fully expected an explanation later.

Her uncle continued, "He helped me see that not only was it not within the power of a six-year-old to stop the evil Nazi force, but that it was pompous for me to think so." He looked into Ms. Catsworthy's eyes, a tear streaming down his cheek.

To the audience, he said, "Don't worry folks, she's in on this," and winked.

The audience laughed and Ms. Catsworthy gave a very cute, face-scrunching smile to show she was being good-natured about it.

"And now, dear Zsofia, the words I've waited decades to say may now be said. I'm sorry to take so long about it."

Another giggle went through the audience as Alistair went down on one knee, still holding her hand. "Dearest Zsofia, I love you with all my heart and soul. I've adored you from afar for low these many years and now would like to ask you to make me the happiest man alive by consenting to be my wife."

A hush went through the room. The only sound was that of a few tissues being pulled out of purses.

"My dearest Alistair," said Ms. Catsworthy, "I, too, have loved you for low these many years and will gladly accept your proposal of marriage. My dearest Alistair, I thought you'd never ask."

With that he swept her up into a huge hug and spun her around and then the two exchanged a deep kiss that Annie noticed left all present stunned.

Annie looked at Nyah and silently mouthed the words, "Old people love, *eeeshh*." Both giggled, but Annie couldn't deny that she was deeply touched by the scene.

The party moved into the ballroom and Annie watched as Uncle Alistair and Ms. Catsworthy began the dance with a waltz.

Annie wasn't sure how such a small band pulled it off, but they played the most beautiful song she'd ever heard. It was both romantic and haunting—the story of the lives of her uncle and his love. "Nyah, do you know what song this is?"

Nyah, too, seemed to be mesmerized but snapped out of it briefly to answer, "I think it's *Dolci Pianti* by Johann Strauss." Annie made a mental note to take a music appreciation class at some point.

As the couple danced together so beautifully, Annie thought the whole room seemed to be caught in their elegance. Their graceful movements seemed well choreographed, as if both had been rehearsing a lifetime for this moment. Annie sighed, thinking of Aaan and resolving to ask her uncle about him.

Annie felt a little better now, infected by the happiness of her uncle, and was surprised at feeling some humor erupt when she recalled her uncle had thought he was seeing a vision, or perhaps that was just his official story so folks wouldn't think him senile and lock him up.

Only a few brave couples ventured onto the floor during the waltz, but after it was over, the band started up with a more modern tune and the floor became full. Even Annie and the other girls without partners danced for several songs. Erik and Roy also politely danced with each girl who didn't have a partner for at least one dance.

Annie thought the evening was fun overall, but was glad to eventually climb into bed, exhausted. She slept much better then she had anticipated with her earlier depression and worry for Aaan.

The next day, everyone slept late and Annie was relieved to find a clean house when she came down. *Wow—Uncle Alistair knows how to throw a party.* Needless to say, he was nowhere to be found. She figured he'd probably be at Ms. Catsworthy's, or the two of them might be out. They'd likely be inseparable now, making up for lost time.

She felt out of sorts and decided to check her homework since the next day would be school as usual. That ended up taking most of the day. That evening, after she'd finished and was watching videos on her computer, she thought she heard her uncle's voice in the hallway. She peeped out her bedroom door to see him disappear into his study. Excellent; she'd catch him now.

She knocked timidly at the door and heard him invite her in. She took a deep breath and entered. "Congratulations, Uncle Alistair," she began.

"Annie, love. Good to see you. And thank you for your kind words." He was beaming with a kind of joy as she'd never seen on him. He came around his desk, and, grasping both shoulders, planted a kiss on her cheek.

"You too, Uncle Alistair."

"Have a seat, child. What brings you to see me?"

Annie sat on a beautifully carved, high-backed, mahogany chair with tapestry cushions, facing his desk. She didn't really know much about furniture, but knew it was very expensive. It made her feel a little formal and she realized she'd never before come into his study to talk to him, only exchanging pleasantries downstairs. She needed to lighten this up. "Boy, you sure do know how to throw a party," she began. He smiled. "And we sure are glad you made it home okay."

She blushed. He smiled good-naturedly, then said, "Okay, Annie, spit it out. You can ask me anything, child." He was in such a great mood that Annie was put at ease.

"Well, I want to ask you about that angel, Aaan."

"You know something about him?"

"Well, you see, sir, it's a long story but he's kind of my friend. And I asked him to go and rescue you." Annie decided not to complicate matters by admitting that she had been in Italy, too. He had been so drugged he hadn't realized it. He'd probably find out later, but that wasn't what she wanted to discuss now.

Alistair raised an eyebrow. "Yes, he mentioned that the two of you are acquainted. But how?"

Annie bit her lip. "Well, you know how you lost one of those STAG controls a while back?" She tried to look at the ceiling, anywhere but at his piercing grey eyes.

Alistair grasped the arms of his chair, his face losing color. "Annie, is there something you need to tell me?"

Annie silently nodded and then went on. "Well, I kind of—found it—and used it to explore a cave. And I found this on the wall." She held out a copy of the translated writing. "Well, not exactly this, it was in Latin and I translated it." She gave him a moment to scan the page.

"Annie, this is incredible. This is him," he said.

Annie blurted it all out rapidly before she lost her nerve. "Yes, sir. I saw him in the cave in Tennessee last summer, and then, when you disappeared, well, I decided to ask him for help. I mean, he seemed nice and all. He called me his Tiny Bold Maiden, and I felt very safe with him. You see, he has always felt left out because he was half-angel and half-human and he never really got to go with either group in the afterlife and he always thought he was supposed to prove himself or grow or learn, or something. To somehow earn getting to go to Heaven." Annie felt herself tear up at this.

"Fascinating. This was a cave near your grandmother's?"

She nodded.

"I've never met the lady, but if she's anything like her daughter and granddaughters, I'm sure she's a delightful individual."

"Well, he lives in a cave on her property—actually, on the border between hers and someone else's," Annie's emotions heightened. "Oh, Uncle Alistair, I'm so worried about him because when he rescued you, he saw his father. And that's not the worst part. His father's the demon."

Alistair's brow furrowed in deep concentration. "He rescued me? I knew he came to comfort and advise me, but didn't know he did anything else."

She quickly filled him in on the details of the rescue, leaving out the fact that she'd been involved.

"I had no idea. Yes, I remember a man named Pietro. He seemed to be the leader of the cult. A cruel man. How do you know so much?"

Annie felt sheepish, "Okay, I admit, I used the STAG control and went, too, but that's not the important thing. The important thing is this," she said, gesturing toward the paper, "Daanak is Aaan's dad. He's a fallen angel, and Aaan's mom was mortal, but got killed in a flood and he thinks she went to Heaven. But the thing that worries me is that no one has seen him since the rescue. The last time anyone saw him, he was with his father." At this she began to sob, struggling to keep her composure.

Alistair handed her a monogrammed handkerchief and knelt in front of her, patting her shoulder. "I see. This dear being that saved my life—in more ways than one— may have been captured by a demon. Oh, dear."

"And Red told Erik about Aaan and that I have a STAG control and he said I had to give it back." Annie peeped up at her uncle timidly to gauge his reaction. "But then I may never see him again. And I think I might … be in love with him." The tears flowed freely now, though her sobs were silent. She squeezed her eyes fast together.

Alistair seemed overcome by emotion as well and embraced her warmly, allowing her to cry onto his shoulder while he remained kneeling in front of her chair. "There, there, Anya. No one's going to stand between you and your true love, least of all me. Yes, the STAG controls absolutely must be kept safely locked away and I'm very relieved to know that the lost one has been located. But you may use it any time you need it. And you know what? You're going to go to Tennessee to see if he's back in his cave very soon. By Christmas, if not before. I will make it a number-one priority and will happily accompany you if needed. I would dearly love to thank him in person. If it hadn't been for your friend, I'd have never had the courage to face my own demons and I now vow to do everything in my power to help him face his."

He wiped a tear from her eye and embraced her again. "Oh, Anya, thank you, thank you, thank you—truly if it hadn't been for you and your courage and wisdom, this happy day might never have come for my darling Zsofia and me."

Annie loved her uncle. She left the study feeling much better and knowing that Alistair would keep his word. He was a man of brilliant potential and would figure out a way to help Aaan. She was able to have hope now.

CHAPTER 17

# *The Wedding*

O nce Uncle Alistair made his decision to marry Ms. Catsworthy, he wasted no time. Red knew that as fond as he was of gatherings and celebrations, he was eager to make up for a lot of lost time. In fact, Red wouldn't be surprised if he disappeared with Ms. Catsworthy to live for a period of time in the transformed state where the body didn't seem to change or age in any way. Red knew this wasn't entirely understood or documented, but suspected the two could spend a decade together and not age more than a few hours, if at all, while transformed by the Sight Stone, as it was now called.

But Ms. Catsworthy was not interested in a quick wedding and Uncle Alistair would leave no stone unturned to make her happy. Ms. Catsworthy wanted a proper Jewish wedding in honor of her family who had perished at Auschwitz. But this would mean Uncle Alistair would have to convert to Judaism, which would take a considerable amount of time. Given their ages, and the fact that he was a professor of religious studies

227

with world-renowned expertise in Christian literature, a long publication record, and firm opinions on religion, he hadn't been entirely comfortable with adopting to any organized religion enough to qualify for membership at this late stage of his life. But he had considered it because he so wanted to please his darling in every way.

Eventually, the two lovers had been able to work out a compromise, partly by calling in a few favors and arranging to have the ceremony at the National Cathedral just after Christmas. As its mission and reputation was to promote spiritual harmony and work toward reconciliation among faiths, Alistair and Ms. Catsworthy were able to get approval for a beautiful ceremony that suited both of them. It wasn't officially a Jewish wedding, nor a Christian wedding, but had elements of both, and it wasn't at all difficult to find a rabbi and a priest willing to participate. It was quite a conversation starter for many in Washingtonian society, so, try as they might to keep the affair low-key and only invite family and close friends, the wedding threatened to grow out of the couple's comfort zone.

Red was excited to help plan the wedding. She daydreamed a little about her own wedding someday to her beloved Viking ghost, but quickly dismissed the thought. It just wasn't cool to think of marriage while in high school. She loved being in love with such a wonderful person as Erik and was thoroughly enjoying the courtship right now.

She was happy, though, for her beautiful Hungarian friend, who'd been through so much and deserved this happiness. She poured over pictures of wedding gowns with Ms. Catsworthy and found helpful websites for her since the elderly lady wasn't quite computer savvy.

Ms. Catsworthy had spent most of her childhood in London and had window-shopped all the bridal salons on Sloane Street, South Kensington, and Chelsea. She had a vision of what she wanted and though time didn't permit having a gown special-made, Red left no stone unturned, or website unexplored, until they found the perfect collection of gowns in a bridal shop in Chelsea.

Seeing Ms. Catsworthy's eyes light up when she first saw the pictures was such a joy to Red. It was worth all the hard work and Red felt a warm glow inside as Ms. Catsworthy gasped, bringing both sets of fingers to her mouth to stifle a scream, and then began to excitedly shake her hands.

Red, afraid Ms. Catsworthy would hyperventilate, quickly called the phone number to ensure a dress would be available right away, without the usual six-month period of cuttings and fittings—she knew the process from the bridal shows on television.

As the phone rang in London, Red began to wonder whether the shop would be open. She checked the computer screen for the time; it was almost ten on Saturday morning. She couldn't remember how many hours the time difference was and began to feel that the inquiry might have to wait until Monday.

She ventured a sideways glance to see Ms. Catsworthy, sitting on the edge of the wooden desk chair in Red's bedroom, staring mesmerized at the picture of the dress on Red's computer screen. She began to feel sweat trickle down the back of her neck and cast a silent plea for help into the ether at the same instant that the phone was answered.

"Hello, Phillipa Lepley Studio," came the efficient and yet highly cultured voice with an impeccable British accent.

Red looked upwards toward the ceiling. *Wow. Thanks!* She explained the situation and painted a very eloquent picture of Ms. Catsworthy as a worthy Holocaust survivor for whom happiness was coming late in life.

Red could tell after a few minutes that the elderly lady across the Atlantic was hooked. She began to reminisce about the bombing of London during that time and said she was certain they could accommodate her friend.

Red handed the phone to a beaming Ms. Catsworthy, and after several minutes of excited conversation, Ms. Catsworthy asked Red, "Dear, what is an e-mail address and do I have one?"

Red suppressed a laugh and decided it was time to take the phone back. Red gave the information to the lady and was assured that she'd momentarily receive photos of dresses that for one reason or another were available for immediate shipment.

After ringing off, true to her word, within moments the lady had sent the first group of photos to Red's inbox. She showed Ms. Catsworthy how to view the photos and used her iPhone to find a list of local tailors who would be able to alter the dress to fit Ms. Catsworthy perfectly. The first two were booked for the next few weeks. She was beginning to think she'd have to locate her mom's old sewing machine from their boxes still stacked in the basement, when finally a very nice gentleman in Potomac Village assured her that his business could accommodate any alterations within the necessary time frame.

By the time she got off the phone with the tailor, Ms. Catsworthy's countenance had changed from excitement to fretfulness. She'd identified three dresses that were equally desirable and just couldn't make up her mind. "Oh, how I wish I could see them in real life," she said.

They needed Annie, Red thought. Annie tended to be very opinionated on such matters as fashion. To Red, each dress was a fine choice and she had difficulty understanding how it could stress someone out to have three good options. She simply wouldn't sweat the difference. But Annie tended to be able to cut through such fogs and proclaim the best option in a way that left people wondering how they could've been so blind in the first place.

She went to Annie's room and found her sitting on her bed, mulling over the printout of the cave writing with her earbuds in, so she didn't hear Red knock. She looked up with a glare of annoyance. Red was saddened that Annie was so dismal these days and hoped to lighten her mood by engaging her in Ms. Catsworthy's happiness while also providing help—two birds with one stone.

"What?" Annie showed her annoyance in the customary way Red recognized.

"We need your help. Ms. Catsworthy is going to have a cow if someone doesn't help her pick out a dress. We have some options on my computer. Can you come now? Please?"

Annie grudgingly complied, though Red knew she was always up for giving an opinion on fashion.

Red was greatly relieved when the process seemed to be working. Annie was able to help identify the features of each gown Ms. Catsworthy liked and zoomed in the pictures so she could get a better look at each feature.

Red stood back and allowed Annie some space, since it seemed to be engaging her finally in something other than worrying over Aaan. And Red had to admit she was impressed with Annie's ability to identify and organize the important aspects of what Ms. Catsworthy wanted in such a way that it made sense even to Ms. Catsworthy, who was still an emotional wreck.

Eventually, by identifying the desirable features and figuring out which gown had the greatest number of desirable features, they thought they had a choice. But then Red looked at Ms. Catsworthy's face as she beheld the picture of the chosen and knew it hadn't worked. So she watched as Annie quickly typed a response to the lady in London explaining the features desired by the bride.

Red began to worry the shop would close soon since it must be after five by now over there. But to their delight, a second batch of pictures arrived within minutes. Based on Annie's input, the proprietor had marked one in particular as a dress she thought would best fit the bill.

And it only took one look at Ms. Catsworthy's face to realize this was the dress. Ms. Catsworthy actually cried when she beheld it—her wedding dress. Red ended up crying with

231

her and couldn't help but give her a hug; she also called in their mom to see the dress and was glad she did because she was equally excited and supportive.

She quickly called the lady back to secure the dress. She could ship the dress that very day, the owner said.

Over the next few weeks, Red was glad to note that Annie's talents were frequently sought by Ms. Catsworthy. It seemed Ms. Catsworthy had been so grateful for Annie's help in choosing the dress that she had begun to rely on her to help with every wedding decision, from flowers to catering. Red knew Ms. Catsworthy also appreciated her artistic eye, so Red offered her opinion from time to time and stepped in when needed. But she allowed Annie to become Ms. Catsworthy's go-to person. Red thought it kept Annie sane. Otherwise, all she seemed to do was sit in her room and brood over the cave writing.

Red confronted her with this one day while the two were alone in Annie's room, watching a new music video. "Annie, what's up with all the brooding over Aaan? I mean, he helped Uncle Alistair. It all turned out great. In fact, it seems like his presence there saved the day and so he's kind of like a hero."

"Yes, but no one's heard from him since then. What if his dad captured him, or worse yet, talked him into joining him?"

"Annie, didn't you read all he's been through? He wouldn't do that. Trust me." Red really wanted to make her sister feel better.

"You think he's okay?"

"Of course, silly. Listen, Aaan's a big boy. He's been through a lot. I don't think a person changes after hundreds of years."

"I just wish I could see him to make sure he's okay. Uncle Alistair said he wanted to go visit him and thank him and said he would at Christmas if not before, but now he's so immersed in his upcoming wedding and getting his research back on track, that I don't know…"

"Hmmm." Red thought a minute. "Annie, I have a plan. Just wait there." Excited, Red went directly to her uncle's study and knocked. She was immediately invited inside and closed the door behind her.

Half an hour later, Red knocked on Annie's door. Annie, somewhat out of character, actually answered the door rather than deliver her usual rude response.

"Annie, Uncle Alistair has something to ask you," Red said with a mischievous twinkle as she stepped aside to allow her uncle to address Annie.

"Anya, dear," he began, "I have a favor to ask of you. It seems that I'll need to ask your forgiveness for failing to follow through on a promise I made to you to go and thank your friend, Aaan."

Annie's face fell, evidently thinking she wasn't going to get to see him after all.

He continued, "But your sister tells me your parents have decided to spend Christmas at your grandmother's since she has a cold and won't be able to travel at this time." Red saw Annie's face begin to light up—Red was pretty sure she'd assumed they would be stuck here because of the wedding.

"I wish to ask you to deliver these two wedding invitations for me." Uncle Alistair produced two beige envelopes of the highest quality stationery and handed them to Annie.

Annie looked at the handwritten addresses. Red knew one was to her grandmother and the other just said "Aaan."

Annie smiled at her uncle and seemed to be speechless.

Uncle Alistair urged, "So you'll deliver them for me? Your grandmother may have to send her regrets due to her health, but I will be most disappointed if our friend Aaan cannot attend my wedding." He wore a delightfully warm sideways smile and a slight arch of one bushy eyebrow.

Annie jumped up to hug her tall uncle, who seemed to loom over her. "Oh, Uncle Alistair, I would be delighted to do you this favor." They both laughed.

Red felt proud of herself for doing this. She and the whole family had been so caught up in the wedding preparations that they'd overlooked her little sister, whose heart was breaking with worry for her friend. Now she'd get to see him—at least, Red hoped. She didn't want to think about the possibility that he might not be there.

The weekend before Christmas arrived too soon for most of the family, but not nearly soon enough for Annie. They packed into her dad's Volvo wagon and drove to Tennessee, conveniently vacating the mansion as many old friends of Uncle Alistair's began to arrive for the big wedding. Uncle Alistair and Ms. Catsworthy would be hosting a Christmas celebration for them. For fear that the pets might be neglected with all the preparations and celebrations, Tatyana, who was staying in town for winter break, had agreed to come and check on Buddy, Midnight, and Roxy, as well as Snagglepuss and Fluffmuffin.

As they drove southward, Annie reflected that this might be the last such family visit to Mamaw's for Christmas, since Red would be going away to college next year. But strangely, Annie felt it was as it should be. Red seemed very happy with Erik and Annie was pretty sure that relationship would work out. One never really knew how people could change, but Red and Erik certainly seemed really into each other.

Annie glanced over to see Red smiling as she texted—probably to Erik. *Well, it's still a little much, though maybe not quite so mushy as it was at first,* Annie reflected and then closed her eyes for a nap.

They arrived after dark, which they'd expected since today was the winter solstice. As they pulled into the driveway, the exterior lighting revealed a crunchy covering of ice on the brown grass of her grandmother's yard.

Annie knew it would be too awkward to try to see Aaan tonight, and rather than risk anything that might mess things up for him, she politely hugged her grandmother, tried to eat a few bites of dinner with the family, and excused herself early. She thought her absence would be barely noticed with all the excited chatter her parents, Mamaw, and even her sister were engaged in over the upcoming wedding. She'd already asked her mom to deliver her grandmother's invitation and determine whether Mamaw would ride back with them for the wedding. With that obligation taken care of, she vowed to try and get some sleep before tomorrow—the big day when she got to see him again—at least, she hoped.

The next morning, Annie was out of bed as soon as the sun broke through the window. The quality of the first light rays seemed a little too bright, and as she pushed aside the curtain and peered out, her suspicions were confirmed—a beautiful white blanket of snow covered the ground. Annie felt this was a good sign. Snow somehow made her think of purity and goodness—and Christmas. It was perhaps the first time this Christmas season that she had a feeling of seasonal excitement.

She nudged Red, who slept soundly. *None of that*, Annie thought; she'd waited long enough. She shook her sister's shoulder more forcefully and continued until she was awake. "What the ..." Red said groggily.

"It's time. You need to transform me." She handed Red the STAG control Uncle Alistair had allowed her to take. "Are you awake enough? I need for you to do the Angel—I mean, Sight Stone transformation; you know what I mean—the ghost transformation. You need to zap me and then be ready to transform me back in a couple of hours. It's six-thirty, so at eight-thirty—no, let's make it nine, they'll still be asleep—at nine, come in here and be ready to point the STAG control at that curtain, and transform me back. And if anyone asks where I am, say I went outside to walk in the snow. Okay?"

"Okay, okay," Red said irritably, obviously wanting to go back to sleep.

"Just press here and then you can go back to sleep. And remember, nine o'clock, okay?"

"Okay."

Red pressed the button. Annie transformed and wasted no time in flying up through the ceiling and then toward the Swan Hole.

Annie could tell it was still almost dark. The world around glowed with the essences of all things and it was beautiful. The other times she'd been in this transformation had been in broad daylight, except for the time she'd been inside the cave. The whole world now looked magical, like the inside of the cave. Something sparkled below in addition to the slightly pulsating glow from the ground as she flew down the country road. She thought it must be ice—or snow, probably a combination of both. It looked like one of those old-fashioned sparkly Christmas cards, except it was as if someone had turned on a blacklight to create a glow. It reminded her of driving through the Christmas lights the park service set up every year in one of the Maryland state parks. When she was little, her parents would drive slowly through the vast light show and open the sunroof, allowing Red and her to stand with their heads protruding through the roof and view the lightshow as if they were flying through the scene—like now.

As she approached the Swan Hole, she noticed that in addition to the sparkles on the ground, glistening icicles hung from the mossy overhangs above the pool. The ferns had dried, but their shapes still draped downward, covered in snow, around the falls and the hillside on the steep side of the creek. The small falls still roared.

As she alighted downward, she stood for a moment and breathed the icy air deeply, not really feeling the cold but shivering nonetheless from the frosty essence of the scene. The icy world seemed so clean and cool that she had an urge to bite an icicle. But she refrained; she had other things to do. Plus, they were the wrong-sized molecules, she reminded herself.

It was time to enter the cave, but Annie was hesitant. As much as she wanted to see him, what if he wasn't there? She didn't want to think of that. Still, he had seen his father, and his father may have talked him into joining his evil schemes. Or worse.

Annie had to stop for a moment, breathe deeply, and suppress these negative thoughts. She looked up to the dawn sky for courage. He was her friend and she was here to help him. And if he wasn't here, she'd find him—somehow. Despite the negative thoughts, she somehow felt his presence nearby, like when she gazed at the etching she kept in the top drawer of her dresser.

She slowly ghosted to the small opening and for a moment wondered if she should call to him first. Shouldn't she knock? But how?

She placed her mouth to the small opening and said timidly, "Aaan?"

No answer.

She felt a small amount of panic rising in her throat. She didn't know if her voice carried enough to be heard over the sound of the waterfalls, and she knew the only way to find out if he was there was to plunge right in.

She closed her eyes and pressed first her face through the wall surrounding the small opening, and then her shoulders and the rest of her body.

She opened her eyes, both afraid to see and not see him. She looked around. The cave looked just as it had before. Her eyes went quickly to the throne and then the couch-like shelf.

No Aaan.

Her heart fell. *Oh no.* She knew her eyes would have filled with frustrated tears if they could.

Frantically now, she zoomed around the room, peeking behind each column and recess, and then entering the tunnel.

"Aaan," she called as loudly as she could. "Aaan!"

She'd never seen beyond the initial opening of the tunnel and didn't know how far back it went. In a short distance, the tunnel opened into another room, this also filled with sculptures and sparkling colorful stones, but, again—no Aaan.

Annie hardly noticed the artwork. She desperately looked for a further expansion of the cave, but found none.

She wasn't ready to give up, but began to feel an oppressive panic.

She ghosted back out into the larger room. She tried to look around for evidence that he'd been there recently. But how could such evidence exist? He probably didn't eat, so there was no garbage. She wondered if he knew about iPods. She should make sure to get him one, if she ever saw him again.

She searched around the room again and then decided to go outside and search around the falls—who knew? Perhaps he could be outside for some reason, though she really didn't think so.

The weight of her grief made pressing through the cave wall seem more substantial than when she'd entered. Like some elfish, green, mossy bed, there was a vegetative smell mingled with the smell of mud—of soil. She could smell the mud as she pressed through it and wondered briefly how she could smell normal molecules in this state but didn't dwell on it. She could just stop right here and stay until he came back—inside the earth, part of the ground, smelling the primeval mud smell. This scent would always remind her of him, she knew. This was the smell of home. Of where he was. She hesitated a moment before pushing on out into the approaching morning light.

She flew upward over the falls, calling his name as she ascended. About thirty feet up over the falls, she stopped climbing when she thought she'd have a good view of the area around the cave. She made a treading-water motion with her arms to stabilize her position and then looked directly below.

Something akin to an electric shock almost knocked her backwards as she caught sight of him below, looking directly at her, a beautiful smile on his face. Her heart pounded with panicked exertion. No matter how she prepared herself, it was always a shock to see him.

He was sitting on an overhang, facing east toward the growing light. He casually raised a hand in greeting.

"Aaan," she squealed as loudly as she could.

He was immediately floating in front of her. "Tiny Bold Maiden, um, Anya," he said in smooth tones that caressed her name as if it were made of silk.

Annie was momentarily speechless. "I—I thought you were gone." She hoped her tone didn't betray the horror she'd felt at this possibility. Her arms still nervously treaded air.

"No, still here, though I do not sleep for decades as before." He looked wistfully toward the rising sun. "In fact, I haven't slept at all in some time. So I try to enjoy the beauty around me. Come, sit with me. I was just watching the sunrise. It promises to be particularly beautiful today." He looked into her eyes as he said the last sentence, making her heart thud.

"Okay," was all she could manage.

He took her hand and she felt electricity course through her as if her entire being was focused on that hand. He led her to the rock where he'd been sitting. She sat and he gently sat beside her.

"Watch over there." As he said this, he pointed with one hand as the other rested protectively behind her back, encircling her in warmth. With his proximity, she wasn't sure she could even focus enough to decipher what she was supposed to be watching. But he seemed so enthusiastic that she tried.

And she was glad, for it was a beautiful sunrise. The ever-changing bands of neon orange and pink were enhanced by an approaching blanket of silvery clouds. "Red sky at morning…" she murmured absentmindedly.

"What, Anya?"

"Oh, it's just a rhyme I learned in school. 'Red sky at morning, sailors take warning. Red sky at night, sailors delight.' "

Aaan nodded, grinning with an adorable sideways grin. "Yes, I have heard that—

and lived it. The day will bring some weather, perhaps more of this beautiful blanket of snow. I notice beauty in the world lately much more than before."

Annie smiled, her heart pounding. "This sunrise certainly is beautiful. Thank you for showing it to me."

"This will forever be our sunrise. I will etch it into my soul."

Annie was mesmerized by that sentiment and wasn't sure what to say next.

"But I am being perhaps too sentimental," Aaan said. "It is just so good to see you, my little friend."

Annie hadn't realized how hopelessly consuming were her romantic feelings toward him until that moment, when he called her "friend." She'd been feeling drawn—

perhaps even seduced—into his essence. Drawn irresistibly in. But now it was … *friend*? It broke the spell and allowed her to remember why she was here.

"I came to invite you to a wedding." She tried to sound chipper and a touch nonchalant, but knew she came across sounding as nervous as she felt.

"Oh," he said with some hint of alarm.

She realized that with his history, he must be used to women getting married at her age and quickly corrected him. "It's for my Uncle Alistair. The one we asked you to rescue on Thanksgiving?"

He seemed to be back in his previous good humor. "How could I forget?"

"Well, it seems you helped him work through some issues he had because of the Holocaust and feeling so guilty for betraying a friend that he didn't feel worthy enough to marry."

"Well stated." He looked amused, and she wondered if he was making fun of her, but his warm smile soon made her forget this line of thought. He prompted, "And who is the lucky lady?"

"Oh, yeah. Ms. Catsworthy. She was the sister of his friend that died in the Holocaust, and she has been his close friend his whole life. We always wondered what the deal was with her coming to America with him and living next door. I guess they've both loved each other for decades, but he didn't feel worthy to do more than look after her and she thought he was still in love with her sister. Anyway, Uncle Alistair's very grateful for your counseling him. He says he's eternally grateful to you and would be honored if you would be present at his wedding. It's this coming Friday, December 27, at the National Cathedral. I couldn't bring the invitation since I'm transformed and the paper would fall apart but can figure out a way to bring it before I leave. Or, I guess I could put it in some special place outside of Mamaw's house and you could get it." She hesitated, unsure what to say next. "You think you can come?"

He gave her a stunningly handsome smile. "Let me check my calendar," he said mischievously. "Didn't think I knew about such things as calendars, did you?" He smiled and took one of her hands in his. "Anya, I would be honored to attend. I would not miss such a joyful occasion. Thank you very much for personally delivering the message and I do not need a paper invitation. In fact, I think I would go anywhere you invited me." He laughed softly, as though remembering a very pleasant thought.

Annie was totally swept away and thought she'd pass out. She probably would have just sat there, staring into his eyes, except she was so nervous she pulled her hand away and scampered up. "I gotta go now. My sister's expecting me back so she can transform me before my parents or grandmother wake up. I'm not supposed to be doing this transformation, but Uncle Alistair let me do it again to invite you."

After saying the last sentence, she smiled at him, a little proud of herself for succeeding in her task. "He's going to be so glad I found you."

"Then it is settled. I shall see you at the altar on Friday. What time is the ceremony?" He looked amused.

"It's at ten a.m. Remember, the National Cathedral. Do you need a ride, or—how do you travel?"

He laughed openly now. "No, I do not need a ride. I am able to transverse distances on Earth easily. Now, if the wedding were on Saturn, then perhaps I would need a ride."

Annie knew he was teasing her and she was enjoying it. But she was also beginning to feel an urgency to get back. Red would be frantic if the time was up and she wasn't there. She wasn't wearing a watch and had to guess how much time had passed. Plus, as much as she enjoyed being in Aaan's presence, it was almost too intense. "Okay, then. See you Friday."

By Friday, Annie had never been so nervous. She felt like this was her first date, even though she knew it wasn't. She'd invited Aaan, in a sense, but it was really her uncle who had invited him.

She didn't know if he'd be visible. She'd seen him in two forms, both ethereal, his spiritual essence and the angelic form he had adopted the day she and Red had asked him for help. If he appeared only as a spiritual essence, likely no one would see him unless they had some kind of special sight. If he appeared in his angel form, she somehow didn't think that would go un-noticed by the other guests. She could see the *Washington Post* headlines now: "Washington Visited by First Angel of the Apocalypse."

She didn't know how many options he had at his disposal. So she reasoned she needed to prepare herself for the possibility that she might not see him at all.

But he'd see her. Of that, she was sure. An electric kind of excitement surged through her at the thought, causing her to spring from her bed and commence her most intensive beauty routine ever; all the years of magazine browsing were now to be put to use on her skin, nails, and hair. She decided to even ask her sister to work on her hair with a curling iron—a definite first.

She found Red equally excited, since this would be the first opportunity for Eric to see her at her most elegant. Annie, Red, and their mom had all purchased new dresses the previous day. Annie commented on how Red's silver, spaghetti-strapped dress made her breasts look full and her waist small, and Red beamed, admitting that she was looking forward to seeing his eyes when he gazed on her in her finery. And she couldn't wait to see how handsome Erik would look in formal attire. Annie thought again of Aaan.

Annie decided this was fun as she and Red scurried about between their rooms and the bathroom, sometimes almost colliding.

But her priorities suddenly changed, as did Red's, when their mom came up to announce that Ms. Catsworthy had called to ask if the three Greene women would be kind enough to assist her in her preparations. Annie felt the pull of an ancient tradition to help the lovely woman on her wedding day and completely abandoned her own preparations except to make sure she was zipped and had remembered her shoes.

Annie was sure her mom and sister felt as honored as she did that the dear lady saw them as her bridesmaids, though there were no official bridesmaids in this ceremony. Her request to help her get ready, however, told them they were treasured in that same way.

They spent the remainder of the time primping the beautiful lady. No princess had never looked finer, Annie thought. She painted Ms. Catsworthy's toenails and Red her fingernails, while their mom did her hair. They made sure Ms. Catsworthy was lotioned, fluffed, smoothed, powdered, perfumed, and buffed until every inch shone like the brightness in her lovely eyes. And it took all three to finagle the dress over her head and properly position the train behind her.

Annie was elated when finally, the shoes were strapped on and the finishing touches made. The four ladies embraced and then walked carefully out to the waiting limo. She knew Uncle Alistair and her dad had driven ahead so that Uncle Alistair wouldn't see his bride before "the appearance" during the ceremony. Annie and crew took great care to pack the train of the dress into the car once Ms. Catsworthy was seated.

Upon arrival at the cathedral, Annie's dad and Erik were waiting in front to assist the ladies. One glance at Red told Annie that she was in awe of her handsome Viking, standing tall and straight. Even his longish hair and beard looked regal in his immaculately tailored suit. Red didn't seem to be able to take her eyes off of him, nor he off of her.

Annie and her mom helped Ms. Catsworthy with her dress until she was safety inside the narthex, the area just outside the cathedral entrance. Then they kissed her before being escorted to their seats by Annie's dad.

As Annie entered, her eyes scanned the occupants. She saw her uncle and they exchanged a tiny wave. He stood at the front of the aisle, more handsome than she'd ever seen him, near the beautifully decorated *chuppah*, the canopy beneath which Jewish marriage ceremonies were performed. It was a wonderful Jewish tradition formerly unfamiliar to her, but Uncle Alistair had explained it. She saw many gaily-dressed people she didn't know. A small brass band awaited a signal to begin from the musician, whose fingers were making magic on the gigantic pipe organ, playing some classical piece she recognized but couldn't name—she'd try to remember to find out later.

But she didn't see anyone who even vaguely resembled Aaan. Feeling a twinge of disappointment, she consciously lifted her chin and gritted her teeth. She reminded herself of two things. First, he'd be here, she just might not see him. And second, it was Ms. Catsworthy's and Uncle Alistair's day and that was the most important thing. And she was glad those two beamed with happiness today.

Red and Erik had taken the end seat of one of the front pews, followed by her mother and father, and Annie sat beside her father. She left a space at the end of the pew, just in case. She hoped the ushers didn't seat someone else there. This row was supposed to be reserved for immediate family.

As these thoughts occurred, she heard the signal as the processional music began and her heart fell slightly. It was too late now for someone to come up the aisle and sit beside her, because any second now, the procession would begin.

People around her began to turn to look toward the brass band. She, too, looked in that direction. Then, as she turned her head back toward the aisle to watch for the procession, she was startled to see that the seat next to her was now occupied. *Aaan?*

Annie couldn't look. She had to stare straight ahead. The proximity was just too close to even venture a bold glance. Her heart pounded.

From the corner of her eye, she saw an arm with a light grey, almost silver, jacket and black gloves. She got the sense of a tall man—a *very* tall man.

She felt the side of his arm against hers and the contact sent electric currents through her body. She watched as he began to pull each finger of the left-hand glove with his other hand and then slide the glove off.

A massive masculine hand was visible. This hand, now engaged in removing the right-hand glove, had a slight glow, not from the whiteness of the skin, for it was colored more of a bronze tone, but from some inner glow.

*Oh no—he's glowing!*

She ventured a sideways glance and saw equally glowing eyes the same silvery color as his suit. He was looking directly into her eyes.

She wasn't sure she could speak.

"Anya, you are a true vision of beauty. Oh most *fayre nymph*, more lovely than a summer's day," a deep voice whispered as he leaned into her ear.

That did it. She was definitely going to faint.

"Aaan?"

"Yes, Tiny Bold Maiden?" She was sure she heard a hint of amusement in the tone.

"You look very handsome, too." She took a slightly bolder look at him now and smiled shyly. She was sure she saw his breathing change when she smiled. "But you're kind of … *glowing*," she tried to say this into his ear, emphasizing the last word.

"Oops." The illumination immediately subsided and he looked normal. "Please tell me if you see that occur again. It is hard for me to tell."

She took a moment to actually look at his face. She'd never seen such a handsome face. The chiseled features, the dark curls, the silver-colored eyes. *Oh my. What eyes.* And how tall. He must be seven feet tall, taller than any other man she knew. Actually, a *lot* taller than any other man she knew.

"Aaan."

"Yes?"

"I didn't realize that you were so *tall.*"

"Oh." He sounded apologetic rather than flattered.

She hadn't meant to imply that she was complaining. Did she just see that? She could've sworn she saw him shrink a few inches in height.

"No, I mean, I like it."

"Oh, you want me to…" he pointed upward.

"No," she said quickly. "You're perfect now."

She glanced around to see if anyone had seen them. Luckily, at that moment the bridal-entrance music began and all rose in honor of the bride. Annie looked up the aisle and observed the smile on her uncle's lips and joy in his eyes as he watched his bride walk down the aisle.

She looked at Ms. Catsworthy and noted that the lady only had eyes for her uncle. With every step, she beamed. Annie wouldn't have been surprised if she'd just given up the slow step routine and gone running into his arms.

As the vows were exchanged, Annie noted that every member of Alistair Hamilton's family seemed to enjoy a time of serene happiness. On that morning, every member was beside the person they loved most. The beauty of the music, the majestic grandeur of the cathedral, the warm wishes of all those around her, and her angel at her side—she knew this beautiful memory would never leave her.

Annie was in such a state of euphoria from all the sensations of beautiful music, happy people, and proximity to the one she adored that she felt her love for him would be unmistakable when he looked at her face. She was almost afraid to look at him as the last strands of music died. But the happy couple had processed out and everyone began to stand and collect their belongings.

She slowly turned toward him as she rose, expecting to get to have a conversation at their leisure as they left their seats. Her mind was filled with observations she wanted to share and questions about his own perceptions of the wedding and cathedral. She dared to hope that she might hear more about her *loveliness* or hint of his pleasure in sitting beside her.

But he merely stood before her in the aisle beside their seats, bowed, kissed her hand and said, "Until we meet again, fair maiden." Then he walked away.

She felt like she had been doused with ice water, her mouth hanging open in an unspoken retort.

Then she shook her head to clear it. Needing to move to allow others out of the row of seats, she moved into the aisle and stood watching him retreat swiftly, too swiftly, down the aisle.

Then it occurred to her that his retreat seemed too purposeful. Questions filled her mind. *What's going on?* She needed to know and didn't want to just stand there like a simpleton.

The crowd of people leaving their seats were rapidly filling the aisle and separating her from him. She tried to follow to ask him to join them at the reception luncheon. Maybe he just didn't understand modern customs and thought he was supposed to leave. She tried to push through the crowd as fast as she could but it was slow going. She saw him ahead in the entrance to the cathedral, evidently congratulating her uncle and his bride. Her heart gave a lurch as she saw him turn back around to look at her. He flashed a heart-wrenching smile and blew a kiss. She tried to wave to him to stop, but it was too late. He had turned and disappeared into a darkened recess leading away from the narthex.

She bolted as fast as she could without toppling any little old ladies to catch up, only to find that the direction he'd taken led to a locked, heavy, wooden door, short with a rounded top. It was so short that it probably led to nothing more than a broom closet. She knocked anyway and tried the handle, but it was firmly locked. She pounded on the door until her knuckles ached. No one else was in this area; the crowd was still moving in a different direction to file outside.

Disappointment flooded Annie. As she rejoined her family, she knew she'd have to make a superhuman effort to avoid tears and appear happy on this special day.

She barely noticed when her uncle did the traditional wineglass breaking and called out "Mazel Tov!" She tried to pay attention because her mom nudged her. She somehow made it through the rest of the celebration, though it was a blur.

# CHAPTER 18

## The Heart of an Angel

Aaan returned to his cave in a perplexed state of joy over his newfound friend and lady-love, equally mixed with an aching sadness and breaking heart at having to leave her behind at the cathedral. He knew she hadn't understood why he had to leave so abruptly. How could his darling understand that this was simply forbidden?

He still remembered, across all the ages, the face of she who was goddess to him. The one who taught him to love. Ila. His mother. So many times when his father had gone away after a night spent with her in their jungle-paradise love nest, he had watched her cry. How his heart had broken for her. She'd had no one to talk to, and was outcast from even her own kin. Her kin thought she had slept with a demon and that her sons were the spawn of the underworld. How wrong they had been. She had been a tower of strength, and her love for his father, Daanak, had been the most beautiful being he had ever beheld.

Back then, his father had been a golden warrior for good, a bright ray of hope to all he encountered.

Aaan had been but a boy when his mother explained why he and his brother Zaak were different, why the other children didn't want to play with them. Why they were so much taller than the other children their age. She told him about meeting his father, of feeling a presence watching her as she bathed in what she thought to be a hidden pool. How she had swum up from a dive, her face breaking the water's surface, to see the golden sun shining overhead. Temporarily blinded by the light, she hadn't seen an enormous crocodile's slanted pupils gliding above the surface toward her until it was only feet away. She had screamed upon seeing the massive mouth open to engulf her but had known her screams would be in vain. Just as she was bracing, expecting to feel sharp teeth tearing into her flesh, she had felt herself lifted up, flown out of the water by colossal arms as strong as those of one of the temple statues.

Daanak had saved her. The two fell in love, irrevocably, unashamedly, all encompassing. Daanak had taken her as his bride and she had born him a son, then another.

He stayed with her every possible moment. He had his own work in the angel realm, and knew this coupling was forbidden, so he tried to hide their love to protect Ila.

But try as he might, she ached for him every moment he was away. She always lived in a state of fear that he would be punished. She said being ostracized from her clan was a small price to pay for time spent with the one whom her heart adored. So he had continued to come to her.

His father had been with them when the flood began—Aaan remembered that part vividly. Aaan heard him tell his mother he would take her and their sons with him, to fly them above the advancing waters until it was over.

But something went wrong. Aaan had never been sure what happened. One minute he was with them and the next he seemed to be dragged away by invisible forces.

Aaan had mulled over that day so many times, trying to make sense of it. He suspected a unit of angels, perhaps a unit assigned the task of preventing any angelic interference with the destruction, had pinned back Daanak's arms and pulled him from the scene so that all he could do was watch—and learn to hate.

Aaan had watched his mother drown, unable to get to her in the churning water. He knew she had died thinking his dad would be back for her.

Aaan could not do that to Anya.

But Aaan was overcome by despair and sheer helplessness as he thought about not being able to love her. Oh, how he wanted to love her. How could this be wrong? Maybe it wasn't, since he was only half-angel, but he didn't know for sure and there was no one to ask.

And he could not risk her life.

If there was a way across that barrier, he had to find it—a way to love her without pulling down deep Heaven upon their heads. He could not forget her.

But his mother's panicked face as she drowned crept into his thoughts, as it had countless times before across the eons of time.

He wrestled with the idea of disappearing and leaving Anya alone. Is this what he should do? Could he?

And then he had an unbearable thought: what if he had already set in motion events that would destroy her? Had their innocent encounters already been noticed by others in the angel realm or other ethereal worlds? Had others above sensed the great love he now carried for her?

He would not allow himself to think in that way. There was goodness somewhere. *All will be well*, he told himself. His long, lonely existence argued that punishment was possible and brutal, but he could not allow that to defeat him. He would find a way.

# Endnotes

[1] Quote from: Francesco Colonna. 1499. *Hypnerotomachia Poliphili*. English translation by Robert Dallington, *Hyperotomachia: The Strife of Loue in a Dreame*. May 27, 2006, EBook #18459 (Y2:82). http://www.gutenberg.org/files/18459/18459-h/18459-h.htm.

[2] Quote from: St. John of the Cross, 1578-9. *Ascent to Mt. Carmel*. Translated and edited by E. Allison Peers from the critical edition of P. Silverio de Santa Teresa, C.D. Published by: Grand Rapids, MI: Christian Classics Ethereal Library. http://www.ccel.org/ccel/john_cross/ascent.pdf.

[3] Quote from: George MacDonald. 1895. *Lilith*, Chapter XXXIX--That Night. Chatto and Windus. London.

[4] Quote from: Jane Austin. 1813. *Pride and Prejudice*. T. Egerton, Whitehall. London.